# CRIMES OF THE LEVEE

## JOHN STURGEON

Black Rose Writing
www.blackrosewriting.com

ISBN: 978-1-61296-266-5

PUBLISHED BY BLACK ROSE WRITING

www.blackrosewriting.com

Printed in the United States of America

*Crimes of the Levee* is printed in Palatino Linotype

To my mother,
an angel,
and to my wife,
who should be one.

# CRIMES OF THE LEVEE

My mother was a whore. I was not aware of this fact until my father told me about it moments before I killed him. I have never seen my mother, nor do I know if she is still alive, but I am looking for her and will until I am dead. My father, the late Jacob Fine, had been a bagman for the two aldermen of the First Ward, Bathhouse John Coughlin and Hinky Dink Kenna. Aldermen had been the official title given these two, but they were royalty, crowned princes of the Levee, and the kings of this shithole that we reside in on Chicago's near south side.

Returning to my father, I mentioned that he did work for the two princes and did quite well at it. He also prospered as a saloon keeper, hotel owner and dabbler in the white slave business. This last venture, and my search for the missing Isabella Rossini, led us to that fateful night when he told me of my mother's occupation and where I put a bullet hole neatly between his two beady, black eyes.

I mention casually that I had a mother and a father, and I guess everyone does, but I was raised at the orphanage at Holy Trinity Church. Holy Trinity was a Catholic institution with a church, school and a small orphanage that never held more than twenty-two people. My father's half of me was Jewish; he had olive colored skin, dark, thinning hair that he combed to one side and a large, well shaped nose. My mother, I can only surmise, was a gentile. I have light, reddish brown hair, a much smaller proboscis and a pale pallor to my skin. In the summer a few freckles, brought out by the sun, find themselves on my cheeks. I could have used my talents as a detective and surmised that she might have been Irish, but was unable to confirm this until the very end.

So I had a mother and a father. So how did I end up at Holy Trinity? My start there began when Father Luigi had to take a piss on the morning of St. Patrick's Day. It would have been further for him to go use the lavatory on the premises than to step outside in back of the church and that was where he found me. I was swaddled up nicely in two woolen blankets and placed in a basket on the back porch. It is said that Luigi completed his piss while looking constantly at my peering, brown eyes that never left the view of the priest as he completed his task. It is also said that I gained my name of Patrick Moses because of the day I was found and the manner in which I was left.

Father Luigi Falcone became my mentor and friend as soon as I arrived at Holy Trinity. There were a number of nuns that watched over me and raised me as an infant, but Luigi was always nearby and when he could finally convince the good sisters that he could take care of me, they let him. He taught me how to read and write, to tie a neck tie, to box and to pray. He taught me all about discipline and when I stepped out of line, I was punished. His thick brown belt sometimes did more teaching than his hard to understand, Italian voice. As tough as he could be, in reality, he was a three hundred pound Guardian Angel.

When I asked what Luigi knew of my mother and father he would only tell me half truths and lies. He told me that he knew nothing of my mother, the half truth, but then he would say he knew little of my father, the lie. He told me that I would know my father soon enough and this became true, but for most of my early life, I considered Father Luigi and the sisters of Holy Trinity to be my family.

When I was twenty-three and a young patrolman on the force I met Francis Keegan. She was a small, petite girl with red hair, pale skin and a constant display of freckles. She was a teacher at the public school in the ward. I fell madly in love with Francis and we were married a year later. The year after that she gave me my son, Charlie. Two years later Bess came along. My life, my values and my understanding of life were defined by my marriage and being a father to Charlie and Bess. This all came crashing down on December 30, 1903 in the flames and smoke of the fire at the Iroquois Theatre. Now, the only thoughts I have of my wife and children come to me in the nightmares that still haunt me with the images of their dark, burnt bodies. I seldom talk of them.

After the Iroquois, you could surely understand why I had thoughts of jumping into Bubbly Creek and sucking the poison water into my lungs or just putting a bullet into my brain, but

God intervened. He sent me a new partner, a large German named Gunter Krause. Things have gone bad for me, some that I can't ever forget or forgive, but for the most part, life has been fair. Gunter's family came over on a boat. He has survived famine, poverty, disease, a distant father and an early life of slaughtering pigs at the Yards. He has gotten away from that and now he, like me, is a Chicago Police Department Detective, assigned to the Twenty Second District's Special Crime's Unit. If I ever get down, Gunter is there to cheer me up. Sometimes, all he has to do is talk about some of the horrors of his past, and it's not that hard to come out of my doldrums.

I suppose I will survive, but I am certain I will never be entirely cured. It may be the district that I live and work in. There is too much that is not human. I have never known my mother and, as years have gone by, I have discovered my father. This does not make me feel better. The First Ward has every vice that you could possibly want and, within its' boundaries, lives every type of two legged miscreant. This, also, does not help my mood. We had just heard of the date of the hanging of Dr. Kluge, and this little bit of information did bring some joy to me and some safety to the ward. I had not yet heard of the missing Isabella Rossini nor had I met the millionaire who would ask me to find out what really happened to his dead son.

## Monday

I am not always a nice man. I am sure this has a lot to do with my job as a detective in the First Ward. It is sometimes difficult to figure out exactly who the crooks are. Of course, we have thieves, pickpockets, madams, opium dealers, crooked gamblers, rapists and even a murderer or two. Dealing with this all day long will not make you nice. It may not do much to keep you sane. The criminals are one thing, you know what they are after, but it's the ward bosses that will confuse you. It is hard to draw a line between legal and what they do. If you want to operate in the ward you had to pay $25 a week to these two hooligans to remain open. Sell liquor and that fee jumped to $50. If you operated a gambling house it might be as high as $100. Coughlin and Kenna run the ward their way. From the Chief to the Mayor, most look the other way. I try to look ahead so I don't step in any of the shit they leave behind them.

I believe in God and I fear him, but I don't always understand him. What kind of God lets all those children burn up at the Iroquois? Why would he let a man like Dr. Simon Kluge kill all of those women? These thoughts baffle me and corrupt me. Father Luigi taught me endlessly about right and wrong and I understand that, but I slip now and then. I don't have the self control that I need for this job, and I fear that it will hurt me one day.

Today promises to be a good day. At eleven o'clock in the morning they will hang Kluge in the alley behind the Cook County Prison. It won't be a good day for Kluge, but it will be some justice for the sixteen women, those that we know of and have found, that Kluge managed to dissect and leave strewn about the city. From what we can tell, all of these victims were prostitutes, and I have had my disagreements with a few of this type, but I have never wanted to increase the openings of their mouths from ear to ear or slash them open from neck to pelvis. Kluge did this without prejudice for about three years. If the bastard doesn't drink a little too much or talk like a school girl, we may not have caught him. At that time, Kluge was very lucky. If Officer Gilman was not present, I had thought of jamming my gun down Kluge's throat and emptying the damn thing. But there was a trial, Kluge was convicted and justice will be served. My only hope is that the hangman will err and Kluge will swing and choke for a bit and suffer before dying.

The morning was mired in a slow, miserable, cold rain. It was only a few degrees warm enough so that snow was not piling around us. The fog that hung in the air allowed for about twenty feet of visibility, even at ground level. It was a perfect day to hang Kluge. I hope they didn't take long to dispense with the doctor. My overcoat and hat were starting to get drenched from standing in the crowded alley near the gallows, but I wasn't going to miss it. For such a seemingly somber event, there was a significant crowd. I saw Mayor Dunne and a number of his cronies; Coughlin and Kenna were there, holding court. There were a number of the elite madams from the Levee. It seemed a gruesome way to spend a morning, but Kluge had murdered no less than sixteen women. He was the reason for the crowd.

The rain fell harder as they led Kluge out of the jail and up the gallows stairs. There was some booing and hissing from the crowd, but the weather helped keep them in check. Someone launched an egg in Kluge's direction, but it landed harmlessly and Kluge never saw it. He eyes were cast downward at the wooden death structure. I was surprised to see him dressed in a dark suit and tie. He would look like a gentleman to the very end. I am sure he looked that way to those women whom he befriended and murdered. Once he was properly positioned under the noose, the Cook County Sheriff, Sean O'Donnell, asked Kluge if he wanted to say anything, but all Kluge did was shake his head. Then a Catholic priest was asked to give him his last rites; Kluge looked calm, the look on his face projecting boredom. I wondered if he approached murder with the same look of indifference. As the priest spoke in hushed tones, Gunter Krause, my partner, sidled up next to me. He is easily six inches taller than me and when I looked up at him and nodded I got rain in my eyes.

"This is a good day for you, Patrick," he said, the German accent still present.

"Not as good as it could have been."

He looked a bit confused. "How so?"

"If we could have caught the son of a bitch a little sooner, we might have saved a few of those women's lives."

He touched my shoulder with his big, gloved hand. "Don't punish yourself over that. We did the best that we could do."

I didn't respond. Gunter was right. We had done the best we could.

The priest was finished with Kluge's last rites and the crowd seemed to take one deep breath. The hangman approached Kluge. He placed the noose over Kluge's head and pulled it tight at his neck. I tried to read Kluge's face for any sign of what he felt. What I saw I would remember forever. Kluge, eyes wide open, smiled and seemed to focus his gaze right on me. I swallowed hard as a hood was placed over his head, ridding the world of the hideous grin. The hangman took a step back, grabbed hold of the lever and gave it a quick pull. The floor dropped and with it, Kluge. His body did a mid-air bounce and then stiffened at the end of the rope. His legs shook for a short few seconds, not much longer. He died quickly, robbing me of my dream that he would suffer.

I heard Gunter give out a deep sigh as the crowd began to disperse. "We used to think of him as a monster," he said, "but he died quite easily."

"Too easy for the likes of him."

Suddenly, Gunter's face wore a big smile. "I forgot. This is quite the big day for you."

"Have I been transferred from the Levee?"

He laughed. "First the hanging and then The First Ward Ball is tonight, and you and I have drawn the distinction of working it."

I spat into the alley. I felt a cold coming on. "I would rather battle a pestilence."

Gunter laughed. "It won't be so bad. You'll get to see so many of your close friends."

Right now, I just wanted to get out of the rain. "That Coughlin and Kenna, making everyone in the Levee buy tickets. That damn party will be crowded this year."

"At least it will be interesting, like going to the Barnum circus."

"Only with more clowns. Now, let's get out of this rain and find something to eat."

"We could go to the Workingman's."

That was Kenna's place. "Again, I'd rather be sick."

*****

The First Ward Ball was Coughlin and Kenna's annual attempt to bring everyone in the ward together in one place. This year's venue was the Coliseum. When I say everyone, I am talking about the prostitutes, pimps, madams, politicians, police and everyone else who could afford a ticket to the event. If you wanted to do business in the ward you had to buy tickets. That was the way it was. When I heard that one hundred policemen had been assigned to work The Ball, I wondered how many would be there for security and how many would be there for the take. I knew none of the reformers would be there, but I knew they would be close by. The *Tribune* had promised to print a list of respectable people attending The Ball, but I doubted it would keep attendance down. There was too much pressure to attend.

If you wanted something in the First Ward you had to go through Coughlin and Kenna, the two aldermen. They controlled everything, including the police brass in the district. My father, Jacob Fine, the top bagman for the princes, had his picture on the wall of the Twenty-Second Precinct, a distinguished honor that cost tremendously. Bathhouse John Coughlin was a big barrel-chested man with a full head of hair and a bushy mustache. He was loud and boisterous, but this was not his most noticeable feature. He often wore garishly colored suits that made him appear like one of Ringling's clowns. Buffoon was a word I heard tossed about privately to describe him. The former rubber at a Clark Street bathhouse had ridden the aldermanic path to fame and fortune. He also wrote ridiculous poems that were often published in the papers. Gunter, a voracious reader, told me you needed a lot of power to get that type of junk published in the papers. Coughlin had that power. His partner, Michael "Hinky Dink" Kenna, was the opposite. He was a little shit, maybe an inch over five feet tall and very slight. He was the serious one, always somber looking, never joking, looking the part of an undertaker. His suits were always plain and dark. To Coughlin, he was the couple's straight man.

The two First Ward bosses had been throwing the Ball since ninety-five. The Ball had gotten bigger each year and this year's was expected to be the biggest. We were ordered to be in attendance in order to make sure nothing serious happened. I was told that this meant making sure no one committed murder; everything else seemed to be acceptable. Coughlin and Kenna wanted no big problems.

This girl that I see, Eleanor Winter, is a prostitute. I had seen her the night before at a den on Wabash Street and she had told me that she would not be attending the ball. Large crowds made her very nervous and, at best, she was a jittery type. We smoked a little and we felt better. I wanted to take her back to my small apartment on Clark, but she had to return to The

Queen's House. Miss Keesher, who ran the place, had been hard on Eleanor lately. She was worried that Eleanor was using too much opium. Miss Keesher threatened to toss her into the street, but Eleanor laughed at this. She was a special girl. It didn't matter if you were white, a Negro, a Jew or even an alderman, Eleanor would entertain you. I knew that the Negro boxer, Jack Johnson, asked for her if he was in town. Her other asset was that she did everything very well. Callers would ask for her frequently. Miss Keesher wasn't going to toss her anywhere.

We were instructed to be at the Coliseum well before the charade started. I made sure that Gunter and I had enough to drink before we went inside, but I had a bottle snug in my inside pocket. I didn't want to be too sober to witness the events. I recall a witness to a few of these parties referring to them as "a second Christmas". That might be, I thought, but it was Coughlin and Kenna who were doing all the taking and doing little, if any, giving. The party began with the Grand Review where Coughlin and Kenna led a procession of all of the madams and prostitutes of the ward in a march around the Coliseum floor. This gave me a great opportunity to view most of the Levee's leading citizens. The madam, Vic Shaw, was there. Her enemies and chief rivals, the Everleigh sisters, Minna and Ada, were in attendance, both dressed lavishly. I saw the gambler, Mont Tennes, walk by with a lovely, somewhat clothed, strumpet on his arm. The brothel owners, Big Jim Colosimo and his wife Victoria looked supremely elegant. The Von Bevers, Maurice and Julia, couldn't match the Colosimos in dress, but they were there prominently. All in all, twenty thousand people crammed the Coliseum. If we could arrest a third of these people we could have solved most of the unsolved crimes of the city, but on a night like this we looked the other way and no one seemed to care.

There were over two hundred waiters in attendance, trying to service the crowd. I didn't think it possible that they could keep up with the demand, but I heard corks popping all night long. I heard later that over ten thousand quarts of champagne and thirty thousand quarts of beer were guzzled by the guests. It was no wonder that most people were well south of sober and their behavior would have turned reformer's hearts to stone. Most of the women were barely dressed and few acted like ladies. I saw a number of the Levee's finest ladies bending backwards over railings to have champagne poured down their throats. Amazingly, there was little violence, although one madam was said to have impaled a male guest with a large hat pin.

Watching the guests and listening to the two bands perform was enough for me. It was getting late, and I had a headache and my nose was plugged. I was getting ready to leave when I saw the two aldermen approaching where Gunter and I stood. Kenna was dressed in a typical dark suit, white shirt and dark tie. The tiny alderman wore no smile on his face as he trailed Coughlin. He could have been at a wake. Bathhouse John wore a huge smile along with green dress suit, mauve vest, pale pink gloves, yellow pumps and a silken top hat. I know I stared longer than I should have, and I know Coughlin saw me.

"It's a great party, Detective Moses," he said. "I hope you are having some fun."

I nodded my head. "Thank you, Alderman Coughlin. Thank you for the invite."

This drew a laugh from Coughlin and a further scowl from Kenna. It was then that I noticed my father, Jacob Fine, trailing the two ward bosses by about ten feet. He was dressed as darkly and plainly as Kenna, but his face was pink and his forehead was dotted with beads of sweat. His thinning, dark hair was matted to his head. He, too, was not smiling.

"Patrick," he said. "I hope you are finding some time to get out and enjoy life."

There was no handshake or other acknowledgement. Just these few words to try and lead my life with.

"I'm having a great time, Mr. Fine." Even though we both knew our positions in the relationship there were never words like son or father mentioned. There were three people, four if you counted my mother, who knew the truth.

My comment drew nothing more than a blank look from Fine as he hustled to catch up with his two leaders.

"Of the three," Gunter said, "I think Jacob Fine might be the least trusting."

"I can't argue with you over that, my friend." With that, I shook Gunter's hand and bade him farewell. "I want to get a good start in the morning."

As I rode in the cab, through the dark streets, back to my apartment, I wondered about Eleanor. I wished I was with her, wherever that was. Other than that, I didn't have much to look forward to. I took a deep breath. With Kluge waiting for admission to hell, I was without a case. I looked out the window and noticed for the first time the Christmas lights in some of the windows. Maybe I really didn't need to get a good start in the morning. Maybe it was time to relax a bit, enjoy the holidays. Would it matter? I doubted it. How wrong I was.

## Tuesday

The awakening I received the next day was not one that I would expect. There was a loud pounding on my door accompanied by the sound of a woman calling out my name. My head felt as if I'd had more to drink than I had, but I think a good reason for this was that I had not slept well. The pounding on the door was not helping. As I got out of bed slowly, wrapping the blankets around me, I realized how cold the room was. I was sure the rats in the basement were warmer. I moved quickly to the door and opened it. There stood Kelsie Casey about to pound and shout my name again.

"Patrick," she said quickly, "you've got to come right away. It's Eleanor. She is not doing well."

Kelsie was a pudgy little brunette who also worked at the Queen's. She wore a heavy coat and hat, and I could only see her tiny face peering up at me. "Where is she, Kelsie?"

"She's at the Queen's, in her room. I've got a cab waiting for us."

It didn't take me long to dress and soon we were out in the Chicago cold and trudging as fast as the horse would take us to The Queen's House on Dearborn. Not to be confused with anything majestic, like the Everleigh Club, the Queen's was an old place, clean, with nice girls. Eleanor and many of the girls were too good for the place, but Miss Keesher paid well and that was all that mattered to them. In the wee hours of the morning the place was without clientele and most of the girls were probably sleeping. Kelsie led me up the stairs to the third floor where Eleanor kept her room.

If I hadn't been able to see her chest rising, I would have assumed she was dead. She looked peaceful with a calm look on her face. Her clear complexion along with her red hair showed her beauty. This angelic display was offset by the mess of vomit that lay close to her face. I grabbed her arm and try to rouse her, but that was useless. She looked fine, but I couldn't wake her. I became alarmed.

"Take the cab and go to Doc Mitchell's on Wabash. Tell him it's a favor for me and bring him back here," I said to Kelsie. When she left the room, I returned to Eleanor and took her hand again, but there was no reaction to my touch. I held onto her hand and waited.

The fifteen minutes that it took Kelsie to return with Doc Mitchell seemed like hours. Like me, the good doctor had to be awakened from sleep and he looked the part. His dark eyes were tired looking, crevices grooved neatly under them, and his hair was a mess. He had helped me with a number of problems, and he had a reputation for helping the prostitutes in the Levee. I doubted this was the first time somebody woke him up. He asked Kelsie and me to leave the room while he examined Eleanor. We stepped out into the cold hallway.

"Will she be alright, Patrick?" Kelsie asked.

"Doc is a good man and he owes me; she'll be fine," I said. I was sure about the first two points of my answer. It was the third part that had me worried.

"I heard her come in about three; I was up in the parlor, reading. I couldn't sleep. She didn't look very good. When I went up to bed I checked on her and that was how I found her."

"You did the right thing in calling me. Was she with anyone when she came in?"

I saw the look on Kelsie's face. "Gussie Black helped her in and up to her room."

The mention of Black's name made my stomach clench. Gus Black was a lowlife faro dealer, cocaine user and dealer of drugs. He lived on the third floor of a building owned by Eugene Huston and his wife Lottie, the King and Queen of the Cokies, the biggest dealers of cocaine in Chicago. Black had his eyes on Eleanor for a long time, but why she befriended him I'll never know. I had warned her more than once about him, but she kept up with him. Hearing his name now only made me want to kill the little weasel.

"Does Miss Keesher know anything?" I asked.

"Not that I know of, but with all this commotion, I wouldn't be surprised to see her soon."

We waited about ten minutes before Doc came out of the room. He silently motioned for us to come in. Eleanor was laying on her other side, away from the vomit, and her chest was still rising and falling rhythmically. Doc had pulled the covers down to her waist and had raised the sleeves on the night gown she wore. He pointed to a spot on her white arms about halfway up on the forearm. The track of four fresh needle pricks was unmistakable.

"I'm afraid Eleanor has graduated to a higher level of satisfaction," he said.

The look on my face must have conveyed stupidity, and I said nothing.

"It's heroin, Patrick," Doc said. "I think she will be fine and she just needs to sleep it off, but she is lucky. In her condition, she could have choked to death on the vomit. She may have a bad headache when she awakes, but she will survive."

I thanked Doc for coming out and shook his hand. As he was leaving and we were exiting Eleanor's room, we ran right into Miss Keesher coming up the stairs. I knew she was close to sixty and I usually saw her in a nice dress, hair done up and face complete with makeup. At this time of the morning with a nightshirt on and her hair under a cap, she was a bit unbecoming.

"Mr. Moses, I warned her about this," she said directly to me. "I told her if this happened again, this drug use, she would not be welcome here."

It was my good friend, Doc Mitchell, who saved the day. He grabbed Miss Keesher by the arm, he had known her for years, and told her that Eleanor had come down with a bad case of the flu.

"Oh," she said. "So she is only sick?"

"Yes," I said. "Kelsie heard her moaning and calling my name. She came and got me and I sent for Doc."

Miss Keesher thought about that for a moment and nodded. "Okay, I see, but I'm telling you, Mr. Moses, no more drugs for Eleanor."

She turned quickly and was down the stairs before I could even respond. Doc said goodbye and also went down the stairs. Kelsie and I checked on Eleanor again, but she was unchanged. I pulled the covers back up, tucking her arms underneath them. Kelsie said she would get one of the black maids to clean up the mess Eleanor had made. I took one more look at her, the look so peaceful on her face. Doc was right. She would be fine. That would not stop me from visiting Gussie Black.

*****

When the cab dropped me back in front of my building, the air had not warmed, but the sun was breaking through some thin clouds in the sky. It promised to be a cold December day. I paid the driver and was about to enter my building when I heard my name being called. I looked to my left and there was a nice brougham parked near the curb, a short, stocky man with a long overcoat and top hat stood next to the coach. Under the hat, I couldn't make out his face or its features.

"May I help you?" I said.

"Detective Moses," he said, "Mr. Field would like to have a word with you." His voice was rough, scratchy.

It was then that the door to the coach was pushed open. I could only see the gloved hand and arm of the person doing the pushing. I stepped forward, past the driver, and looked into the cab. There sat the king of the merchants, a solemn faced Marshall Field. There was a lamp flickering on the inside of the coach and it gave off some light, but it allowed to me to see Field clearly enough. He, too, wore a top hat and heavy, long coat. His skin was pale and the hair on his head and in his mustache was purely white. It was his eyes that got me. Nothing, but supreme sadness, was projected by those eyes.

"Detective Moses, I am sorry for the timing of our visit, and I thank you for seeing me," he said. His voice was flat, tired. "When you hear the reason for my visit I am sure you will understand why we need to be discreet."

I had seen Marshall Field once before when Francis and I walked the aisles of his palace on State Street, dreaming of the days when we could afford any of the wares that he sold. From up close, I was speechless. He was as close as you could get to true royalty in this city, right up there with Swift, Armour and Palmer. "It is an honor to meet you, sir," I said meekly.

He smiled weakly and then coughed a bit. He withdrew a handkerchief from the inside of his coat and wiped his mouth. The look on his face remained stern. "Detective Moses, I have a business proposition for you."

I had absolutely no idea what kind of business Marshall Field would need me for. "What kind of business proposition?" I asked.

"You are familiar with my son Marshall's death?"

Only a complete fool would not be familiar with Junior's death. Some say one of the girls at the Everleigh Club shot him. Others say he killed himself. The "official" version, supposedly secured when Marshall, Senior threatened to pull his ads from the local papers, was that young Marshall shot himself while cleaning his gun. When it happened, I heard all the stories and liked the Everleigh angle myself, but the story died so quickly that no one knows for sure. "I am familiar with it," I said.

"What are your thoughts on the matter?"

"My thoughts? I haven't had many since it happened in November. My recollection is that he shot himself accidentally while cleaning a gun." That was the story that Field had wanted in the papers so I went in that direction.

"That is one contending theory," he said quietly.

"Theory, sir? That is what I heard and read in the papers."

He laughed lightly. "Ah, yes. What you read in the papers." He coughed again, this time harder, and wiped his mouth. "I am not really sure what happened to Marshall that night. He was in his house the night he was shot and he did die at Mercy Hospital, but I am not sure how he was shot or how he got back to his house on Prairie. When all of that Everleigh Club stuff was going around I called the publishers of the papers and told them I'd pull all of my ads if they continued to publish that rubbish. They all abided by my wishes, not wanting to lose the advertising revenue. Now that things have quieted down, I need to know the truth. I'd like to know what happened to my son that night."

I cleared my throat; this cold was becoming a constant bother. For the first time, I felt nervous. "Have you spoken with the Chief of Police?"

"As you know, the police concluded their investigation and could find nothing other than the death was an accident. Now, I know that in the Levee, it may be hard to ascertain the truth. You might never get it. It's tough to trust the people down there, even the police."

Smart man, I thought. "Why are you talking to me? I am a police detective."

"Detective Moses, I did some research on you and discovered two things. You are a man of incredible investigative talents. This has been demonstrated many times. More importantly, you are a man of impeccable honesty."

I felt myself blushing and felt foolish. "I try to do well on both of those things."

"Those are the two biggest reasons why I am asking you to investigate Marshall's death. Of course this will need to be an unofficial inquiry. My staff and all of the staff at Marshall's house have been notified that you will be investigating and they will cooperate in any way you need them to. Are you interested?"

I shifted nervously on the seat, not saying anything.

Field reached into his coat and removed a manila envelope with a clasp on the top. "Here is a retainer of one thousand dollars. There will be another two thousand when you have concluded your investigation. Of course, all of your expenses will be reimbursed."

"Of course," I said.

"Once again, are you interested in taking this case?"

I wanted more time to consider this proposition, but the huge sum of money swayed my thoughts. I looked deep into those sad eyes. "I will be glad to look into this for you."

*****

The meeting with Marshall Field had been nothing less than a surprise. Even though I was exhausted and this nagging cold was trying to get deeper into me, I was unable to sleep much in the hours after the meeting. This didn't help me get to the precinct on time and the desk sergeant, Connelly, told me I was wanted immediately on the second floor. This was where the brass had their offices, so my first thought was that I was in some trouble or some word of my agreement with Field had been leaked. As I started for the stairs, I noted the picture of my father on the precinct wall. I didn't genuflect or anything of that nature. Many held my father in high regard. I didn't.

When I got upstairs, I found Gunter Krause sitting outside of Captain Morgan's office, wearing a severe scowl on his face. I noticed that the Captain's door was closed.

"I'm glad you could make it in today," Gunter said.

"I had a bit of a problem with Eleanor. Did I miss something?"

"Not yet. Morgan has a visitor from downtown and they both want to talk to us. I was told to wait out here until they opened the door and invited us in. That's why I'm glad you're here so that when they come looking for us, us is here to see them."

"I told you. Eleanor had a rough night and I had to have Doc Mitchell pay a visit."

I could see the muscles in Gunter's face relax. He liked Eleanor and was worried about her as well. "What did she get messed up with this time?"

"Maybe heroin and probably Gussie Black."

Before Gunter could respond or I could explain further, Captain Morgan's door came open and Morgan was there, waving us into his small office. Morgan was a tall man, the tallest in the precinct, and he had a long, droopy mustache that hung below his chin. He also suffered from a chronic bad back that kept him hunched over most of the time. He wasn't the one in the precinct who would win an award for having much sense, but he was a nice enough fellow. He also trusted Gunter and me and left us alone. This was worth more than a really smart cop who wanted to know our every move. Morgan's only true fault was that he listened to much of what Coughlin and Kenna told him.

I hope when I reach Captain that they award me with a larger office. Morgan's space barely had enough room for his desk and chair. When you added in the three wooden chairs that now sat in the room it became very crowded. In one of the chairs sat an intense looking officer in full uniform. The chevrons on his coat told us he was a lieutenant. He stared coldly at Gunter and me as if we had shit on our faces.

"Lieutenant Shipley, this is Detective Gunter Krause and Detective Patrick Moses," Morgan said, pointing to us with the introduction. Shipley said nothing nor did he offer his hand. We took the other two seats. I took the seat furthest from Shipley. I didn't like our friend from downtown.

Morgan shut his door and took his seat slowly behind his desk, evidence of his back pain on his face. I wasn't sure who was running the meeting. "Lieutenant Shipley has a new case for you."

"First of all," Shipley said in a high pitched voice that defeated the intense stair, "from the mayor and the Chief of Police, we want to congratulate you both on the capture of Dr. Kluge."

We both nodded and mumbled our acceptance of the accolades.

"That was great police work, but we now have a problem that appears to be getting out of control in the city. It does appear to be a city problem, but it also appears that the problem is centered down here in the First Ward, particularly the Levee district."

"What problem would that be?" I offered.

Shipley had to lean forward a bit to see me around Gunter's large mass. "It is the problem of white slaving."

I had heard the term many times and what I knew of it meant the moving of prostitutes into the city from other cities and states. Prostitution was legal. Brothels always needed prostitutes. I didn't understand what problem it was that Shipley was referring.

"There is a great problem in the city where we believe that up to five thousand young women, and sometimes even girls, each year are taken against their will and forced into a life of prostitution."

Both Gunter and I sat forward in our chairs. "Did you say five thousand?" Gunter said.

"That's an estimation, and we have had a very hard time of gathering facts in the cases that we have, but we did have in our custody a young woman, Veronica Long, who claimed to have been picked up at Union Station by a man named Mike. He promised to take her to dinner, help her find a job and to introduce her to number of new friends. Instead, Miss Long was abducted, held in captivity, drugged, raped repeatedly and then sold to a brothel in the Levee. She was constantly threatened with her life if she mentioned one word of this to anyone. It wasn't until she was picked up near Lincoln Park that we were able to get her story."

"Excuse me," I said, "but you said you did have her in your custody?"

"That is correct, Detective. Miss Long died several weeks ago. She had a terrible case of influenza, along with syphilis, and was feverish for most of the time we could talk with her. She finally succumbed."

"How in God's name did she get to Lincoln Park?" I asked.

"We think the brothel owner or his agent delivered her there when it was discovered she was both ill and diseased."

"That was nice of them," Gunter said, "but why the wait of a few weeks to talk with us?"

"As I said, we don't have as much information as we would like, but what we do know is that most of the stories we get have these women being held or at least filtered through the Levee before they are sold off to a brothel."

"Well," I said, "the numbers are astounding, but I'm a bit surprised that we haven't heard much of this white slaving before."

"It's not anything the department or the mayor is proud of, but it is a real problem. When a body of a young, unidentified woman was found under the El tracks near Wabash and Eighteenth her body was taken to Ralston's morgue and the normal death notice posting was made. There were nearly five hundred inquiries, trying to discover if this woman was their missing relative. If you will recall, there was a fire last year at an old chop suey joint on Custom Place. The building needed to be demolished. In the ruins were found the bones of seven young women, all unidentified. In the far western town of Wheaton there is a cemetery that holds four hundred and fifty one bodies of young women that we have shipped to them for burial. Again, all of these women are unidentified."

"So where are these women coming from?" I asked.

"Many come from right here, taken off the streets, some not unwillingly, I might add. Others come from cities like Milwaukee or St. Louis. Some from as far as New York. It is becoming a countrywide epidemic."

"So you would like Detective Krause and me to help you clean up a countrywide epidemic?"

The intense look from Shipley was back again, but then he smiled. "No, Detective Moses, I am only relaying to you the extent of the problem. On a large scale we are very concerned about local women being drawn into this trap. That is our big concern. Our smaller concern, but no small matter, is why I have come to see you."

Shipley reached into a black valise that was by his side, resting against his chair. He withdrew a picture and handed it to Gunter. I was able to clearly see the picture as Gunter held it in his two, large paws. The woman depicted in the photograph was somewhere around twenty years old. She had dark hair, worn in this picture on the top of her head, dark eyes and a thin, deceptive smile. She was dressed in a light dress which made her skin look darker. Clearly, there was a small, crescent shaped scar on her chin. Other than this blemish, the woman was beautiful. "She's lovely," Gunter said.

"This is Isabella Rossini. She is the daughter of Frederico Rossini who is the brother of Alberto Rossini, the current Italian Ambassador to the United States. It appears Miss Rossini took a train to St. Louis to visit with some family there before the Christmas holidays. At the St. Louis Union Station she was supposed to rendezvous with the family members. We know she was on the train from New York and got to St. Louis. Sometime in that city she disappeared. Our fear, and the family's fear, it that she has been abducted. They have been awaiting a ransom demand. We don't have that concern because we believe she was abducted and taken into Chicago and is being held captive as a white slave."

"What makes you think she got to St. Louis?" I asked.

"Several witnesses, workers at the station, saw her clearly and she was with a tall, well dressed man. Many of these people have all stated that they saw this couple board a train for Chicago. That train was set to come into the Illinois Central station."

I ran my hand through my hair as I absorbed this information. "Why would this woman come all the way to St. Louis and just suddenly hook up with this stranger and get on a train for Chicago?"

"Good question, Moses," Shipley said. "Miss Rossini is a bit impetuous and argumentative. She lives with her father in New York. Her mother is dead. The relationship between father and daughter is tense at best. The family believes she was charmed by the kidnapper, their words, and led astray by him. She may have thought this was some way to gain her freedom from her demanding father. The family believes she was tricked into being kidnapped. We think she has been abducted by white slavers."

I looked again at the picture of the pretty woman in Gunter's hands. There was something about her smile that made me think of agreeing with the family's assessment, but why would this good looking woman, from a prominent family, just disappear with a stranger. "What is it that you would like us to do?" I said.

"Like I said," Shipley started, his high pitched voice nearly cracking. "We believe she was abducted by slavers and ended up in Chicago. It seems the slaves get routed through the Levee before being sold off. Miss Rossini disappeared five days ago. We think she is still down here in the Levee in captivity. We would like you to find her."

I saw Gunter's eyes widen; I laughed out loud. "You said you would like us to find this one woman down in the Levee?" I asked.

"I did."

"If she's down here, and that's a big maybe, the people that have her probably have her pretty well hidden. I doubt they will make it very easy for anyone to find her."

"I assume you are correct, Moses. I'm also here to advise you that this is your number one task, your lone priority, at this time. We want you to put all of your energy into finding Isabella Rossini."

There it was, clear as a bell. Headquarters had the idea that there was a tremendous problem confronting the city, five thousand women taken into captivity each year. This was a huge problem, at least the way Shipley described it. Now they wanted Gunter and me to find one of these women, if she was even down here. It seemed daunting. I didn't know what else to say.

"We will give this matter our full attention," Gunter said, answering for us both and that was how we ended up with the case of the missing Isabella Rossini.

*****

My usual reaction to a new case was one of mixed excitement. The challenge, as always, was to solve the crime. This factor, in most cases, was what produced the excitement. I didn't feel this way with Isabella Rossini. Lieutenant Shipley had stated that somewhere near five thousand women from Chicago went missing each year due to this scourge he'd called "white slaving". This was not an insignificant number, but when you factor in the 384 resorts, 278 shady hotels, 47 disorderly dance halls and 44 places that sold cocaine, opium and morphine illegally as the *Chicago American* suggested Chicago possessed, the possible places that Isabella Rossini could be was near infinitum. That was, if she was in Chicago at all.

Witnesses in St. Louis placed Isabella on a train for Chicago that was due to arrive at the Illinois Central station. I dispatched Gunter to that terminal with the picture of Isabella in his possession. I wanted him to ask as many people as he could if they had ever seen her. While Gunter was off on this mission, I went to the best place I could think of for street information. That would be the newsstand owned by Louie Pagano. This small stand was located at the corner of State and Adams. Louie went by the nickname of Big Louie even though he stood at exactly five feet tall. He told people that he'd once been a jockey, riding thoroughbreds. When he was around twenty a horse had kicked him in the head when Louie had fallen during a race. From that point on Louie had been legally blind. You might want to know how he could manage a newsstand with the inability to see. This became easy for him when he acquired a large German shepherd who was aptly named Little Louie. The dog became his eyes, uncanningly knowing the exact amount of change a customer would place on the counter in return for a paper. If anyone tried to cheat Big Louie, Little Louie would growl, bearing his fierce looking canine teeth. This had never failed to settle all disputes.

Most people liked Big Louie and they talked freely with him. His always friendly manner and his disability aided him. People told him almost anything. That was why he was such a great source of information. Of course, he didn't dispense with any of his knowledge for free. The papers he sold, the information he released, the book making, opium sales and his activity as a pimp were the ways he made his living. I wasn't thrilled about a number of his operations, but I was only interested in the information that he had. He seldom failed me in that area.

It was just before one when I made it to Big Louie's stand. The day was a bright, windy cold one and there were a number of people out shopping for Christmas in the downtown area. State Street was clogged with horses, electric cars and automobiles. All the stores in the area were done up with holiday decorations. I hadn't failed to remember that my new client's immense store was only a few blocks away. I found Big Louie tucked inside the stand, trying to stay out of the wind and cold. Little Louie was on the outside of the stand, guarding against any possible theft. The shepherd recognized me as I approached and let me rub the top of his enormous head. I said hello to Big Louie who hadn't detected my presence.

"Ah, my good friend, Detective Moses, what brings you to this part of town?" he asked. "I doubt you have made the little trip to buy a paper."

"I've come to see my good friend, Louie," I said, "but am also in search of some information."

He smiled first and scratched his chin which had more than a day's stubble on it. "Information can be hard to put a price on sometimes."

"How about if I tell you what I'm looking for and you let me know how much it will cost?"

Big Louie seemed to ponder this for a few seconds and then he smiled. Under the hat he wore, it was hard to see his unfocused eyes, but I had a clear view of his teeth. Most were yellow, with a line of black across the top. One, just to the left of center was completely missing. In his seeing days, a barroom fight had cost him this incisor.

"I think that is fair," he said after his short contemplation.

"I'm interested in the business of white slaving, what you know about it and who might be running it."

The term seemed to cause Big Louie to flinch. "This is a disgusting business. Some of the reformers will tell you of the sins of prostitution, but that is legal. There can be nothing legal about what these white slavers are doing. It seems, in some ways, to be worse than what the south did with the Negros."

Now he had my interest. "So it really does exist?"

"Where have you been, Moses? Are you so involved in the terrible number of murders that plague this city that you forget that we have other signs that prove that we can lower ourselves close to the bottom of the depths of depravity?"

Louie's outburst caught me off guard and brought a low, gurgling growl from Little Louie. The cases that I'd worked usually involved homicides and there was no shortage of new customers. I guess I did pay little attention to the vices of prostitution or even drug sales. "I have been a little caught up a bit with murderers," I said defensively.

"Yes, that's true," Big Louie said reflectively, "but one can't sit on his laurels in this city too long even if they include the arrest of the notorious Dr. Kluge."

"Okay, I confess. Chicago is an open town and a lot doesn't appear to be a crime. I was unaware of the true meaning of the term "white slaving" until this morning. I am in need of further education. Please enlighten me."

Big Louie smiled. "This game of white slaving has become a rather large enterprise and rather lucrative to the men and women who play in it."

"I was told today that there may be upwards of five thousand women each year who are dragged into it."

"That could be," Big Louie said. "No one had ever given me any number like that, but I have heard quite a bit."

"What will it cost?" I said, referring to the fee I knew I'd have to depart with to get the needed information.

"In this case, Moses, there is no fee. I was raised a Catholic and I do still believe. I dabble in a few things that are questionable, but I am not ashamed. What these white slavers do is so deplorable that I look forward to someone putting a stop to it. If I can help, maybe God will forgive a few of my lesser sins."

I didn't view what I was doing as any form of confession or act of penance, but if Louie saw it that way, I was fine. "I appreciate any help you can give me."

"You've got to come closer to hear this," Louie said. "I want this to remain between the two of us."

I was only about four feet away, but I stepped closer, into the covered part of the newsstand. Little Louie eyed me cautiously, should I even think about acting against his owner.

"This practice of white slaving has been around this city for years," Big Louie said. "Today there is a tight ring of people that run it here in the city. I've heard a few names thrown around, but never any big ringleaders."

I wondered if Louie knew more than he was saying, but didn't want to give up any of the leaders right away.

"These slavers will pick up these young women, and from anywhere. Train depots seem to be a great place to grab the young immigrants as they come into Chicago looking for work. The slavers promise they'll find the women work, but first comes the offer of maybe dinner and dancing. These women are so enamored with the good looking man who has suddenly taken them under their wings that they fall for the story. They do end up going for dinner and maybe a dance, but then they are drugged and taken away to a private holding area. These are called stockades. There is one called The Ranch out in Blue Island. At these stockades the women are held captive, continue to be drugged, are repeatedly raped and trained in the ways of satisfying a man. Once they are beaten and fully trained they are sold off to the brothels, sometimes for as little as a few dollars. At these brothels, none of the top class resorts, I promise you, the women are still drugged and are still captive. They cannot get away. Only if they become sick, die or diseased are they released, and this is usually too late. The women are wasted away to nothing by then."

I am sure they I stood there with my mouth hanging open. Shipley had relayed some of this information earlier, but now it seemed that Big Louie was making it all seem true. "Do you know some of the places where these slaves are being taken?"

"I've heard a few, but you don't have to imagine where they are. All along Bed Bug Row, that's where they thrive. Try the Saratoga, Victoria, Sappho, Black Mays, Silver Dollar and the House of All Nations. These are a number of the places I'd heard."

I was jotting down notes as fast as Louie spoke, my hand without its glove chaffing from the cold. A customer stopped to pick up a *Tribune*. Louie thanked him while Little Louie made sure he put the correct change for the paper into the dish.

"It's really turned into a tremendous problem for the city, a shame, if you ask me. I hear that they will pluck these women from anywhere. Ice cream shops, chop suey places, theatrical talent agencies, employment bureaus, salons that cater to women and dance halls are a number of places that allow these slavers to prey on the women. It has truly gotten out of control."

I continued to write, my hand cramping with the cold. "What about the operators? I need some names, Louie."

Big Louie again seemed to be contemplating handing over this information. His willingness to help with the elimination of white slaving appeared to stop with the handing over of names of operators. He rubbed hard at his chin, causing the already pink skin to go white for a moment before regaining its crimson hue; again, Little Louie let out a suppressed growl. I thought I may have all I was going to get.

"The two names I can give you are the ones I have heard the most about. You know how if you hear a person's name over and over again than it must be a fact."

"I understand that," I said, holding my breath, hoping to get the names.

"There is a guy, Mike Hart; I hear he owns a piece of the Marlborough Hotel. I also hear that he is into this slaving quite a bit. The other person I can think of is a woman. Her name is Mary Hastings and she runs the Sappho. From what I understand, these two will do anything for a dollar and this means ending a young woman's life. That is what sickens me, Moses. These people have no value for human life."

I could see the pain on Louie's face, without the benefit of reading his eyes. "Is there anything else that you can tell me?"

He paused for a bit. "That's all I have for now. I will keep my ears open; you know my eyes aren't very good, and I will tell you if I hear anything else."

I thanked him for the information and gave Little Louie a good rub on his neck and head. As I was about to leave, Louie called out my name. "You need to be careful, Moses. I gave you two names, but I think these are bit players in a much bigger play. In Chicago, especially the Levee, there may be big actors involved. The bigger the fish down there, the more dangerous it will be for you."

Again, I thanked Louie for the information and his last bit of advice. Even though he insisted on wanting to help for free, I put two dollars in his basket. Little Louie barked twice; Big Louie only smiled.

*****

Of my many faults, I would deem impatience and stubbornness to be at the top of the list. Both of these traits seemed to get me in my fair share of trouble. Father Luigi was quick to point out, when I younger, that that these faults would cause me problems and they had. I should have waited for Gunter before I ventured on to my next call, but I couldn't wait. With the information that I had from Big Louie, I decided to get over to the Sappho on Custom Place to visit with Mary Hastings, the owner and alleged white slaver

Bed Bug Row was a line of twenty-five cent crib joints that lined Custom Place on the east side of the street at Nineteenth Street. Prostitution was legal in town, but this was as low as you could go. It almost seemed gloomy as I walked along the brothels that made up the Row, but this was because I knew what was behind the windows and doors that were now closed to the weather

When I walked past the Victoria, a young lass in a lacy, pink robe pulled the curtain aside in the second story window and rapped on the pane. When I looked up at her she smiled at me and quickly opened her robe to expose a pair of rather large breasts. I returned the smile and tipped my hat, but kept on moving down the Row.

At the King's Palace another young courtesan opened the front door and yelled out to me. What she yelled, I won't repeat here, but she was not asking me in for a cup of coffee. I didn't dignify her with a smile or the tip of my hat and, in return, she called me a dirty bastard. I took exception with that comment. I might have been a bastard, but I took pride in my own personal cleanliness, and I was not dirty.

I came upon the Sappho just as a gust of wind roared down the street, almost blowing my hat off and causing me to lose my balance. I regained my hat and righted it on my head as I looked up at the Sappho. The building was three stories in height, a gray stone, streaked with the dirt and grime of the city. All of the windows of the place had curtains covering them and none of the brothel's ladies were propositioning me as I walked up to the door and rang the door bell. I rang three times and waited.

I was about to ring again when the door was opened by a short woman, partially dressed in a tattered gown. The woman was not clean and either she or the premises smelled. I detected noticeable knots in her black, stringy hair and she had more than a few red welts upon her face. That this wench was a representative of the faire you could have at the Sappho sickened me. What I wanted was an interview with Mary Hastings. I figured the sooner that this was accomplished, the better off I would be.

"What can I do for you, kind sir?" the woman asked, smiling and revealing a set of rotten teeth.

I pulled out my detective badge and showed it to the whore and her smile went away. "We're doin nothin wrong here, officer."

"I'm sure," I said. "I would like to talk with Mary Hastings, the owner. Tell her it is a private matter."

Some of her courage returned along with the putrid smile. "I am not sure she's here just now, officer."

"Please tell her that Detective Moses would like a moment of her time and that it will go better for her if she talks to me now and I don't have to come back."

She nodded and made her way down a long, barely lit hall off to my left. From where I stood, the foyer, I suppose, I could tell the building was in ill repair. Where there was paint on the walls it was chipped. I could even see that the chips were dirty. The walls had no paintings or other coverings. The floor was wood, the varnish old and cracked. There was a cheap dirty rug that covered a good portion of the wood. To my right was a white, painted staircase that led to the rooms on the second and third floor. I quickly decided that the first floor was the only floor I would ever want to be on in this building. One never knew when they would have to make a hasty retreat. The only other thing I can tell you about the building was that it was deathly quiet. I didn't know if the occupants could tell I was with the police or if this was just a quiet time.

I bided my time for more minutes than I thought necessary and watched a cluster of cockroaches move from one hole in the wall, along the floor, and into another hole. I was about to go down the hall in search of someone when I saw a tall woman approaching me. She was extremely thin, wearing a brown dress. Her hair, dark with streaks of gray, was on the top of her head. She might have been fifty, but wore enough powder on her face to conceal the truth. She wasn't pretty, nor was she unattractive. She also wasn't smiling.

"Mary Hastings?" I asked.

She looked me over a bit before responding. "I have made my payments for the month," she said. She put her hands on her hips and gave me a defiant look.

"I'm not here inquiring about any type of payments," I said, not sure where this conversation was going.

"I gave Big Jim the payment myself. There shouldn't be any problems coming from the police and, as far as I know, we haven't done anything wrong."

I shook my head. "I don't know about any payments and I'm not here about any violation that has been reported to us."

"We are not supposed to have any trouble from the police."

"I am not here to give you any trouble, I hope."

She relaxed her arms and dropped them to her sides. "Then what are you here for, Detective?"

"I am looking for a young woman."

She smiled. "Most young men are."

"I don't mean it that way," I said. "This young woman has gone missing within the last five days. She is a young Italian woman, twenty years of age, very pretty. Her name is Isabella Rossini."

Mary Hastings' eyes narrowed. "Why would you think that she is here at Sappho?"

"We were given a tip that she might be in one of the places along Bedbug Row."

"Have you checked with the other resorts?"

She was cagey. "We were also given a few names of proprietors where she might have gone to work. Your name came up."

Again the narrowing of the eyes which caused a showing of other lines on her face through the powder. "We have not had any new girls come to Sappho for some time, especially the last five days. Definitely there is no pretty, young, Italian girl."

I nodded lightly. "How do you secure your girls here?"

"What do you mean?"

"I mean how do the girls that work for you come here?"

She laughed. "Like any other job, Detective. They inquire if we have any openings."

"So you never go out into the street and try and procure girls to come and work for you?"

"We've never had the need to do that. We always have plenty of girls who want to work for us."

Again, I nodded. My short discussion had yielded nothing. I had to probe a little harder. "Do you know of a brothel in Blue

Island called The Ranch?"

She tilted her head to one side, the eyes glancing upward. "I have not heard of that resort."

"What about a man named Mike Hart?"

"Sure. I know Mike. He and his wife own a portion of the Marlborough Hotel. I've known Mike for many years."

"Are you familiar with the term white slaving?"

Again the nagging pause, suggesting that she needed time to frame her every response. "That is not a term that I am familiar with."

Another dead end. I was sure that Isabella Rossini was not at the Sappho, and I was also sure that Mary Hastings was not going to tell me anything about the business of white slaving. Other than interviewing some of the girls in the resort, I was wasting my time. I decided that asking the girls of the Sappho was about the only way to get any answers, but also decided to wait on that pursuit. "Well, I appreciate the time that you have given me," I said at last.

"It's been no bother, Detective. It's just that I have paid Big Jim, and I don't want any problems."

I was also sure that Big Jim was Big Jim Colosimo, a precinct captain, and lackey for Coughlin and Kenna, but I had no idea what payments he was receiving and why they would insure that the police wouldn't visit a brothel or question the owner.

*****

After concluding my short and useless conversation with Mary Hastings, I found myself with a couple of hours before I was due to rendezvous with Gunter. I also found myself within walking distance of the former residence of Marshall Field Jr. on South Prairie Avenue. The walk was actually a bit longer than I thought and a cold one. It gave me a little time to think about Junior's death and how much I hated the nagging cold I had that was clogging up my head.

It had only been a little over three weeks since the death of the merchant prince, but the story had died down to not more than hushed whispers. The known facts were that Junior had been shot on November 23, 1905 and died four days later on November 27$^{th}$. What was unknown was exactly how Junior had been shot and that was why Senior had hired me. There were at most three theories about his death. The first, and least scandalous, had him shooting himself accidentally while cleaning a gun in preparation for a hunting trip. The second, a bit more damaging to the family's reputation had Junior taking his own life. The third reason, the reason that Senior had hushed all of the town's newspapers, was that Junior had somehow gotten himself shot at the Everleigh Club in the Levee.

I had heard the Everleigh Club theory as had most Chicagoans, but this rumor, like all the rest had been squashed by the father. That I had been hired by Senior to find the "truth" behind his son's death meant that Senior wasn't accepting the accident or the suicide reasons. This meant that he was more inclined to favor Junior being shot somewhere where he wasn't supposed to be and then dying in his own house. This all seemed to make sense to me. My first idea was to start with the staff and servants at Junior's residence to see what they knew. If the *Tribune* had it right, they were the first people to attend to Junior after the shooting, whatever the reason was that he got shot.

When I first laid eyes on the Field mansion at 1919 Prairie, I was convinced that Big Louie was right about my attention to matters. Maybe I was too attracted and focused on all of the murders that took place in the Levee to see some of the other things around me. As I looked up at the house, if you could call it a house, that young Field had resided in, I was stunned. The structure was bigger than the entire church, school and orphanage at Holy Trinity where I was raised and grew up. It looked to be three stories tall, a brownstone, with a basement. It was a very long building which I later learned had over forty-three rooms and near thirty thousand square feet. The windows on the first floor stood over eight feet tall and the afternoon sun reflected brilliantly off of them. The entire property was contained within a four foot tall iron fence, but I found that the latch on the gate was easy to open. A short walkway led me to a cement staircase, eleven stairs in all, up through a tall archway and the front door. If nothing else, my interest in the house alone was piqued. Even if no one of value was present, I wanted to see the inside of the residence.

The large oak door that faced me had a heavy, brass door knocker in the shape of a lion's head. This knocker was right in the center of a large Christmas wreath that adorned the door. There was also a bell, but the lion's head knocker intrigued me. I raised the knocker, it was very heavy, and gave the door three solid raps. From where I stood, there didn't seem to be anyone home, but it was worth a try.

Not more than a minute went by that I heard a latch on the front door being pushed to one side and the stiff, cold door being opened. The woman who faced me was dressed in a dark blue dress, with some white trimming on it. The hat she wore, more of a bonnet, was completely white. She was an odd shaped woman, at best. From the waist up she was slender, with no noticeable breasts. From the waist down, her hips widened disproportionately and provided her with a large backside. The hair on her head that I could see was dark as were her eyes. She peered at me cautiously. I could she was nervous, maybe even scared.

"May I help you sir?" she asked in a hushed voice.

I flipped open my badge and introduced myself. "Mr. Field told me that the staff should expect my visits," I said.

She smiled weakly. "I am sorry, sir," she said. "I thought you might be another of those vultures from the papers."

"No vulture here. I was hoping to begin my investigation into the matter of Mr. Field's death. I was hoping to find some of the staff that attended to him on the night of the shooting."

I saw her blush and it wasn't from the cold. "I am the only one who is here at present. Mrs. Field is out for the day with the children and will not return until about six. Mr. Thomas Lowe, our butler, and Mr. Robert Gant, our cook, do not work today."

"And who might you be?"

"I am Ms. Emily Penfield. I am the nurse for Marshall Field the third. He is not always a healthy child."

"I see. Were you on duty the afternoon of the shooting?"

Again the nervous blushing of the face. "Mr. Lowe and I were present when Mr. Field shot himself."

A cold wind blew from the west and chilled me. The cold in my system did little to help matters. "May I come in out of the cold for a moment?"

"Oh, I am sorry," she said. "Please do come in."

She opened the door wide enough for me to enter and I was soon overwhelmed by the glittering of gold and silver that assaulted my eyes. The entire foyer was done up magnificently with Christmas decorations. I could not have found a greater contrast in the whole city than I presently had from the Sappho to the foyer of the Field mansion. First of all, the foyer was massive with a beautifully painted and carpeted staircase that led upstairs and a hall that led to other rooms on the first floor. To my right was what I was told was a sitting room, complete with a grand piano and one of the house's fourteen fireplaces. The foyer itself had a large, Persian carpet that covered the polished, wooden floor. A sparkling chandelier, bigger than anything I'd seen, provided most of the light for the entrance. A number of oils covered the walls, separated by golden sconces with electric bulbs, shaped like candle flames, flickering away. I am sure if I got down on the floor and checked diligently, I would not find a speck of dust. Certainly, no cockroaches resided here.

"Detective Moses, you wanted to discuss the night of the

shooting?" Ms. Penfield said, retrieving me from the trance the foyer and sitting room's sites had put me in.

I recovered and remembered why I had made the visit to Prairie Avenue. "I am sorry. I was just taken back by some of the beauty of the house."

"It is a very beautiful house," she responded coldly. "The night of the shooting, sir?"

Her bluntness put me back on track. "Can you tell me what you can recollect about that day?"

She drew both of her hands to a bow on her dress at her waist. She began to wring them together as she started to speak. "As I have told the police before, I was on the second floor when the shooting took place. I was getting Marshall the third's room together for the night. It was then that I heard the gunshot, very loud, and then Mr. Field's cry for help."

"One gunshot?"

"I'm sorry," she said as if she hadn't heard me.

"Was there just one gunshot?"

"Yes, just one shot and then Mr. Field's cry for help."

"What exactly, if you can remember, did Mr. Field say?"

She paused, the hand wringing continuing. "He was just crying for help and there was so much anguish in the cry."

"Anguish? Please tell me what you mean?"

"His cry told me, at least, that he had done something awful, and, in this case it was true. He had killed himself, and I always thought he knew that as soon as the shot was fired."

What would be your first thoughts after shooting yourself, I asked myself? "What happened then?"

"I am ashamed to say that I did not act right away. I hesitated a few moments, and then I heard a few more muffled cries, and then I made my way to Mr. Field's bedroom. When I got to his bedroom, I found Mr. Lowe trying to help Mr. Field back into the chair from which he had fallen."

"Mr. Lowe, the butler?"

"Yes, sir."

"Was there any conversation amongst the two men?"

"Only Mr. Field saying that he had done a stupid thing, shooting himself while cleaning his gun. He was getting ready for a hunting trip to Wisconsin."

"What kind of gun was it?"

She looked at me as if I asked her if she was a woman. "It was a hand gun, a revolver."

"So you know guns?"

"I know a handgun from a rifle and was told it was a revolver." There was a tad bit of bitterness to this answer.

"Continue please."

"Well, Mr. Lowe finally was able to get Mr. Field righted in the chair. I could see that Mr. Field was in a tremendous amount of pain. Mr. Lowe asked him if there was anything he could get for him, but Mr. Field only responded that he needed a doctor and right away. Mr. Lowe went to the phone in the room and called the doctor."

"What was the name of the doctor that he called?"

"I am sure that this is all in the public record," she said. She was holding the bow with her two hands so tightly that the area around her knuckles was white.

"I am sure it is, but this is a new investigation, my investigation, and I'd like to hear the answers from the participant's mouths?"

She cocked her head to her left. "You view me as a participant in this matter?"

"The wrong word maybe, but certainly an important witness. The name of the doctor, Ms. Penfield?"

"At first, he tried to call Dr. Frank Billings, the family doctor, but he was away in Downers Grove. Then he called Mr. Dibble, Mr. Field's brother in law. Mr. Dibble said he would be right over and instructed Mr. Lowe to call a number of physicians. I heard Mr. Lowe making these calls."

"What were you doing while Mr. Lowe was making these calls?"

"I was attending to Mr. Field. He was in great pain and was very pale."

"Was there much blood?"

"Excuse me."

"Could you see much blood on or anywhere around Mr. Field?"

This question caused her to think for a bit. "There wasn't much blood that I could see, as far as I can remember."

"Where was Mr. Field shot?"

"On his side, near the ribs."

"In a gunshot wound, wouldn't there be quite a bit of blood?"

Her eyes narrowed. "I am a house nurse, sir. I am not that familiar with gunshot wounds or the amount of blood they produce."

Unfortunately, I was not a nurse of any type, but I was familiar with a number of gunshot wounds and, in most cases, there was blood to be seen, both on the victim and near them. "What happened then?"

"Mr. Dibble arrived first, followed by two doctors, Doctor Bevan and Doctor Harry. Mr. Dibble called Mercy Hospital and told them that Mr. Field would soon be arriving and would require an emergency operation. At this time, the two doctors were looking over Mr. Field, trying to make him as comfortable as they could. Eventually, one of the doctors called a private ambulance and told them to hurry over to help transport Mr. Field to Mercy.

"It was also about this time that Mrs. Field arrived home with the children and I'm sure you can imagine the shock and panic that ensued. I took the children into the sitting room on the lower level while Mrs. Field stayed with her husband. At about this time, the ambulance arrived and Mr. Field was put onto a stretcher and carried to it. The ambulance was soon on its way to Mercy."

"Who went with the ambulance?"

"Mr. Dibble and, obviously, Mrs. Field. The two doctors went in a separate coach and Mr. Lowe went back to his duties. I stayed with the children through the night until they all went to bed. At that time I retired to my quarters."

"And you don't know much of what happened when Mr. Field left the house or while he was at Mercy?"

"Very little. Only what I heard repeated. There was an operation, the bullet was recovered, but there was too much infection and internal bleeding to save Mr. Field."

I was writing down notes, and as I did this I reflected on my feelings of Ms. Penfield's answers. There was something missing, maybe emotion, in the way she spoke, but the fact that her recollection was good made me think that this story was the truth or that it had been practiced quite a few times.

"Are we finished, Detective?" she asked.

I put up one finger, perhaps rudely, to silence her. "A few more questions," I said. "What kind of man was Mr. Field?"

This question brought about a loud expulsion of air from my host. "I will tell you the same things I told the newspaper vultures. Mr. Field was a good man, a kind man. He was generous, a good person to work for, a good father and a good husband."

"Did you ever see him in a depressed sort of mood?"

"Of course," she said quickly. "I have been in the Field's employ for over three years. In that time, I'm sure I saw Mr. Field down a bit, but that was not even close to his normal mood. If you are asking if I ever thought he was down enough to try and kill himself, the answer would be no."

"That's fine. I understand. Now, one more question. Do you know or have you ever heard of Mr. Field making any trips down to the Levee district?"

It was not a blush this time that crossed Ms. Penfield's face. It was more like a match had lit her up with a crimson glow. "That is a preposterous question, Detective. Mr. Field would never be seen alive or dead in that disgusting area."

I wasn't sure if Marshall Field, Jr. had ever been seen alive in the Levee, but I wondered if he'd come close to being seen dead there. There was something about the lack of blood at the shooting scene that made my back teeth grind and ache.

"Are we finished now?" Ms. Penfield asked, the red glow gone from her face, replaced by a look of disdain.

"We are done, Ms. Penfield," I said, "for now."

*****

As I started down the eleven steps from the mansion and carefully closed the gate on the iron fence, a rather fat man, bundled in a heavy coat, top hat and scarf made his way towards me. He had on a leash a very small white dog that seemed to be pulling him along. As the dog got close to me he jumped up on my pant leg and his owner pulled him back harshly.

"I am so sorry, sir," the fat man said. "This damn dog, my wife's baby, has never been properly trained."

"No harm done," I said.

"Trying to get the true story of what happened?" the man said with a laugh.

I thought he was referring to my job as a detective, but then realized he took me for a reporter. "Just trying to see if any of the facts have loosened up in the past few weeks."

The little dog gave the owner a strong pull away from us and, again, the owner jerked him backwards. "I don't know what the great mystery is."

"I beg your pardon."

"There's no mystery. It's a well known fact that Mr. Field was a regular down in the Levee district on Wednesday nights. He was a frequent companion of Ernest Lehmann. They went down there almost every week for roulette, drink and who knows what else," he said with a wink.

I was stunned. "You know this to be a fact?"

"Of course, I never witnessed any of this. I have never been to the district myself."

"Of course."

"I do know Mr. Field was a regular in the Levee and that he was seen a lot with Mr. Lehmann. Now how he got himself shot at the Everleigh Club, I haven't a clue."

The little dog gave another hard jolt and this time the fat owner gave in and followed him along the sidewalk.

"Your name, sir," I called after him.

"Oh, no," he said over his shoulder. "I would never hear the end of it from Martha if my name were to get in the papers."

With that he was gone up the street with his little dog. Who he was I would never find out, but what he said was new information. Not only was it new, but it contrasted completely with what Ms. Penfield had told me about Marshall Field Junior's reputation. It would soon be time to find Mr. Ernest Lehmann and for possibly a trip to the Everleigh Club.

*****

I met with Gunter at five o'clock at Clancy's, a small pub that was located on LaSalle Street near Madison in the heart of the city's financial district. Clancy's had a good sized mahogany bar where the drinking patrons sat. Gunter was seated at one of the dozen tables which gave diners a little more room and privacy than the bar. At this early hour of the evening, Clancy's was starting to fill up. Business was good with Christmas coming. Small ornaments decorated the area just above the bar. When I found Gunter he was leaning back in his chair, smoking a thick cigar and was lost in some deep thought.

"Don't hurt yourself," I said as I walked up to him.

"What do you mean?" he said abruptly. He seemed agitated.

"With all of that deep thinking. I don't want you to hurt your brain."

At least this drew a short smile. "Have a seat, Patrick. Cigar?" he said, offering me one that looked similar to the one he was smoking.

Gunter knew I didn't smoke cigars or cigarettes, but it was always his manner to offer me one. I waved him off quickly and sat down. A sprightly, little waitress took my order for a beer.

"We need to talk," he said.

"I thought something was bothering you."

"I just don't know what to think.

"About what?"

He took a drag on the cigar and let three small rings of smoke out of his mouth. "While I was walking the IC station today, talking with anyone who would talk with me, I was thinking of the absurdity of this case."

"What case?" I asked, knowing full well the answer.

"This Isabella Rossini case," he said, a bit too loud. "The father thinks she was kidnapped and the department thinks she was taken by white slavers. You and I are given the task of finding one missing girl down in the Levee." Gunter was talking fast and when he did his German accent muddled a few of the words, but I got most of it.

"She is the niece of the Italian Ambassador."

"I never cared too much for the Italians."

"I see. I take it that things didn't go very well at the train station?"

"Not very well. I talked with ticket agents, track workers, porters, a few engineers and even an Italian or two and no one has ever seen Isabella Rossini."

"And this is why you are upset?"

He shook his head vigorously from side to side and took another puff of the cigar. The waitress brought my beer and I took a sip. "I just think that we are being used by the department and the city as a political move. We have an excellent arrest record for the violent crimes we've investigated and they put us on this babysitting adventure. They are wasting good manpower on this case."

I felt my face redden. "So you don't think that Miss Rossini deserves two detective's attention?"

He shrugged. "Not two detective's with our experience."

I took another sip of the beer. Gunter stared at me expecting a harsh response. "That may be," I said, "but I look at it differently. First of all, I was ordered to take the case. Secondly, that is someone's daughter who is missing. The first thing I thought of when I heard that Isabella had been taken was Bess. If someone had taken my little girl, I can't imagine the anguish I would feel. I can't imagine Isabella's father's worried mind right now. I feel for him. I worry for Isabella. It is my job to try and find her and I will. If you don't think this case is worthy of your full attention then I suggest you see the captain and ask to be reassigned."

Gunter's jaw dropped a bit, and I thought the cigar might hit the table. "I didn't mean that, Patrick. I just think that there are more serious crimes in the city, especially the Levee, that require our attention. I think detectives with less experience than ours could track this case."

He sat back again and crossed his arm over his chest. "That may be, but I have learned a few things. I had a discussion with Big Louie and he gave me a tutorial on the business of white slaving. It is not, as I thought, a business of moving prostitutes from one city to another for employ. Like Shipley said, it involves the kidnapping, drugging and abuse of young women for the purpose of turning them into trained courtesans. It is, as Louie suggests, a very big business. He claims there are some big players involved, but he gave me none of their names. He did tell me of a Mary Hastings, the operator of Sappho on Bed Bug Row, and Mike Hart, a partial owner of the Marlborough Hotel. These two are involved in the slaving."

I saw Gunter uncross his arms and lean forward to hear better. I had his attention. He was relaxing. "I went and saw Mary Hastings, but the conversation was vague. The only thing I learned, and she repeated it more than once, was that she had paid some protection money to "Big Jim". To me that's Big Jim Colosimo, Coughlin and Kenna's man, but to what extent the money was supposed to offer protection I don't know."

"Do you think that she was telling you that the protection money would cover anyone looking into this white slaving?"

"That's what I thought. Mary Hastings told me that they had done nothing wrong and had paid protection."

"So you think this white slave talk is a real situation?"

I realized for the first time how tired I was and that my friend, the head cold, was not abating and I needed some sleep. I took another sip of my beer. "I was skeptical at first, but when I talked to Louie, I could feel his passion as he described his disdain for the practice. It is real and I have two real names to look into."

"But you have already spoken to this Hastings woman."

"Spoken to her. What I have not done is to interview the women in her employ. That will take place when you and I make a second visit to the Sappho."

Gunter smiled, this time a toothy grin. "And what of this Mike Hart fellow?"

"He is on my list as well, but first there is a stockade that we need to visit and soon."

"A stockade? What in the Kaiser's name is a stockade?"

"According to Louie, these are places where the women are held and drugged. They are then subjected to repeated rapes from professional rapists. When the girls are broken and submit they are the sold to the brothels down in the Levee. It's all a very systematic process."

"So how do we find this stockade?"

"We go to Blue Island, a place called The Ranch. Louie gave me the name, and I asked Mary Hastings about it. She denied any knowledge of the place and as soon as I asked her, I realized my error. I am sure the place will be cleaned out in days if not already."

"Then we are off to Blue Island tomorrow."

"You'll arrange for our use of one of the motor vehicles?"

"I will."

"That is where we are headed."

I stopped talking and picked up the menu the waitress had left for us. Gunter always liked the beef stew. I liked pork better, but couldn't eat it in Gunter's presence due to his experience with slaughtering pigs in the Yards.

"You know," he said slowly, "I am sorry that I lost my temper and devalued the importance of this case. I didn't know what you had found, and I really thought we were over qualified to handle it."

"That's okay", I said. "I know you'll give the matter your full attention."

"And you will still come for dinner on Friday night. Margaret is looking forward to seeing you again."

Margaret was Gunter's beautiful wife. They had two children, a boy and a girl, who would be about the same age as my children had my children lived. They had invited me to dinner on several occasions and I had finally consented to going. "I will be there."

"Wonderful. Margaret is making a beef roast"

I smiled. When you lose your wife and children in a horrific fire it is sometimes hard to find yourself in the holiday spirit. Seeing their blackened, burnt bodies in the morgues that held them never left my mind. Tinsel and lights on a tree would never erase that memory or make me forget that they should still be here, but I wasn't going to be rude. What could one dinner with Margaret and Gunter's children do to me?"

*****

By the time we had finished our dinner and drank several beers it was after eight o'clock. We were able to flag down a cab on LaSalle, but when Gunter asked me if I wanted to be dropped at my apartment, I told him to have me dropped at The Queen's House. I knew that Eleanor was fine or I would have heard differently, but I wanted to see her. Her late night escapade from the night before made me want to ask her a few questions.

The Queen's House was busy as could be expected. Miss Keesher was playing the host in the lobby of the brothel, looking quite beautiful in a long, red gown. The smile she wore as she talked to her customers went away when she saw me. When I told her I was there to see Eleanor she told me it was okay to go on up to the third floor. She quickly turned and returned to the men in the lobby.

Eleanor was sitting up in her bed with a lamp on the table beside her lit up brightly. It looked like someone had helped her clean up. She wore a pink nightgown, with the long arms pulled down over the needle marks I'd seen earlier that morning. Her hair had been cleaned and tied back away from her face. The color in her face had returned. She looked healthy. The linens on the bed had been changed. There was a sweet, scented smell in the room.

"My, you look lovely," I said.

"A little different from this morning, I take it?"

"You know I was here?"

She smiled. "Kelsie told me you came right away and got the doctor for me. She also told me that you and the doctor calmed Miss Keesher down. If you hadn't, I might not be working here any longer."

I only nodded. She looked so pretty, so vulnerable. I was suddenly afraid that I might lose her and I wasn't sure I could deal with any more loss.

"Are you upset with me, Patrick?"

"Why, because you came down with a bout of influenza?"

She smiled again. "You don't have to lie, Patrick. Kelsie told me everything. She told me that you knew I had been with Gussie and that he had brought me home. She also told me that the doc figured out that I had used heroin and he had told you."

Again, I nodded sheepishly. "Am I allowed to ask why?"

"Why was I with Gussie or why did I use the heroin?"

"Both, I guess. You know I don't care for Gussie Black and you know that heroin is not like opium. You know it can be very dangerous."

For the first time since I'd known her, I saw a tear at the corner of Eleanor's eye and she reached for the handkerchief that was on her bedside table. She dabbed the tear away and looked to me. "I don't have a good answer for you. I don't suppose there is one. You tell me all the time to avoid Gussie. You tell me he's no good for me, but, you know, I like him. He makes me laugh a lot and he helps me relax. I know last night didn't work out very well, but I had such a good time."

"Including using the heroin and returning to your room in a near comatose state?"

"Don't be harsh, Patrick. I am not your wife and sometimes I wonder exactly what I am to you," she said, and I immediately felt like an ass. "I know Gussie would never do anything to hurt me. It was me who wanted to try the heroin. Gussie told me that it would take me to a greater level of awareness, far greater than opium. And, do you know, he was right. I never felt so good. I was gone from here, away from the Levee. I was no longer a prostitute. It was peaceful."

"You don't have to be a prostitute."

She laughed, quite loudly and put her hand over her mouth to smother the laughter. "How many drinks have you had this evening?"

"Just a few. I had dinner with Gunter."

"Well, than I guess I can't blame your coming speech on the alcohol you've had to drink."

"What coming speech?"

"The one you usually make when you are drunk and with me. The one where you tell me that you'll take me away from the Levee, we'll get married and we'll have children speech. At first, I believed it, but then I realized that you only spoke those words when you were drunk. I had never heard you say them when you were sober. I knew over time that you would never take me away and that we would never be married. I came to realize that I, nor anyone else, could ever replace your Francis.

It was when you were with me and when you were sober and talked of your loss that I knew nothing could replace her or your two children."

I wanted to say something. I wanted to respond, but the words were stuck in the back of my throat. What I wanted to say was that she had figured me out. "I know I may have said some things when I was drunk that I didn't exactly mean, but you must know that I care about you immensely."

She took my hand. "I know that, Patrick, but I also know that it's a little like a big brother caring about his little sister, except for the time you are in my bed."

I blushed. "I am your friend and I want you to be safe. I have warned you about Black and the trouble he will bring you. Miss Keesher tells me if she finds you are using drugs again she will put you out."

"You worry too much about Gussie. We are friends, nothing more. I will do my best to keep safe. It's tough down here. As for Miss Keesher, I will try and do my best to stay employed."

Always the stubborn one, Eleanor was going to continue to do things her way, no matter how many times I talked to her. "Will I be able to see you soon?"

She smiled once more and shrugged. "Why not? You are one of my closest friends, but you have to give me a day or so to get back on my feet."

"Of course," I said.

"Promise me one more thing, Patrick."

"If I can."

"I know you will see Gussie and talk to him, but that is the extent of it. I don't want you to hurt Gussie."

As my stomach tightened and the tart taste of bile hit my throat, I nodded. Eleanor knew of my hatred for the little faro dealer, and she knew I might hurt him. She had made it clear before and again tonight. If I ever hurt Gus Black our relationship would be over.

*****

Eugene and Lottie Huston, the king and queen of the cocaine dealers in Chicago, owned a three story brownstone on Twentieth Street about two blocks west of Dearborn. The elite drug dealers had an exquisite apartment on the first floor of the building. The second and third floors had been divided into two apartments each and these units were rented out. Gussie Black lived on the third floor of the Huston's building. I only found out what I know about the Hustons because of my investigation of Gussie. If Gussie had stuck with faro dealing, I could have possibly tolerated him. What Gussie did for the Hustons was deliver cocaine all over the city for them. Apparently, Gussie had no fear and would go anywhere in the city to deliver, even some of the toughest spots. This impressed the Hustons and they tried to help him out when they could. I didn't really know all that much about the Hustons, but I was told that Lottie was a college graduate, spoke five languages, composed music and painted. She didn't sound like many of the drug dealers I'd seen.

It was about nine-thirty when I got to the flat and it was a dark, cold, cloudless night. Winter looked like it had finally arrived and was ready to stay. Eleanor knew that I would speak to Gussie and she had warned me about getting tough with him, and I had promised that I wouldn't hurt him. I didn't think I'd have to. I was sure he'd get my message without me putting a hand on him.

I walked up the flights of stairs to the third floor and found Gussie's apartment. I pounded on the door, waited a minute and pounded again. I tried to listen closely to see if I could hear any movement in the flat, but the only sound I heard was when I tried to clear my stuffed nose. My discussion with Gussie was going to have to wait until another time, but I wasn't upset. I knew I'd get another chance.

As I was walking down the stairs, and having reached the first level, the door to the Huston's apartment opened and Eugene and Lottie stepped into the hall. Both of them wore heavy coats, gloves and hats. They looked to be going out on the town. Eugene was both a tall man and wide across the shoulders. Lottie was much smaller than Eugene and I could see under the hat that she was a very pretty woman.

"Can I help you, sir?" Eugene said. I didn't know if he liked the idea of a strange man lurking about in the hallway of his apartment building.

"I was trying to reach Gus Black."

"I see," Eugene said. "Mr. Black is out on business right now, and I wouldn't expect him to be back here before midnight."

"What business do you have with Gussie?" Lottie asked. She both looked and sounded more suspicious.

I reached into my pocket and removed my detective's badge and flashed it to the couple. "Official police business," I said.

"Gussie's not in any trouble, is he, Detective?" Eugene said.

"Not any trouble. I just wanted to ask him a few questions about some people that he might know."

"Do you think we might be able to help you?" Eugene asked. Lottie looked concerned.

"I don't think so."

"Can we tell Gussie who called for him?" Lottie asked.

"Yes. Please tell him that Detective Patrick Moses was here to see him. I will call again at another, more reasonable hour.

With that the Hustons left the building and got into a waiting cab that proceeded in the direction of the downtown area. I wasn't far from home and was tired with a clogged nose. I started walking in the direction of my apartment and my bed.

## Wednesday

The following day was bright and cold, like the day before. The temperature never got above twenty for the entire day. It would have seemed that this would have been a nice day to take an automobile ride into the country towns to the south of Chicago, but I was sadly mistaken. The automobile we were issued had seen better days. It was dented in several spots and it looked to me like the rear tires were crooked, at least compared to the front tires. I was glad that there was a roof on the vehicle; this kept some of the cold out. The crack in the windshield did not help with the cold or the noxious fumes that emanated from the vehicle's engine. To my luck, it seemed the fumes were blowing through the crack and right into my face. Thankfully, I had a plugged up nose, due to my lasting cold, or I might have perished from the smells. To top this all off, any type of level road, once we left Chicago proper, was non-existent. Once we were outside the city, we bounced, swerved, dipped and dove our way to Blue Island. The freezing temperatures also added some nice spots of ice which allowed us to experience some lengthy slides. Lastly, the car's engine seemed to roar with noise, the sound of a wounded bear.

I knew two things about Blue Island. It was the home of some of the largest brick makers in the Midwest and there was a store there called the Lieutenant's Store on Central Street. This shop was started by a Civil War veteran who had only reached the rank of lieutenant. He couldn't figure why he would call the store a general store. There were two other interesting things about the store. The owner, Chester Gallanty, knew everything about Blue Island, so he could help us find The Ranch, and he also sold gasoline which would help us get home, if we survived the initial trip.

Chester Gallanty looked to be close to sixty-five or seventy when we found him working behind the counter of his store. There were more wrinkles on his face then you could count and a nasty scar across the bridge of his nose. His gray hair, which was shoulder length, hung loosely across his back. When he smiled, his mouth showed that he was clearly missing most of his teeth.

"I was with General Lee right up until the end at Appomattox," he said, a Southern accent still present. "Now that was a sad day. We just never had the men or the ammunition. It was never really a very fair fight."

"How did you end up here?" I asked. Gunter had very little knowledge of the War Between the States.

"I went back to Virginia, but there was nothing there. With Reconstruction and everything, I knew I had to come north. I asked my daddy to stake me a claim and he did. I came up north to Illinois and started this store."

The store looked like it had a little bit of everything and we didn't notice any other stores in the area. "It looks like you've done pretty well for yourself."

He smiled, showing his wide gaps. "I have done pretty well," he said. "Now, what can I do for you two gentlemen?"

"We are looking for a resort called The Ranch."

He got a quizzical look on his face. "The Ranch, a resort?"

"You know where The Ranch is?"

"I know where The Ranch is, but it ain't any kind of resort."

Gunter and I looked at each other. "What can you tell me about it?" I asked.

"As far as I know, it's a home for orphaned girls. I've never been up there, you here, but that's what that owner told me."

"Do you know the owner's name?"

"Sure, good lookin fella, walks with a bad limp. Goes by the name of Mike James. He's been in here a few times. Doesn't talk much."

"How do you get there from here?"

"Well, that's easy. Just continue right up Central until you come to the fork in the road. Veer left and follow it about four miles and you'll run right into it on the left side of the road."

"What do you think?" I asked Gunter when we were back in the automobile.

"An owner named Mike, saying it's a home for orphaned girls? There's something strange going on up at this place."

We did as Gallanty told us and were soon looking at an old farmhouse, two stories tall and badly in need of a lot of repairs. The house had once been a light blue, but badly needed paint, some windows were broken and there was a hole in the roof. The road that led up to the house was unpaved, and it was hard to tell if any traffic had been this way in a while. The trees and bushes that kept the house partially hidden from the main road were leafless. As we stepped outside of the auto and climbed the stairs to the front porch it felt colder here than it had in Chicago. It also felt very lonely.

"This Goddamn place looks deserted," Gunter said.

"It does," I said taking a step towards the front door. I could see that it was open by a couple of inches. I drew my revolver and poked the door open with it. I could tell that every window in the place had an inside covering over them. There was very little light in the house. I stepped inside and Gunter followed after drawing his weapon.

"Doesn't look like much of a resort," he said.

"Doesn't look like much of anything."

The first to thing to hit us was the smell in the house, old, lingering, maybe from death. The first floor had a main sitting room that had some old furniture, nothing you would want in your house, and no decorations of any type on the walls. The furniture was an old settee and two old, cloth stuffed chairs. None of the pieces matched. Across from that room, there was a small dining area and here there was a wooden table and four chairs. Again, nothing adorned the walls. Off the dining area, was a kitchen, and there were some dirty dishes, mostly plates and cups, piled high on a table by a small sink. When I stepped into the kitchen, I saw two mice scurry behind a cluttered cabinet. On the opposite side of the kitchen was a staircase that led to the second floor.

"The bedrooms must be up there," Gunter said.

"Nobody here, but the mice," I said, starting up the stairs. At the top of the stairs, through the dim light, we could make out one door straight ahead of us and two on both the left and right, equally spaced and all closed. Still we were the only ones making any sounds in the house.

I walked to the first door on my left and could see that it was closed and latched with a dead bolt lock that could only be opened from the outside. Moving my gun to my left hand, I drew back the bolt and pushed the door open. There was still no light and there was hardly any sound. What the room had was smell. It smelled like piss, vomit, excrement and death all mixed together. The little bit of light there was showed a heap of piled blankets that lay on the bed. I moved closer, gun extended in front of me, and I saw what looked like a human female head and then a face. There was a face, but as I got used to the light I could see that it was the face of a ghost. I had Gunter tear down the shade that was covering the window in the room as I grabbed the wrist of the woman in the bed. I could feel no pulse and when the light flooded into the room I could see that the woman, now just a young girl, was dead.

"Jesus Christ," Gunter said. "She looks like she might only be fourteen or fifteen."

I let go of the girl's arm and it dropped onto the bed and then slipped off the side, hanging limply. "I hope she died peacefully because I don't think the time she spent in this room was all that enjoyable."

"Should we check out the other rooms or do you want to get back to town and get the local police involved?"

I stared hard at Gunter. "Is this a little worse than the pigs you slaughtered at the Yards?"

Gunter knew I was upset, but only responded with a curt nod. We left the first room and made it down the hall to the second room, also locked with a dead bolt. Again, I pulled the bolt aside and pushed the door wide open with a loud bang.

"Who's there?" a young girl in the bed said as she sat up quickly.

I held my gun trained on her while Gunter pulled down a shade on the lone window in this room. The smell was not as intense in this room and it consisted mostly of a stale body odor. The light reflected on the bed and showed another young girl, maybe fifteen or sixteen, very thin with dark brown hair and squinting brown eyes that darted from Gunter to me and back again. She looked extremely frightened.

I put my gun in its holster and pulled out my badge to show to the girl. "We are Chicago Police Detectives, "I said.

"You're with the police?"

"Yes, from Chicago."

With this, the young woman began to sob. I moved closer to her and could see she was only dressed in a filthy, white sleeping gown. On one arm the gown rode up and I could see the needle tracks clearly. As I got closer to her, she backed away from me.

"It's okay," I said. "We're here to help you."

She stopped crying and looked at me for a second. Gunter still stood by the window. "You are really here to help us?"

"As much as we can. What happened here?"

"Mike won't know that I told you this?"

"Mike, the owner? He'll never find out."

She looked relieved. "Most of the girls here that I could talk to were taken from the Illinois Central station and driven here. We were promised that we would be set up and given a job. Instead they took our clothes from us, locked us in these rooms, drugged us and raped us. After a while some of the girls were taken away from here. I think they were taken into Chicago." She said this all quickly through tears and sobs.

"You could communicate with the other girls?"

She nodded slowly. "We could talk through the walls when Mike and the other man left the house. It was the only way we could communicate. Can you tell me how Tricia is?"

"Who is Tricia?" I asked.

"She was in the room over here." She pointed in the direction of the room with the dead girl. "I haven't heard her say much of anything the past two days."

I avoided her question about her friend. "When was the last time anyone was here to see you girls?"

"It's been a couple of days, maybe two or three days ago. They took two girls away then. I thought Tricia and I would go next. How's Tricia?"

"Who's next door on the other side?" I asked.

"Roberta. I think she's a foreigner. She's got a thick accent and doesn't like to talk much. You're not telling me about Tricia. She's not okay, is she?"

"No," I said. "I'm sorry. She's not okay. She didn't make it."

A grim look crossed her face.

"Why didn't you girls try and get out of here when the men left the house. There had to be something that you could do."

She looked at me for a second, puzzled, and then raised the blanket that was covering her legs. On her left leg was a manacle and attached to this was a chain that led to the bed post and a second manacle. I could see both were soundly in place.

"We'll get you out of there in a minute. We just want to go check on Roberta."

She looked startled. "You won't leave me alone in this house?"

I took her hand. It was cold and had a strange feeling to it. "We won't leave you alone. We're just going next door to check on Roberta." She said nothing, only nodding.

Gunter and I moved to the room at the end of the hall. As with the other two rooms, we pulled the latch aside and were quickly inside the room. Gunter pulled the shade off the window in this room, throwing light on the bundle on the bed. There was a dark haired girl lying on the bed. I thought for a moment that she was dead, too, but when I took her wrist, I could detect a pulse. I tried to wake her, but couldn't. I also moved the blankets away from her legs and saw the now similar looking manacles.

"This one's alive," I said. "We have to get her some help."

"Why don't we check the other two rooms and then I'll drive back into town for help, the sheriff and something to cut these women free," Gunter said. I could tell he was clearly stunned by what we had discovered and was probably wishing he was back in the Yards.

We left Roberta and checked the other two rooms on the floor. Both of these rooms proved to be empty, but each had loose manacles and night gowns tossed on the floor. It looked as if the last occupants had been moved out. I told Gunter to head into town for help, and I would keep the girl in the room and Roberta company.

I heard Gunter start up the automobile and hoped he wouldn't be gone too long. Roberta needed immediate help and, to be honest about it, I didn't want to be alone in that house in case the owners returned. The girl on the bed had sat up. Although I could tell she wasn't in very good shape herself, she looked to be a very pretty girl.

"What's your name?" I asked.

"Sally. Sally Crowe."

"How old are you?"

"Sixteen. I was born and raised in Indianapolis, but I didn't like it much there. I thought if I came to Chicago, I might find some fun and adventure. This turned out to be some fun."

"Do you mind telling me what happened?"

A sad look covered her face and I thought she might cry again. I wasn't trying to upset her, but maybe any discussion of her ordeal would do just that. "I was at the Illinois Central station; I'd just gotten off my train, and was looking for some way to get into the heart of the city. That was when Mike approached me and told me about a job he might have for me."

"Tell me about Mike."

"He said his name was Mike James. He was tall and very good looking, but he walked with a bad limp. He had such a nice smile and was so handsome. It was hard not to be attracted to him. He was so nice."

"He offered you a job?"

"It was to be a domestic job, helping a wealthy woman with her two small children. Mike claimed I would live in a very nice house with the family."

"I take it you never saw any of this family?"

She smiled a bit. "He drove me into Chicago. He had a very nice automobile. He showed me a number of the sites, the impressive tall buildings and Marshall Field's store. It was really very nice. Then we went to dinner. I remember he ordered me a steak and allowed me to have a glass of wine. That's really about all I remember. He told me we were going to go dancing, but I don't remember that. When I woke up the next morning, I was here." I saw her chest rise suddenly and fall. She let out one sigh and then tears rolled from her eyes.

I reached into my suit for a handkerchief and gave it to her. She wiped away the tears and continued. "They took away all my clothes and I was only given this nightgown. Every day Mike and this other man would check on me. They shot something in my arm with a needle and then removed my nightgown. That other man, the big one, would have his way with me. I don't think he could talk. He could understand what Mike said to him, but I never heard him mutter a word, much less a grunt. While this was going on, Mike would only watch. The only thing I hoped for was that I would pass out, but that didn't always happen. When the big man was done they would leave the room and I would cry myself to sleep."

"Did they feed you?"

"Oh, we were fed, but the food wasn't very good, but you had to eat it. That was all there was."

I nodded. My stomach felt tight. "What did they ever tell you?"

"Nothing much. They told us this was the best thing for us. We would soon be going on to our jobs, important jobs. They also told us that if we ever said anything to anyone about how we had been treated we would be killed. Did they kill Tricia?"

"I don't know exactly what happened with her," I said sadly.

"She had more fight in her than I did. When they went in there she was always screaming and shouting. I never had that kind of fight. I didn't think there was much I could do."

It appeared to me that Tricia had resisted her attackers and maybe they had given her too much of whatever drug they were administering. Maybe her captors had given up on her. "Did you ever see any of the other girls?"

She shook her head from side to side. "No and I could only talk to Tricia and Roberta. There were other girls. I heard them screaming, but I never talked with them."

So much for her seeing Isabella Rossini. Had Isabella been one of the other girls in the rooms across the hall, the empty rooms? "How long do you think you've been here?"

She wiped away more tears. "I'd say three weeks, maybe a little more. I tried to keep track, but it was tough. I kept losing track."

I took her hand. It still had a cold, clammy feeling to it. "It's okay now. We'll get you to a doctor and contact your family."

This soothing talk I gave really caused the tears to flow. "It's just my mother and my little brother. I just didn't get along with my mother. I wanted something more. Now I want to see them both more than ever, but promise me you won't tell them what happened. My mother can never know what happened to me."

It pained me to do what I did, but I told her we wouldn't

say anything to her mother. This was a lie. Sally was a minor who had been kidnapped, drugged and raped. I couldn't see that it was possible, in any fashion, to keep this from her mother. It also appeared that Sally was a runaway, trying to find a better life. This had not turned out the way she had wanted. I had lied to her and told her that we wouldn't tell her mother. A minor promise I couldn't keep. What I could do was track down her kidnappers, Mike James and the "big man" with no name. I made a promise to myself, and a silent promise to Sally, that I would put both of these men behind bars or see them dead.

The wait for Gunter to return seemed like an eternity. I sat on the edge of the grimy bed, amidst the dirty blankets and held Sally's hand. She would be somewhere between rambling, incoherent phrases and crying. She talked about Christmas, it had to be soon, and wouldn't Santa be coming? She wanted to know if we were sure that we couldn't do anything for Tricia. Why, she asked, had I lied to her? In the middle of one of her crying stages, she blurted out that her mother was a "fucking whore." Physically. I was certain, with proper medical attention that Sally would survive. Mentally, I was well aware, that she was possibly damaged beyond any hope of recovery.

It was well over an hour before Gunter returned to the farmhouse. I heard the clatter of the automobile while it was still a quarter of a mile away. Shortly, following his arrival, came two horse drawn ambulances and one horse drawn hearse. Following the three coaches came the sheriff, a large fat man, who had a belly that hung well over his belt. He had one eye that crossed terribly, and a huge beard complete with traces of his last few meals. While Gunter and I helped the ambulance and hearse drivers load the patients and deceased into the vehicles, this law officer strutted about like some kind of rooster, mumbling under his breath. It was only when the coaches were fully loaded and on their way back to Blue Island did the sheriff address Gunter and me.

"How'd you boys know what was going on up at this here house?" he said. I noticed now that he was chewing tobacco and he let fly with a large quantity of brown spit.

"We got a tip from someone up near Chicago," I said.

"Seems a little odd that someone in Chicaga would know anything about this kind of set up way out here in the country."

I saw Gunter's eyes narrow and I was certain he might try and strangle the sheriff. "Mr. Sheriff," Gunter said, holding back his temper. "What seems odd to me is that this was occurring within a couple of miles of your own town and you knew nothing about this." As I mentioned earlier, when Gunter got upset his German accent became more pronounced.

"You're not from around here, are you boy?" the sheriff said, spitting a wad of brown juice too close to my shoes for me. I don't know if it was the term "boy" or spitting so close to us that got Gunter, but he soon hand his ape like hands on the sheriff's throat, and there was little time for me to hesitate. I yelled at Gunter to stop, tried pulling him off the sheriff, who had now been driven to the frozen ground, and finally settled on cuffing Gunter behind the ear with my revolver. Gunter grabbed the side of his head and rolled off the sheriff. I was almost too late. The fat ass sheriff was turning blue, I thought from the throttling Gunter had given him, but then I realized he had swallowed his tobacco wad. I did what I thought best and stomped viciously on the sheriff's chest. The tobacco wad was forced out of his throat and flew out of his mouth, straight up in the air, only to land on his nose and splatter across his face. Gunter was back on his feet.

"Why did you hit me, Patrick?"

"You were going to kill this son of a bitch."

"That was the idea."

The sheriff was still lying in the dirt, trying to catch his breath, when Gunter and I got back into the automobile and started our return trip to Chicago. It was late in the afternoon and had been a long day. Mike James, I had thought, was Mike

Hart, but he would have to wait until tomorrow. We knew he owned part of the Marlborough; we knew he had to show up there eventually. We'd been driving in the clattering vehicle for over an hour, the sun was down now, and we realized only one of the car's front lights worked.

"I owe you an apology, Patrick," Gunter said.

"I'm the one that hit you with my gun."

"It's not that," he said, "but my head still throbs."

"You don't owe me anything."

"I do. I never believed this white slave nonsense. After roaming around that train terminal all day and finding nothing and even after hearing what Big Louie had told you, I doubted the story. The long drive we made today, I thought was a waste of time. When I saw those girls, the way they were locked in those disgusting rooms, worse than we treat jailed prisoners, I felt sick. Even the pigs in the Yards were treated with more dignity than those girls. Who does something like that to human beings? I thought Dr. Kluge was an animal. What other kinds of human animals do we exist with?"

I said nothing. I had no answer for Gunter, and I wasn't sure he wanted one. The light of the day was fading as we bounced along, but it was good enough. The day had been a tough one and as it ended for Gunter, there were tears of anger brimming in his eyes.

*****

After the long day and the bitter cold, once we had returned the automobile to the precinct, we both went our separate ways. Gunter went home to his family. I retreated to a local eatery for something to eat and, more importantly, something strong to drink. It was good to get out of the cold finally; the eatery was warm and well lit. The place had the expected holiday decorations up and the clientele seemed in a boisterous pre-Christmas spirit. I was as far from that feeling as possible. I had no appetite even though the mutton stew tasted very good. The whiskey burned its way down my wind damaged throat, but failed to warm me. The cold I had been hanging onto was part of the reason for my mood, but as the night wore on the memories of what we had seen at The Ranch gnawed at me. Those were people out there, those young women who had been shackled to those beds. They weren't animals. Who takes a young girl captive, drugs her and then rapes her. Gunter had made a reference to Kluge, but he was right. This was almost worse. I only ate a few bites of the stew and after my second whiskey failed to take me out of my gloom, I paid my check and headed for my flat.

There was nothing I wanted more now than my apartment and the warmth of the blankets on my bed. If I could just sleep peacefully, this one night, tomorrow would start out better than today had ended. Tomorrow, Gunter and I vowed to track down Mike Hart and to look into the girls who spent their lives with Mary Hastings at Sappho. Tomorrow promised to bring answers. When I reached the door or my apartment, I immediately noticed something was amiss. Around the doorknob was tied a piece of red cloth with hints of gold running through it. I undid the cloth and stepped into my apartment where the light was better.

The piece of cloth turned out to be a scarf. There were gold lines and small stars woven within the cloth. In the center was a diamond and within the center of it were two initials, MS. Most of the prostitutes that Dr. Simon Kluge had murdered were from the lesser class, the women of Bed Bug Row or even less. I had seen this scarf before, but it had been blue, but it was an exact replica aside from the color. The scarf had been worn by Maria Scott, the last victim of Kluge, who had worked at Madam Vic Shaw's place on Dearborn. I had seen the blue version of the scarf taken off Maria Scott by the coroner at the county morgue. That scarf had been torn in places by the knife wielding Kluge, but had hung on around Maria's neck. What bothered me know was how this red copy had shown up on my doorknob and why? There was one more question. Who had put it there?"

I sat on the edge of my bed still holding the scarf. I had only removed my hat. The scarf was made from some cheap material; it was certainly nothing of value. Did that matter, I thought? Was someone trying to pull a prank on me? I was in no mood for humorous gags. I stood and removed my coat, still holding onto the scarf. I sat again and untied and slipped off my shoes. I lay down on the bed still in my clothes and looked at the scarf. What message had been delivered to me? I closed my eyes, and soon, I was asleep.

I didn't dream that night of Kluge, dead prostitutes or of the evil we had seen at The Ranch. What I dreamed of was my father or, in particular, how I figured out that Jacob Fine was my father. It had not been that hard to do. For as long as I can remember, and I'm sure before my recall, Jacob Fine would make frequent visits to Holy Trinity. It was without fail that after these visits I always presented with some sort of a gift. I can remember getting new shoes, a coat, a hat that didn't fit me, and I didn't like, candy and books. These gifts that were given to me specifically made me a bit of an outcast with the other members of the orphanage and caused a number of fights. This led me to learn to box and by the time I was twelve, everyone, including those older than me, kept their distance.

I also noticed than when the orphanage needed something repaired my father would make a visit, inspect the damaged or used up item, and replace it. If for some reason there was ever a shortage of food, my father would have cart loads delivered to the door. No child at the orphanage ever had a Christmas where they didn't have a gift. I begin to act a little like a trained animal. When I saw my father appear I expected to receive a gift. As I got a bit older, I began to question this. Why had this man, whenever he showed up, had a gift for me?

"How come when Mr. Fine comes to the orphanage, I

always get some kind of a gift?" I asked Father Luigi, the day after I had received a fine cotton shirt.

The fat, Italian priest rubbed his chin. "Mr. Fine seems to have taken a special liking to you?"

"If he likes me so much, how come he never speaks to me?"

Now Luigi gave me a stare that showed that I had crossed a line, the line that included questions you weren't supposed to ask. "Mr. Fine is a busy man. Be grateful, Patrick, that someone has noticed you and had taken an interest in your well being. Is that not enough?"

"Yes, Father," I said, but I had more questions. I lived at Holy Trinity my whole life until I joined the police force. In all those years, Jacob Fine would visit and I would get gifts. The orphanage always had a benefactor for things that needed repair or to help out when there was a shortage of food. In all those years, I had also seen a number of kids, too many to count, that had been taken from Holy Trinity in the form of adoption. I was never one of those children.

I was in my late teens when I asked that question. "Father Luigi, why do you think that I have never been adopted?"

Again, there was that crossing the line look. "People have inquired about you?" he said. This was not a lie, I would learn. People would inquire and they would be told that I was not eligible to be adopted. I was a ward of Holy Trinity. I was being watched for someone.

On my twentieth birthday we had what amounted to a rather large celebration at the orphanage. It was the one time I can remember that all of the priests and most of the sisters had more than a little wine to drink. It was a joyous affair with singing and jokes all night long. Toward the end of the evening I sauntered over to a drunken Luigi. He had a broad smile on his face. I often wondered what he was thinking.

I had snuck a few glasses of wine and I had a warm glow about me as I approached my old friend. His smile got broader as he saw me approaching. "Ah, Patrick, have you had a good birthday?"

"It has been one of the best that I can remember. Thank you

very much."

"And do you like your new suit of clothes?"

The wool suit I was presented with that day was to ensure that I would look my best as I ventured out into the world. "I like it very much," I said. "What I wanted to know was if I could ask you a question?"

There was no crossing the line look this time. Luigi was probably too drunk for that. "You may always ask me a question," he said.

"Is Jacob Fine my father?" I said.

Now came a look, but it wasn't a stern one. He contemplated me sadly. For some reason, I thought I might have hurt him. He took a drink from the glass of wine and licked his lips. He let out a loud belch. "What do you think, Patrick?"

To this day, that was as much affirmation that I ever got from Luigi regarding my father's identity. I never pressed the issue, but after that day, I spoke to Jacob Fine whenever I saw him. This continued when I got on the police force, first as a patrolman and then a detective. I always addressed him as Mr. Fine and he addressed me as Patrick. That was it, nothing more. But it was on that day, my twentieth birthday, when I found out who my father was.

When I awoke, there was enough light in the room to tell me that I had slept for a while. The Maria Scott scarf was gnarled between my fingers as if I wrestled with it all night long. The light revealed to me that it was just before eight o'clock. I was to meet with Gunter at the Marlborough Hotel at ten to try and find the Hart's. I was wide awake with a couple of hours before I had to be anywhere. This would give me ample time to get over to the Field residence to interview the butler, Mr. Lowe. The other nagging problems of my life, the scarred relationship with my father, and now the Maria Scott scarf, would have to wait.

## Thursday

After my first trip to the Field mansion and my interview with Emily Penfield, I became aware that everything Ms. Penfield told me I could have learned from reading the *Tribune* editions that covered the story. What I hoped to find, maybe because I'd be talking to a man, was a little something more about the dead Mr. Field. Surely a man would have a better insight of another man, and might not be shy about relaying some of those feelings. I was hoping that this was the case when I interviewed Robert Lowe, the butler.

Robert Lowe was a man in his mid-fifties, tall and slender with a long, pointy nose and a continuously bobbing Adam's apple. The thin hair that he had on his head was combed straight back. His eyes were a cloudy blue and they helped give Lowe the indifferent, uninterested look that he had on his face.

"I have been over this so many times with the police that I really think that this is a tremendous waste of time for everyone involved. Not only that, but all of this dredging about just doesn't give Mr. Field any opportunity to rest in peace. I know Marshall Field Senior ordered this investigation and wants us to cooperate, but it just seems such a waste. I did tell everything to the police." Lowe delivered this short lecture to me shortly after having me take a seat at a table in the kitchen and preparing me a cup of tea.

"I am sorry for the inconvenience," I said, "but if you can recall, sir, I was not one of the policemen that you told the story to. I would like to hear it for myself."

His response was an exasperated sigh. "I'm only telling this story again because Mr. Field ordered us to."

There was no one else in the kitchen, but Lowe and myself. There was no one else to approve or disapprove of him telling the story again. I didn't care what his reason was. I wanted the story.

"What happened the night of the shooting?" I asked.

He reflected for a moment, perhaps gathering his thoughts. "It was just after five o'clock on the night Mr. Field shot himself. There was no one in the house besides Mr. Field, Ms. Penfield and myself. I remembered thinking how quiet the house was. Suddenly, I heard a gunshot and then I heard Mr. Field cry out for help."

"How did you know it was a gunshot?"

"Detective Moses, when you spend five years in the army, I think you can distinguish a gunshot."

I had no response to that. "What did you do?"

"Naturally, I ran to Mr. Field's room and found him slumped on the floor. He told me he had accidentally shot himself. I helped him up into the chair he had been sitting in just as Ms. Penfield entered the room. He was in great pain."

"Where was the gun?"

"The gun," he said. "The gun, I believe, I think that Mr. Field was still holding it."

"After shooting himself with it?"

"As far as I can recall, sir."

"What about blood? Did you see any?"

He pondered this a second. "Not right away, but Ms. Penfield was there by now so I went to make some calls. I called the family physician, Dr. Frank Billings, and then I called Henry Dibble, Mr. Field's brother in law. Dr. Billings was out of town, hunting near Downers Grove. Mr. Dibble told me to call some other doctors, and I got a hold of Dr. Arthur Bevan and Dr. Robert Harry. Both of these doctors told me they would be right over."

"As you waited for Mr. Dibble and the doctors to arrive, what did you do?"

"I went over to where Ms. Penfield and Mr. Field were to see if I could do anything to assist them."

"Was there any blood then?"

"What? I'm sure there was some blood on the shirt that he wore. I don't recall."

"Does that strike you as odd that a severe hand gun injury would cause so little blood?"

"I guess I never thought that much about it."

"I see. What about the gun?"

"Yes. That I do recall. When I returned to him the gun was clearly resting on the table where Mr. Field had been cleaning it."

"So there's no real amount of blood to be noticed and the gun is on the table. What did you do at this point?

"Like I said. Ms. Penfield and I were simply trying to make Mr. Field as comfortable as possible. We talked to him, Ms. Penfield held his hand, and it was a constant concern to keep him still."

"And when Mr. Dibble and the doctors finally showed up?"

"There was little for us to do at that point," he said quickly. "The doctors took over examining Mr. Field on his bed and they quickly ascertained that he would need immediate surgery. They gave Mr. Dibble the task of calling Mercy Hospital to explain that Mr. Field would be in soon for an emergency operation. One of the doctors, I can't recall which one, called a private ambulance service to come and transport Mr. Field to Mercy. It wasn't long before the ambulance came and they were all off to the hospital."

"I believe Mrs. Field arrived at home during this wait?"

"She did. She arrived home and immediately became very distraught at the situation. Ms. Penfield took charge of the three children so Mrs. Field could accompany her husband to the hospital."

"At that point you became like everyone else in the city?"

"How's that?"

"You had to rely on what was said in the papers about Mr. Field to know what his latest condition was."

"That is true. Mrs. Field stayed with Marshall until his death. When his father and mother arrived from New York they also stayed at or near the hospital. It wasn't like we had any immediate access to information."

"I see," I said slowly. "How long have you been in the Field's employ?"

"Nine years this past June."

"You've gotten to know Mr. Field fairly well?"

He considered this. "I would say so?"

"I have heard it said that Mr. Field was a wonderful man, a good man to work for, a good husband and a wonderful father."

"All of those things are true to the best of my knowledge."

"But what are some of the things that most people wouldn't know about Mr. Field?"

He tilted his head to one side, the Adam's apple's bouncing picking up some pace. "I'm not sure I understand you."

"Every man has them, Mr. Lowe. They are called vices. Some of us like to drink a little too much, some like to be in the arms of a different woman and others smoke filthy, nasty cigars. I am sure that Mr. Field had a vice or two, and I'd like to find out what they were. Since you were in his employ for so long, and claim to know him fairly well, you could save me a lot of time by telling me what one of his vices was."

His head was now straight and he was looking at me directly. "Like a lot of men, Mr. Field liked to have a drink, but I can honestly say that I never saw him get out of hand."

"That's good to know. Was that his only vice?"

His eyes were lowered to the floor and he spoke quietly. "Occasionally, he liked to play roulette. He would boast to me when he won, but, of course, I never heard when he lost. He didn't speak about this frequently, but we talked about it on several occasions."

I nodded slowly. "And where did Mr. Field go to play roulette?"

I saw the Adam's apple move up and down as Lowe swallowed hard. "Mr. Field liked to play roulette in the Levee. In most cases, I understood that he went to the Everleigh Club."

\*\*\*\*\*

With the new information I'd received from Robert Lowe swimming in my head, I felt myself suddenly energized. From the start with Emily Penfield, to the dog walker on the street, and Lowe, the information I was gathering on Marshall Field, Jr. looked to be saying that something more mysterious than an accidental shooting had occurred. I thought it was time to track down Ernest Lehmann and find out exactly what he knew about Field and his supposed trips to the Levee and the Everleigh Club. I was excited by these thoughts and wanted to move forward as quickly as I could, but my excitement was derailed by my next thought. This wasn't my job. My job, and the case I'd been assigned, was to find Isabella Rossini. So, first things first, as they say. I was off to the Marlborough Hotel to meet up with Gunter and try and see if we could track down Mike Hart and find Isabella.

I had seen the Marlborough Hotel on numerous occasions. It sat on Twenty Second Street between Wabash and State Street. On the opposite side of the street, located on the corner at Wabash was Freiberg's Dance Hall, operated by Solly Freidman and Jacob Fine, my father. From this domain, Solly and my father controlled all of the liquor sales in the Levee. This, of course, meant that if you operated in the Levee and wanted booze you had to buy it from Solly and father. They got their cut of the sales along with Bathhouse John Coughlin and Hinky Dink Kenna. As I said earlier, if you wanted to operate in the Levee, Coughlin and Kenna always got their cut.

The Marlborough wasn't a bad looking place to look at. It was a concrete, five story structure that served two types of clientele. The first floor contained the lobby, bar, dance floor and a reception room. The second floor contained eight luxury suites that were rented out monthly. This was where Mike and Mollie Hart maintained a residence. The top three floors were a little less luxuriant. These three floors provided small, but clean rooms for local prostitutes, that weren't housed at a brothel, to take their customers. There was a separate elevator in the back of the hotel that only serviced these floors. The way I understood it, no one on floors one and two ever saw the folks who frequented and played on the three floors above them.

As soon as I came east of Dearborn on Twenty-Second I could tell something was wrong. There was a large crowd milling about in front of the Marlborough. Amongst this crowd were a large number of police officers, their blue uniform coats easily identifying them. It could be an arrest, I thought, but there were too many people. I picked up my pace as a light snow began to fall. I was within a hundred feet of the crowd when I saw Gunter waving to me. I walked over to him.

"We're too late," he said.

"Too late for what?"

"The Harts. They must have had another appointment."

"What the hell are you talking about, Gunter?"

He roughly took my arm and guided me toward the hotel's entrance. "Come on. I'll show you."

We nudged through the crowd, showing our badges where necessary although many of the policemen knew us. The inside lobby was glowing with bright lights and holiday decorations. No one present was smiling, and I knew something had happened to dampen the holiday spirit. Trailing Gunter, I watched as he bounded up the two flights of stairs to the second floor; it was always a challenge for me, with my short legs, to keep up with the big German. On the second floor there was another crowd, all talking at the end of a long corridor. This crowd was made up of the police, some ambulance personnel, and a completely scared looking man in a suit.

When we got to the crowd I recognized two detectives, both in plain clothes, Sam Walker and Horace Langley. They were talking to the scared looking suit wearer. "Moses, do you have something to do with this case?" Walker said. He was a big, tough looking guy who needed to shave twice a day. We had come onto the force at the same time and our careers had paralleled. I never thought it was a competition, but I knew Sam Walker did.

"We're just here to talk to the Harts on another matter," I said rather dumbly.

"He wants to talk to the Harts," Walker said to Horace Langley, an ugly son of a bitch with a horse face, who had a reputation for beating witnesses.

"You don't say, Sammy," Horace said. "Let him talk to them."

The two cops and the suit man got out of the way and we were let into the Hart's suite. It didn't take long to see whatever Mike Hart was up to he had been making real money. The suite was decorated in a lavish, expensive fashion. I didn't think I could afford a furnishing or decoration in the main room.

"The bedroom is over here," Gunter said.

I followed him into the room where he'd already been once this morning. Again, this room was decorated well enough to suit a king. There was really nothing out of place until you looked at the bed. There was a man and a woman, both in bed clothes, both had their hands and feet bound and mouths gagged. They were lying next to each other motionless. It might have been a serene setting without the bonds, gags and blood and brain matter splattered behind their heads on the headboard. I stepped closer and saw that each had a large caliber bullet hole in the center of their foreheads.

"Somebody wanted to meet with them much quicker than we did," Gunter said.

"I guess he didn't like what he heard."

"Do you think this has much to with The Ranch?"

I was staring at the Harts. Mike Hart had been a good looking man. His wife Mollie, bullet hole excluded, had a beautiful face. They would have been a very attractive couple. They were still attractive, but I knew them only as white slavers. I didn't feel all that badly about their demise, but wished we'd been able to talk with them.

"Patrick, what do you think?"

"Sorry," I said. "I was thinking and, yes, I think someone heard about us finding out about The Ranch and blamed Mike Hart. This was his punishment."

"It could have been something else."

"No. This is too coincidental."

We left the room and stepped out towards the crowded hallway. It looked like the ambulance people were getting ready to take the bodies away. Walker and Langley were still talking to the man in the suit, but they had moved to the side of the hall.

"Have a nice chat?" Walker said and Langley laughed.

"Any idea what happened here, Sam?" I asked.

"Yeah. Somebody gave Mr. and Mrs. Hart a special wake up call," Sam said, smiling widely.

I didn't have time to respond before I saw Gunter's right fist fly past my face and catch the still smiling Sam Walker flush on the chin. Sam flew backwards and his head smacked the wall and then slid down it until he was in a sitting position. "You want some too, funny boy?" Gunter said to Langley. Horace only shook his head as the suit wearing man looked like he might faint.

First, I looked to Gunter, but he just shrugged. Then I knelt down by Sam who was recovering from the punch. I lifted his chin up by my index finger so he was looking directly at me. "Sam, sorry for my partner's behavior, but this has been a tough couple of days. We are looking for a young girl and we think the Hart's may have known where she might have been taken. We wanted to talk with them, but someone beat us to them. Any idea what happened here?"

Walker's eyes were becoming focused. There was a nice bruise forming on his left jaw. "The manager here, Mr. Simms," Walker said pointing to the man in the suit, "always wakes the Harts up by phone. When there was no answer after repeated tries he became worried and visited their suite. This was what he found." Blood was trickling out of the corner of Sam's mouth.

"You see," I said, letting go off his chin and watching it drop. "That wasn't so hard, was it?"

Sam mumbled something, but I didn't understand it. Maybe he hadn't recovered as much as I thought. I turned and headed for the stairs. This time Gunter was following me.

"Where to, Patrick?"

"The Sappho on Bedbug Row."

He must have known what I was thinking because the only thing he said was "Mary Hastings".

The streets and sidewalks had become a mess with the now heavier snow that was falling. We were over half our way to the Sappho before either one of us spoke.

"I probably shouldn't have hit Walker," Gunter said. "This won't help my promotion chances."

"Forget it," I said. "The only thing better would be to shoot the bastard, but the department would never move you up." I had made a joke of this, but Gunter's temper would get him into trouble at some time.

*****

The entire walk from the Marlborough to Bed Bug Row took less than ten minutes, even with all the slipping and sliding we did in the fast falling snow. This time as we walked along Custom Place, peering at the brothels that lined the street no one called out to us. It was still early morning, perhaps very early morning for a prostitute, and even they needed their sleep. When we got to the door of the Sappho there was still no sign of life from any of the buildings and except for a lone carriage that was parked across the street, there was no one milling about. The cold and the snow were shutting the city down.

I rang the doorbell, pushing so hard my finger hurt. I wondered if anyone was awake in the brothel. Before I could ring again the door was opened by a big brute, all forehead, jaws and chin. All of these features appeared twice as large as they should have. The rest of him wasn't small either. He was just a tad less than six feet tall, but wide across the shoulders and broad throughout the chest. In his hand he held a wooden club, about eighteen inches in length.

"Are you expecting trouble?" I asked as I flashed my detective's badge.

The brute stared hard at my badge and then at Gunter's. I could see his grip had tightened on the club; his knuckles were white. "You never know for sure," he said, the Irish accent strong.

"We're here to see Mary Hastings?"

He crossed his big, beefy arms across his chest. "I don't suppose you have an appointment?"

I smiled. "Don't make this difficult for us and do us the small favor of putting the club down."

His arms returned to the sides of his body, but he still held the club. "Mary is not here today."

Immediately, I became concerned, the vision of the Hart's bedroom flashing across my eyes. "Where is she?"

"I saw her last night and she told me that she had to attend to a meeting in the Loop today. She told me she thought she'd be here by noon."

"She told you this last night, about this meeting?"

"She did." The arms crossed over the chest again.

I wondered what meeting Mary Hastings had to go to. Did it have anything to do with meeting the person or people who had earlier visited the Harts? "We'd like to talk to the girls that are in the house at the moment. We are looking for a young lady. Maybe some of your girls can help us out."

He smiled broadly. "I'm thinking that most of the girls are asleep at this time. There was a lively crowd here last night and we closed up late. Anyway, from what Mary told me, we've made our payments to Big Jim and the police shouldn't be bothering us. We've done nothing wrong."

I heard Gunter groan behind me. "This has nothing to do with your operation here at Sappho. We're just looking for one young woman. We think she might have come in contact with either Mike Hart or Mary Hastings. We'll just ask a few questions and then we'll be gone."

"Why don't you try Mike Hart?"

"We did. He wasn't much help?"

The brute seemed to think about this. "I can wake the girls and you can talk to them, but I need to be there. You can only ask them about this missing woman."

This didn't sound right to me. Here was this thug telling us, the police, how we could question his workers. I wondered what these people were told when they paid their collection money to Big Jim. "We just want to try and find this woman."

He motioned to us with the club. "Follow me."

In all Sappho held twelve rooms where the prostitutes performed their duties. On that cold, snowy day we found nine sleeping or partially sleeping whores at home. A couple had a hard time waking from a hard night of drinking and possibly drugs. Most of the rooms were dirty with an old, rotting smell to them. The sheets and blankets that these women slept on were not clean. The women themselves, although young, seemed like they were on their last legs. Most were haggard, sickly looking women, like the woman who'd opened the door for me on my last visit. A few had rashes on their faces and arms. More than a few coughed harshly as they were awoken. It was a pitiful sight, not much better than the shackled women at The Ranch.

The questioning was very simple. When Gunter showed them the picture of Isabella Rossini, the women were asked if they had ever seen her. The unanimous answer was no. With the brute standing nearby I was able to ask each girl their name which they all shared with me. When I asked where they were from a few said Chicago, two were from Milwaukee, one from St. Louis and the one I had talked to before was from Detroit. One girl shrugged and one couldn't remember. These girls, as young as they were, were half dead. They were the used up girls that Lieutenant Shipley told us about. This might be their last stop before they were discarded on the street or maybe dumped into the Chicago River.

The last question I asked each girl, and I was careful how I phrased it, was how they had come to work at the Sappho. I listened to what each girl told me, but I paid more attention to their eyes, but there was nothing there, in any of the girls, to suggest they were lying. They all responded in some fashion that they needed to work somewhere and Sappho had offered them jobs. Sappho, they said, was as good as anywhere else.

Before we left, with no answers of value, we told the brute to let Mary Hastings know we still wanted to speak with her. He grunted some reply, but I knew this was all in vain. I had asked Mary about Mike Hart and The Ranch. Days later the Harts had their brains blown out and Mary Hart had to attend a mysterious meeting. Whether that meeting ever occurred we'll never know. And there would be no more talking to Mary Hastings. Her body was discovered later that day on a stretch of Lake Michigan beach near Madison Street with half of the back of her head blown away. With her death, the only names that Big Louie had given me had died.

Disheartened by the lack of anything substantial coming from our trip to Sappho, we decided to take a break for lunch since it was approaching noon. Before that, Gunter wanted to check with the precinct for any messages. He used a street police call box to make the call. The message he got was that he was to report to Captain Morgan's office as soon as he could. There was nothing in the message about me. This, we reasoned, had to do with the punching of Detective Walker.

"It could be back to the packing houses for me," Gunter said glumly.

I laughed. "Walker and Langley are two of the most despised officers in the department. I'm sure that silently Morgan is praising your actions, but he has to speak to you about it. I'll bet you a pint it's a minor slap on the wrist."

He didn't smile. "You'll still come to dinner tomorrow even if I am sacked?"

I'd almost forgotten the dinner. "I'll be there even if they send me packing with you."

"Do you want to come into the precinct with me?"

"No. I've got something I need to do and I haven't eaten anything today. I will catch up with you there a bit later on."

He nodded and headed back to Eighteenth for a cab that would take him to the precinct. I started walking south. I again found myself not far from the mansions on Prairie Avenue and the homes of Marshall Field Jr. and Ernest Lehmann, Field's alleged partner at the Everleigh Club on the night of Field's shooting.

*****

Like the Fields, the Lehmanns had made their money in the retail department store business. The house that young Ernest lived in was not a large as the Field mansion, but I wouldn't have balked if asked to move in. When I rang the bell to the front door it was answered quickly by a plump, stuffy servant that informed me that Mr. Lehmann was in Milwaukee and would return home in two days. I thanked the surly servant who said nothing further to me as he closed the door in my face.

Suddenly feeling as if I could get no further on either the Isabella Rossini case or the Field matter, I decided to grab a bite to eat and then return to the precinct. Sometimes when I get ahead of myself I find it better to sit and write notes about what I knew and what I thought. This was one of those times. It would also allow me to find out if Gunter had gotten himself into any real trouble.

*****

It was getting late in the afternoon and I was sitting at my desk reviewing the notes I had made on both cases. Of course, I only pulled the Field notes out of the drawer to read or write something on when a thought occurred to me. Gunter was across from me at his own desk having gone unpunished from his encounter with Walker. Captain Morgan has said something to the effect that it was not good form to punch another officer in the face. Before I had returned to the precinct, I had placed a call to Eleanor at The Queen's House and asked her how she felt and if she could go to dinner with me. She told me she felt healthy and strong and would love to go to dinner. She had to be back at the House before nine as a busy night was planned. The holidays had a way of increasing business at the brothels. Her tone of voice and her new condition made me feel better. After our last meeting I wasn't sure what kind of welcome Eleanor would give me. I guess it was a good that I hadn't found Gussie Black.

I was close to finishing up my thoughts for the day and I could see that Gunter wanted to get home, too. Just as we were about to rise to get our coats and leave we were summoned into Captain Morgan's office. Could this be another admonishment?

Morgan didn't look comfortable with his long body sitting in the chair behind his desk. He wasn't smiling either as he told Gunter and me to come into the office and shut the door behind us.

"I understand from Walker that you two were on the way to see the Harts and when you got there you found that they had been murdered?"

I thought Morgan had heard this from Gunter in his earlier talk, but maybe the Captain had only addressed the slugging. "We had a tip that they were involved in white slave traffic, and they had a place out in Blue Island that they held some of the enslaved women captive until they could be sold to the brothels. It's in our early report that we submitted this afternoon."

Morgan was nodding, but he didn't seem to be listening. I could see he was forming another question for us. "And you know a woman named Mary Hastings?"

"We do," I said. "The same person who gave me the tip on the Harts told me that Mary Hastings might be harboring white slaves herself at her brothel, Sappho."

"Who is the source of your tips, Patrick?"

I saw little harm in telling Morgan, my superior, who had tipped me off. "Big Louie Pagano. He owns the newsstand at State and Adams."

Again the silent nod. "Well, Mary Hastings was found down at the beach with most of the back of her head blown away about a half hour ago."

I looked to Gunter. "I guess her meeting didn't go very well."

"I'm worried here, men," Morgan said. "We put you on a case to find a missing Italian girl and suddenly we are faced with three more homicides than we had before the assignment was given to you."

I shifted on the hard wooden chair, not sure what Morgan was saying. "I had only briefly talked with Mary Hastings, and we'd never met the Harts."

"Obviously," he said, "someone didn't care for your snooping around and what Mary Hastings or the Harts might have said. Don't you see the coincidence?"

"With the news of Mary Hastings's demise, I can see it clearly."

"But you have nothing on Miss Rossini's whereabouts?"

"Nothing."

Morgan suddenly stood, his tall frame hovering over us. He tried to stretch his back and there was some awful crunching. His face showed the discomfort he was in. "Be extremely careful with this case. I'm not sure where it's going to lead you, and I don't want any more murders or anyone else's foot stomped on."

Gunter and I both nodded and said a quick "yes, sir", but I only understood part of the message. I could understand the part about no more murders, but the part about the foot stomping confused me. This was a police department investigation. If I stepped on someone's feet to find Isabella Rossini, so what? There was somebody out there in the Levee who Captain Morgan didn't want their toes to get crunched. It wouldn't be much longer before we learned who.

*****

We found ourselves in a little place called the Chicago Room that was located on the north side of the river. The meals in the small restaurant were cheap and the crowd was quiet even as we approached Christmas. The piano player stuck with a steady blend of Chopin and carols, and you were able to communicate without having to shout. When I was with Eleanor, I felt relaxed and noticed the nice touches of Christmas decorations that the owners had put up. I also noticed how pretty Eleanor looked in the pink dress she wore. The dress's long sleeves covered the still fresh needle marks on her arms. It also closed tightly at her neck where she wore a heart shaped locket I had given her on a gold chain. Her neck had a pureness to it, unblemished, white. Her face, other than a touch of rouge on her cheeks, was pure. Her blue eyes were clear and bright. Her red hair flamed on the top of her head. She was smiling.

"You're happy?" I said.

She took my hand. "I am here with my good friend, Patrick, and it is Christmas time. What more could I want."

"You like Christmas?"

"Of course. Who doesn't?"

Since my wife and children perished at the Iroquois, Christmas, like many other holidays, lost some of its glimmer. I didn't know if that void would ever close.

"I'm sorry," she said, sensing my thoughts. "I know how tough the holidays can be for someone who has suffered such great loss."

Eleanor's parents had died somewhere in Pennsylvania when their carriage had slipped down a steep incline and into a swollen river. The carriage driver had been able to swim away from the wreck, but Eleanor's parents had drowned. She had then gone into a Philadelphia orphanage system that was less than adequate. She had escaped this at age seventeen and come west to Chicago, still young, but wiser. She needed work and prostitution beckoned. She'd been at it seven years.

"It is my burden," I said, "But let's try and enjoy the night."

"I only have until nine," she said.

"I will cherish each moment."

She laughed out loud and covered her mouth. "Don't make me laugh."

I was hurt. "I am serious."

"Then I apologize again."

"Stop with the apologies. We don't have enough time in the evening for the discussion to drop into valleys. We have to try and keep it on the peaks."

"Can I thank you for something?"

"Of course you can."

"I want to thank you for not pursuing Gussie. He told me you went by his apartment this week, but have not been back.

His landlords, the Hustons, told him you were there. He is my friend. Throttling him will not do either of us any good."

I wanted to disagree with her. I thought that throttling Gussie would do me a world of good, but our food was served and I had to withhold my comments. Eleanor had a roast chicken with potatoes and vegetables; I had ordered a beefsteak with mushrooms. Both dishes were delicious and we ate quietly, enjoying our meals.

"You didn't make any sarcastic comment about what I said about Gussie," she said, as she finished her last bite of chicken.

"I would only get myself into trouble."

"I won't argue with you there."

I wiped some steak juice away from my chin with my napkin. "He works mostly for the Hustons?"

"Exclusively, as far as I know, except when he deals faro. They have a lot of clients and Gussie does the deliveries for them. I think Gussie probably knows more prostitutes than anyone else in this city."

She had caught my attention. "He gets into most of the neighborhoods?"

"Wherever there are resorts, he goes. West side, north side or the Levee, the Hustons control the flow of cocaine into those areas. Gussie makes most of their deliveries. They trust him."

"There's a case that Gunter and I are working on and we may need Gussie's help."

She couldn't hide the look of shock that hit her face. "You want Gussie Black to help you with a case?"

I put my index finger to my lips to quiet her and checked neighboring tables to see that we were not overheard. "I am looking for a girl. Her name is Isabella Rossini. She is the niece of the Italian Ambassador to the United States. She came here on the train from St. Louis and disappeared. Some people within the department and mayor's office think she might have become a victim of white slave trading."

I saw Eleanor wince and she took a sip of her glass of wine.

"I have heard something of this. Some men have approached Ms. Keesher about the prospect of buying girls from them, but she wants nothing to do with it."

"Apparently, what we've been told is that up to five thousand women are being swallowed up in Chicago each year by these traders. It is becoming an epidemic."

Her eyes were cast down at the table. "Five thousand," she repeated quietly.

"That's the number that we have been told, but, of course, we have no way of verifying it. This one girl, Isabella, is our only concern at this time. We have been charged with finding her, but our only leads have turned up dead." I sounded figurative, but was being literal.

Eleanor grabbed my hand again, squeezing hard this time. "From what I have heard, Patrick, there are some powerful men behind this slaving. Powerful and dangerous men. You need to watch yourselves at all times."

"Do you know the names?"

She shook her head from side to side. "These are powerful men in the Levee, but I don't have names."

My thoughts went to Coughlin and Kenna, but these two dictators were family men. It didn't seem to fit. "Maybe you can approach Gussie about talking to Gunter and me". I smiled. "I would forgive an awful lot of what I think he did."

She wasn't smiling. "I am not kidding, Patrick. I will talk to Gussie and ask him, but he may not want to get involved. These people are very dangerous. I heard about the Hart murders. It was said they were involved in slaving and now they are dead. You really need to be careful."

The fingers in the hand she held were losing circulation, and I had to separate myself from her grasp. I think if she had names she would have told me. I don't think she knew. What she did know scared her tremendously. The term "white slaving" was synonymous with evil. The short conversation we'd had on the topic had turned the mood of the dinner sour.

We finished the meal in near silence.

When I dropped her back off at The Queen's House she kissed me softly on the cheek and then roughly on the mouth. "I will talk to Gussie," she said. "Promise me you'll do nothing stupid."

"I promise," I said. She didn't respond. She pushed open the carriage door, and I watched as she bounded across the walk and up the stairs to The Queen's House.

*****

As the coach returned me to my flat, I had two thoughts which crossed my mind. I had seen the evident terror on Eleanor's face when I mentioned the scourge of white slaving. She knew something about it, quite a bit, I'd say, and she hadn't shared all her thoughts and knowledge with me. When the mere mentioning of a topic shuts down all conversation, there's something amiss with the topic. The other thought I had as the carriage trudged through the day's snow was the scarf that had belonged to Maria Scott. I hadn't mentioned the present that had been left on my door knob to Gunter. It might be just the work of some sick hearted prankster. Still, as we turned up the street towards home, I wondered what I'd find tonight.

I didn't even get to my apartment door before I saw the horse and carriage parked in front of my building. The coachman was seated in his chair, his back to me, bundled up to deal with the cold of the night. I thought someone might be seated inside the coach, but then I noticed the man sitting on the steps to my building. He was huddled up against the wind in a long dark coat and hat. His head was tucked down, making it impossible to see his face. As I got out of my coach and paid the driver, I turned towards the man. He lifted his face and I could see the flattened nose of a boxer, broken many times in this man's youth. It was the face of Father Seamus McCoy.

"It's Father Luigi," the tough priest said to me. "He's had a heart attack."

In the ride to Mercy Hospital, the same hospital that Marshall Field, Jr. had perished in, I could get very little out of Father Seamus. Father Luigi had been at work in the church's sacristy, preparing for the weekend masses when suddenly he groaned loudly, grasped his chest, and tumbled to the floor. Luckily Sister Andrea had been present when this had happened and an ambulance had been called to take Luigi to Mercy. This had occurred around six-thirty. Father Seamus had left Mercy to find me when Luigi was in his bed and resting.

"What kind of shape is he in?" I asked.

"It is hard to say," Father Seamus said.

"Is he communicative?"

Seamus shook his head and I realized he was crying. "He's in and out of consciousness and he mumbles some things. He asks for you. The doctor has stated that he is tough, but that he is in grave condition."

At the time, Mercy Hospital was probably the best and most modern facility in the city. Once we entered the building you could make out the unmistakable smell of antiseptics. We got past the nurse at the reception area rather quickly and Seamus led me up a flight of stairs to the second floor where they had taken Luigi. I had always seen him as a big, tough man, a bit invincible. I was surprised at what I found. Luigi was lying on his back either asleep or unconscious. They had dressed him in an all white hospital gown and I was stunned to see that the chalkiness of his face almost matched the color of his gown. Somehow, he looked smaller in the bed. The room was only lit by a small lamp on the table by his bed. The only window in the room had its curtains drawn. There were two wooden chairs by the bed. Seamus sat in one; I took the other.

The vigil that we began became long and mysterious. I watched Luigi the entire time I was in the room with him, my eyes never leaving his prostate body. He looked so much older and there was little movement. For the most part, there was only the regular rising and falling of his chest, but occasionally there would be a tremendous deep breath and exhaling that would cause Luigi to shutter. When this happened, I feared for my old mentor, but then his body would calm and the breathing would return to near normal. It was nerve wracking, watching this for hours. The room became warm, and I stood to remove my coat, placing it over the back of my chair. Seamus, exhausted from the stress of the situation, had fallen asleep in his chair, his head resting on his chest and occasionally slid from side to side.

At around midnight, with my legs cramping and little change in Luigi, I stepped out in the hall for a stretch. As I walked about, I became aware of two nurses who manned a station on the second floor. They were chattering about the next day's assignments, and I could tell they weren't too happy with where they were going to be working. They were both young nurses, not bad looking, and each had a solid Irish accent. They paid little attention to me as I walked around the area, trying to get the stiffness out of my legs.

"That Doctor Bevan," I heard the one nurse say. "Sometimes he has a bit of a challenge keeping his hands to himself."

The other nurse giggled and covered her mouth. "You're terrible, Katherine," she said when she was able to compose herself.

"Well, it's true. The last time I was near him, I thought I was the patient, he was probing me so much."

Again, the second nurse giggled. "Well, he's here at six, so you'll only have to watch him until ten. Maybe he won't be so frisky in the morning."

"I doubt if I can be that lucky."

"Excuse me," I said. Both nurses turned quickly towards me. I figured they hadn't counted on me overhearing them.

"Yes, sir," the accuser of Doctor Bevan said. She was the prettier of the two with blonde hair and blue eyes. She had a nice smile.

"Is that Doctor Arthur Bevan that you two were just talking about?"

I could see both of the nurses blush as if I had caught them stealing. "Yes, sir. We were only teasing." The pretty blonde now wore a serious look on her face.

"Did I hear you say that he will be here at six?"

The other nurse, a bigger girl with brown hair and a full figure looked at chart. "Yes. Doctor Bevan will be here at six tomorrow. He will be here until about noon."

I didn't respond. One of the doctors who had dealt with Marshall Field, Jr. after his shooting would be available for me to question, and since I wasn't about to leave Luigi, it wouldn't hurt to hear his side of the story. I thanked the two nurses, who looked confused, and returned to my chair at Luigi's bedside. The room had become cold now and I wrapped my coat around me.

Seamus was still sleeping, but no longer quietly. He had begun to snore and it sounded like the growl of a wild animal. With all of this noise, I doubted sleep would come for me, but I was wrong.

I did manage to fall asleep sitting in the hard backed wooden chair, something I'd never had happen to me before. Maybe I was tired or perhaps my lingering cold was wearing me down, but I did sleep and rather well. It was not the noisiness of Seamus that woke me. What I woke to were the loud mutterings of Father Luigi. My eyes popped open as soon as the old priest began to talk in his sleep, but being awake didn't help me. Luigi was going on in Italian.

Father Seamus was awake as well. "This happened the last time, too. He went back and forth between Italian and his brand of English." Seamus smiled.

Luigi had a brand of English that when he spoke it fast, or when he was excited or upset, you might be able to make out every third or fourth word. If you were lucky. I stood and stretched my legs again and sat back down.

There was nothing for maybe ten or fifteen minutes but the slow rising and falling of Luigi's chest. I thought I might drift off again. I closed my eyes for a moment and Luigi started his mumbling again.

At first, the words that came out of his mouth were all in Italian. Neither Seamus nor I understood a word he said. Seamus told me he could go get Father Allegretti, a younger priest who spoke Italian, but I told him to wait for the time being. It was maybe five minutes later that Luigi spoke his first word in English and it was clear and distinct. "Patrick," he said.

I stood up and took one of Luigi's hands in mine. It was cold to the touch. His face hadn't recovered any color, but there were beads of sweat just under the hair that covered the top of his forehead. "Talk to me, Luigi," I said. Seamus stood and took a spot on the other side of the bed.

There were another few minutes of silence, nothing coming from his mouth. One of my two nurse friends came into the room, the blond one, but we told her everything was fine. She told us to get her if anything changed. I was going to sit again and then one of the struggling, breathing episodes began and Luigi's eyes popped open and he looked at me for a moment and said, "Patrick Moses."

I watched as his eyes closed and his breathing came back to closer to normal. I grasped his hand a little tighter. "What are you trying to tell me?" I said, and I realized my voice had cracked.

"Jacob Fine," Luigi muttered and then he went into a long dialogue in Latin. I recognized most of it and then I knew.

"He's saying mass," Seamus said, smiling, but then his smile dimmed.

"What's wrong?"

"It is the funeral mass that he is saying. He is giving a funeral mass and I think he is saying it for himself."

I saw the tears emerge from Seamus' eyes, and for the first

time I felt one or two drain from my own and stain my cheeks. I wiped at them with my sleeve. Be strong, I had been told by Luigi as a young child. Never show any weakness. Was this a weakness? I wanted to know. My old friend was dying and before he went he was saying his own funeral mass. Suddenly he stopped. I knew from the many masses I had served as an altar boy that he had not finished. His breathing looked fine, steady. His eyes were closed. I looked to Seamus, but his head was bowed as he prayed silently.

"In the name of the father and the son and the holy spirit," Luigi said loudly. His hand gave mine a tight squeeze and then relaxed, limp. "God Bless the Irish Rose."

There was another bout of the troubled breaths and then Luigi calmed and his breathing became even lighter and easier. There were no more words uttered. He had said all that he would.

"I can't imagine who the Irish Rose is," Seamus said.

I could imagine, but I said nothing. My pocket watch said it was a little after four o'clock in the morning. I sat again in the chair and I knew I was beginning the last vigil for Luigi. I would stay until the end. I would stay all day if I had to. I'd call the precinct to let Gunter know where I was later in the morning. There was no case that could take me away from Luigi. He was the only family I'd ever had. There was no way I was going to leave him now.

Other than his few changes in breathing patterns, there wasn't much to report for the next couple of hours. When it got to be seven-thirty, I rose again for a walk into the hall. I looked over at Seamus, but he was asleep. I wandered into the hall, getting the building knots out of my leg muscles and found the nurse's station. The attractive blonde was there putting some files in order. She looked up and gave me a polite smile.

"I was wondering if you could tell me if Doctor Bevan has arrived?"

"He has," she said quietly. "If you walk across the hall and walk past the last patient's room there is a small office that the doctors use for record keeping."

I thanked her and walked across the hall. There was a row of five patient's rooms that all looked occupied. At the end of this row of rooms was a small office containing a desk and chair. The desk had a small lamp and a pile of files on it. Behind the desk sat a man of about fifty in a doctor's white gown. He wore glasses and had no hair on the top of his head. He didn't look the type to be frisky with the nurses. As I walked into the door of the office, Doctor Bevan was studying a patient's file intently.

"Doctor Bevan," I said. He didn't seem to hear me or didn't care that I was there. "Doctor Bevan," I said again.

This time he looked up. At first he looked stunned that someone was talking to him this early in the morning. Then he seemed to focus. "What can I do for you?"

I took a few steps forward and was standing right in front of the desk looking down at him. I showed him my badge. It occurred to me that since I hadn't been home in almost twenty four hours, I probably looked like hell. "I'm Detective Patrick Moses. I'd like to ask you a couple of questions about the Marshall Field, Jr. shooting."

He looked up into my face and appeared to be squinting through his glasses. "The Field case? That's been closed for almost a month."

"The department has decided to do a follow up investigation. It's becoming a standard procedure in questionable shootings."

He looked at me as if questioning my lie, but then shrugged his shoulders and sat back in the chair. "I guess this is as good a time as any."

"My friend, Father Luigi Falcone, is a patient here on the floor. When I heard you were here, I thought I'd take the opportunity to question you."

A thin smile with no comments showed me what he

thought of my explanation. I decided to question him before he changed his mind.

"What time did you arrive at the Field residence on the night of the shooting?"

"You should have this in your records, but it was right about five-thirty."

I nodded slowly. "What did you find?"

He looked amused. "Well, I found Field for one. He was in his room on the second floor with that thin nurse, the butler, Mr. Lowe, and his brother in law Mr. Dibble."

"What kind of shape was he in?"

"Not good at all. He was in a great deal of pain undoubtedly caused by the amount of internal hemorrhage. In the end that is what killed Mr. Field."

"The internal bleeding. What about external bleeding?"

He thought for a moment. "There was very little. When I first saw Mr. Field the wound had been cleaned and dressed. There was very little blood."

"Even on the floor or the bed?"

"I don't recall seeing any for that matter. The wound had stopped bleeding when I got there. Like I said, the wound had been taken care of, but, of course, the bullet had not been attended to."

"No idea who cleaned the wound or put the dressing on it?"

"I had always thought it was the house nurse who attended to young Marshall Field. It looked like a professional had done the work and there was no need to ask. Mr. Field's condition and his immediate care was my primary concern."

"Yes, I see. What happened next?"

"By this time Dr. Robert Harry arrived and Mr. Dibble had called Mercy to tell them to prepare for an emergency operation. Dr. Harry did a quick examination of Mr. Field and concurred with my finding. Mr. Field needed an immediate operation. Dr. Harry got on the phone and arranged for an ambulance to take Mr. Field to Mercy.

"After that, everything happened very quickly. I remember Mrs. Field arriving back at home and then the ambulance showed up. Mrs. Field and Mr. Dibble accompanied Field in the ambulance. Dr. Harry and I followed in a coach. It didn't take long to get to Mercy; the horses were pushed to break neck speed. Once we got to Mercy, the operation began as soon as we were prepared. The hospital had done a remarkable job getting ready for us."

He stopped as an older nurse, one I had not seen before, knocked on the door and held a thick file for Bevan to see. "The Brewster file," she said.

"Thank you, Ellen," Bevan said and the nurse handed him the file and left the room.

"Where was I?" he asked.

"You were getting ready for surgery."

"Yes, rather simple procedure if I recall. It took about a half hour."

"What did you find?"

"The bullet, of course."

"I understand that," I said quickly. "What else could you determine?"

"I don't have my notes, but it's still pretty clear in my head. The bullet had entered just below the ribs, missed the stomach, perforated both the liver and spleen, and lodged near his spine. The damage to the liver was severe. His intestines had not been damaged. I'll say it now as I've said before. The gunshot might not have killed him, but for the internal bleeding. It was profuse. That, and the infection, killed him. We located the bullet and removed it."

"You said the internal bleeding was profuse. Is this normal for a bullet wound that had occurred only a few hours before?"

He laughed a little. "We all talked about that. He had bled so much internally that it looked like it had been going on for at least a full day, not several hours."

"I see. Any sign of powder burn? A close gunshot, that of someone cleaning a gun, should leave some trace of burn."

"You would think so," he said," but I saw none. That doesn't mean it wasn't there and possibly cleaned away or covered with antiseptic before the operation."

I nodded. "And you're convinced the gunshot itself wouldn't have killed him?"

"I am. Field died of paralysis of his bowels and lower extremities."

"If he had been treated sooner would it have helped?"

Confusion crossed his face. "We treated him as soon as possible, as soon as we were called to the residence."

"But it is your opinion that the amount of internal bleeding made it look like he had bled for a lot longer than a few hours?"

"I don't know what you're getting at."

"Just your opinion on the amount of internal bleeding. What you thought about it."

He thought this over for a bit. "The poor man is dead and I would never say this to one of those snakes that works for the papers, but it looked like he had bled internally for a while, a half a day at least."

I thanked Bevan who looked irritated at the time I had taken him away from his files. This latest interview, along with what the dog walking neighbor and the butler, Robert Lowe, had told me, convinced me that this "accidental" shooting of Marshall Field, Jr. might not have been so accidental. I had ruled out the suicide angle altogether. The only thing that was left was that someone had shot Field. I needed to find out who and why.

When I returned down the hall to Luigi's room I could see that it was now overflowing with members of Holy Trinity. Word had gotten to the parish that Luigi's time was getting close and they had all rushed over as soon as they could. The room was crowded with weeping nuns and sad looking priests who tried to contain their grief. Luigi had long been a favorite of all at the parish despite his tough demeanor and lack of control around alcohol. I wanted to go into the room, but I thought I had seen Luigi at the best that he was ever going to be. I stood outside the room and let his fellow parishioners mourn his passing. They didn't need me interfering with their visit.

Seamus came out of Luigi's room at a little after eight-thirty and he shook his head sadly. The visitors from the parish had not abated. Luigi's room was still crowded and there was a soft murmuring of prayers echoing from its confines. I still stayed outside.

"I don't think it will be long, Patrick," Seamus said.

"I don't think he is suffering."

Seamus laughed. "I don't think Luigi liked all of the people in that room. He might be suffering if he could see some of those that are blathering over him." I laughed, and as I did, a tremendous scream came from the room. I saw two nurses quickly rush to the room and push through the crowd. Many of the visitors left the room. I saw a look of pain and anguish on Seamus' face. The time had come. A younger doctor, this one with a long beard, entered the room and more visitors exited. Now, it was only the nurses and the young doctor with Luigi. There was controlled silence out in the hall, even with the all the praying going on. I noticed my heart beat had quickened, even knowing the outcome was near. I tried to settle myself, but it was useless. Finally, after no more than ten minutes, the young doctor came to the door and addressed the mass.

"I am terribly sorry," he said in a deep, somber voice, "but Father Luigi has gone to our Father."

I heard this clearly, and I also heard the screams and wails from both priests and sisters. I heard all of this, but all I saw were the stairs to the left that led to the first floor and the exit. I said nothing. I didn't want to speak with anyone. Before I knew it, I was down those stairs and out into the cold wind of the morning and the eight inches of snow that had fallen the day before. I had no idea where I was going, but I started to walk. I barely noticed the snow and cold. I'd left my hat in Luigi's room. I only felt the sting of warm tears that ran from my eyes onto my now cold face.

## Friday

How many hours did I walk about? It's hard to say, and I don't recall a lot of what I did after Luigi's death. Nothing seemed to matter after a while. I remember thinking how cold it was and how much snow had fallen, but was I cold? Did the mounting snow cause me any inconvenience? I don't recall that.

As I considered Luigi's death in my long stroll, I asked myself question after question. The first was probably why had God taken him? After that, it was pure selfishness. How was I to get on without Luigi? For so long he had been my family, my guiding light. Now that he was gone, who would be there for me, as he had always been? My closest friends were Eleanor, who admitted that I kept her at a distance, and who didn't always believe I was truthful with her, and then Gunter. It was hard to say that Gunter was my friend. He was my partner on the force and he had always responded when I was in need on the job. Other than the streets we walked together, I hadn't had much to do with him. Tonight's dinner, a first for me, would be the first thing we'd ever done together that work had nothing to do with the planning. For some odd reason, I was nervous about it. Why? I can't answer. Maybe the thoughts of pure family style moments were something I couldn't imagine for me. I'd have to wait and see.

I wondered about how bizarre it was that Mercy Hospital was on the same street as Marshall Field Junior's lavish house. In fact it was nothing more than a short, six block walk to the mansion, slipping and sliding around in the still fresh snow. I stopped in front of the house and looked up at it. In the still early morning light it looked like a castle. Were these people real? They had so much money and so many secrets. Their son had been shot and had died, but yet they didn't know the real reason why he had perished. Did they really want to know? Would it hurt their precious legacy? Why had Marshall Field Senior quieted the newspapers? Why hadn't he just offered a pile of money to the police to find out what really happened instead of paying me what was probably a pittance for him?

"Fuck you!" I yelled at the looming giant of a house.

I remember making my way to the Levee and started on Bed Bug Row. I walked up and down the street looking at the forlorn brothels, but they were also quiet this morning. I assumed they'd had raucous crowds the night before as Christmas was the following week. Everyone was getting into the spirit, except for me. I wondered about the missing Isabella Rossini. Was this whole investigation a waste of time as Gunter had said? Were we just babysitting this case for political reasons? How real was the white slavery issue? Five thousand girls a year? That number seemed preposterous. Even if it was five thousand, how were we supposed to track down one girl, especially down in the Levee? The area was known for swallowing people whole. Some of these even wanted to be swallowed.

I walked up to the door of the Sappho and pounded hard on it. When no one answered, I pounded again. Still, no one answered. I thought I saw a curtain on the second floor move and was certain I'd been seen. They all knew who I was and I doubted they'd open for me. Maybe they were in mourning for their lost leader, Mary Hastings. Possibly, and more likely, given their mental and physical state, they didn't know what to do.

"Isabella!" I yelled as loud as I could. "Are you here?" I yelled again, but there was no response. I turned and headed up the street.

I was the lone customer in O'Halloran's on Seventeenth, unless you count the drunk at the corner of the bar who slept with his head on the mahogany, drool running out of the side of his mouth. The bartender was washing glasses and looked interested in nothing. I wondered if he saw me. When I ordered a straight whiskey, he calmly poured it without a word. His eyes never reached mine. I had two more whiskeys and laid my money on the bar, but he pushed it back at me.

"Police drink for free," he said.

"And they should," I said. "You don't know the half of it, the garbage we encounter down here."

He finally raised his eyes, but they were vacant as he looked me over. He poured me one more double shot and I threw it back quickly, burning my throat.

When I got to the Everleigh Club on Dearborn, the skies were clearing and I knew it would be a cold, sunny day. I didn't care. The whiskey had both warmed me and dulled my brain. I wasn't sure I'd been rationale when I'd started out, but I was certain now that I wasn't right. The two double brownstones that housed the most elaborate resort in the Levee stood before me. I giggled as I thought of walking up those steps and asking Ada and Minna what had really happened to Marshall Field, Jr. on the night he was shot. I was a police detective. If I asked them they had to tell me the truth. Right? I laughed again and headed back towards Twenty-Second.

The Marlborough looked closed up. There was no one in sight at the hotel. They, too, could be mourning the loss of the Harts. I wandered what the maids thought when they had to clean the blood and brain matter off of the Hart's headboard. I thought I might have asked for a raise. I'd get somebody like Debs to fight for me. I won't clean up blood and brain for less than a nickel more an hour. I laughed out loud.

I camped at a bar named Tilley's across from Freiberg's Dance Hall and contemplated my next move. While I did this pointless pondering, I had four or maybe five more double whiskeys. I don't recall too much of what I saw, said or thought while in the tavern. I had only one thought. Luigi was dead. What would it matter? That thought? Go across the street, confront my father, ask him about my mother and then kill him. Easy enough. I got up from the bar- this time the barkeep did not reject my money- and walked out to the street. The dance hall across the street was quiet. Was my father, Jacob Fine, even in there? I removed my revolver from its holster. I was in the middle of the street and I'm sure I looked like one of those gunslingers at the O K Corral. The sun was nearly blinding me as it poked through and over some of the buildings. I waved the gun at Freiberg's and maybe I shouted, but maybe I didn't. However stupid it sounded, I was an officer of the law. Walking into Freiberg's and murdering my father, regardless of my rationale, wasn't right. I holstered my gun and moved back towards Clark Street.

Soon Lee's was a chop suey joint that I went to frequently. I had never eaten there. The meat they served didn't look like beef or chicken. The reason I went to Soon Lee's was not the first floor eatery. I went there for what existed on the lower level, below the street. Here was the hop joint that I came to when I needed to be alone. Soon Lee was quiet and he was discreet. He knew that I was a police detective, but that didn't matter. Maybe it helped. I also was not a charity case. My money was as good as the next person.

I walked right in and nodded at Soon Lee. He was a small Chinaman, complete with pigtails. He was sitting by himself sipping his morning tea. He got up from that table and led me downstairs. I remember paying him and the pipe being pushed near my lips. As I began to smoke, I recall seeing him smile and I felt good, secure. This was the last thing that I remembered.

*****

When I awoke I was in my apartment. My overcoat and my suit coat had been placed neatly over the chair near my bed. My shoes were untied and on the floor at the foot of the bed. My tie was on the floor in a twisted heap. This one article of clothing looked like the only thing out of place. I was still in my shirt and trousers and had the blanket pulled up to my neck. I had to remember to check my lease when I renewed it to make sure that heat actually came with a "heated apartment".

When I sat up in the bed I got my first good thumping from the hangover headache. I looked at my watch and it said five-forty-five in the afternoon. It was already dark outside. I had over an hour before I needed to be at Gunter's for dinner. I rotated my neck from side to side, trying to get some of the stiffness out of my neck and shoulders. When I righted my head, I saw the small gift wrapped package that was lying on my small desk. I didn't remember bringing it in the room, but I also didn't remember even getting home. I got out of the bed, shivered and sneezed, and felt like my cold was blocking any attempt I had at breathing. My head pounded nastily at the temples and my stomach lurched, but I got through it. I grabbed the box and sat back down on the bed.

The box, without specific measuring, was a square, looking to be about four inches by four inches. It was wrapped in a mostly red holiday paper that did not appear cheap. A small green bow adorned the box on top. There was nothing else, like a name tag, that told me the gift was for me or who it was from. Like a small child, I shook the box, but could barely make out anything rattling about in it.

I carefully took the bow off the box and placed it on the covers beside me. This procedure told me nothing more of the mysterious package. I removed the wrapping from the gift and was faced with a plain white box. I took a deep breath and removed the top as I felt my heart beat quicken. Whoever had packed the box had lined it with preformed cotton. There was a square piece that covered the rest of the box and its contents. I slowly removed this piece and looked deeper into the box.

I wasn't startled or shocked by what I saw. My reaction, perhaps caused by the whiskey, opium and hangover was one of complacent expectation. There before me was a complete, not too shriveled, female index finger. Where the digit had been cut from the hand the wound was a mixture of brown and black colors. There was almost no smell. When I saw the colored polish that the finger possessed, a light green, chipped here and there, I knew where the finger had come from. When we came upon the body of Estelle Perkins, a prostitute who worked out of Easy Life, she had all the usual cuts and markings of a victim of Dr. Kluge. The only thing significantly different about Estelle was that her right index finger had been lopped off.

I took the finger out of the box and it felt cold to touch. Maybe it had been recently frozen. I placed it on top of the box lid and could make out that it was from a right hand. Someone had given me- I couldn't remember- or left me a brightly colored package containing the missing finger from Estelle Perkins. I placed the finger back in the box and covered it with the top. I returned the box to my desk and sat back down. My head was no longer thumping and my stomach felt intact. Whoever had done this to me had caused my symptoms to abate. That much I was thankful for. What bothered me was who was leaving these little trinkets for me.

If it had just been the Maria Scott scarf you might think it was someone who had some knowledge of the case and had come into the possession of the scarf by some means. Now that the incidents totaled two, and the second occurrence had revealed something more personal than an article of clothing, my interest was heightened. Who would have access to Estelle Perkin's finger? This was too obvious. It could have been the killer, but Kluge was dead. It could have been an accomplice. Did Kluge even have one and who was he or she? The one thing that gnawed at my brain was one last question. Could it have been the killer and we hadn't caught him? We were damn sure it had been Kluge acting alone. I massaged my temples one last time and needed to get ready for dinner with the Krause family. Like the scarf, the finger would have to wait before I could give it any attention.

*****

At the door of Gunter's apartment I was greeted by a small Christmas wreath. I knew what I was in for once I got into their apartment. After all, it was the Christmas season and Gunter and Margaret Krause had two small children. I was certain that the apartment would be full of the coming of Christmas cheer. I was in no way ready to celebrate this holiday, or any for that matter, but I promised myself, as I knocked on the door, that I would not ruin another person's Christmas because of my sour mood.

I had seen Margaret Krause twice before. Once it had been from a fair distance; the other time that I had met her we shook hands as Gunter introduced her. I remember that both of those times I couldn't take my eyes off of her; she may have been the most beautiful woman I had ever seen. She had pure, white skin and hair that a raven would have been jealous of. Her eyes always seemed to twinkle. When she opened the door to their apartment, I swear I had to catch my breath. I knew that she supplemented their income by making dresses and the one she wore now, red, a little off the shoulders, did little to hide her luscious figure. I was transfixed.

"Good evening, Detective Moses," she said, smiling. "Won't you please come into our humble abode?"

I handed her the bottle of wine I had picked up on the way over. "This is for you," I said. I felt like a thirteen year old.

"All for me?" she said. I could see she was about to laugh.

"For dinner. For all of us, except the children."

Now she did laugh. "Of course. Please do come in."

I stepped past her and into the apartment. As she took my coat from me I surveyed the small apartment. There was one large room where we stood, a kitchen area, a water closet and a room that had its door closed. I assumed this was the bedroom. In the large, main room there was a small bed crammed into one corner for the children, a dining table set for five, two sitting chairs and a lamp. In front of the window was a small

Christmas tree, adorned with lights and ornaments. In front of this tree sat two small children, a boy and a girl. They had been looking wondrously at the tree and its decorations. Now they were looking at me.

As Margaret returned from where she'd hung my coat, the door to the bedroom opened and Gunter came in the main room. He looked to be wearing the same suit I had seen him in the day before. He also wore a serious look on his face.

"Patrick, I am so sorry about the death or your good friend, Father Luigi." I thought he was just going to shake my hand, but soon I was held in a great bear hug. If I didn't know better, I'd have thought Gunter was trying to crush me. Finally, he let go. "Patrick has suffered a great loss," he said to Margaret. "His good friend Father Luigi has passed on."

She wore a puzzled look. "I'm sorry, Patrick," Margaret said. "I didn't know or I wouldn't have acted so silly. Perhaps someone should have told me before our guest arrived."

"Don't you have to be looking after the roast?" Gunter said coolly to her.

She turned and moved into the kitchen area, not responding. "Children, come now and meet my good friend, Patrick Moses," Gunter said. It was then that the fantastic smells from the kitchen first hit me.

The two little urchins got up from in front of the tree and walked shyly towards me. The young man, maybe eight or so, boldly stuck out his hand. "It's nice to meet you Mr. Moses. I am Jonathon."

I shook his little hand. "It is my pleasure, sir," I said and Jonathon smiled.

The little girl didn't come as close. "Hello," she said. "I am Emily."

I bowed from the waist. "An honor, miss." She blushed and turned away.

"You may go back to your tree," Gunter said and the two children were gone as quickly as they arrived.

"Come, sit," Gunter said to me. "Let's talk."

We took seats in the two chairs and Gunter poured whiskey into two glasses that were on the table. We each took a glass and sipped the whiskey. "I am so sorry for your loss. I know what Luigi meant to you and there is probably nothing I can say that will make it better for you."

I nodded and sipped my whiskey again. After the previous night, this was no easy task. "How did you hear?"

He gave me a shocked look. "You called me. You told me that Luigi died and that you would not be in. Don't you recall that?"

I didn't, but I lied. "Of course. It's been such a long day. I'm exhausted."

"I can't imagine," he said. "I hope he went peacefully."

I didn't know the answer to this. I was not in Luigi's room when he had died. "I believe it was peaceful."

He refilled my glass and his and we each took long sips. "Now, it is only the living that suffers."

I was going to comment, but Margaret called out to us that the dinner was ready. Gunter sat at the head of the table with Margaret at the other end. I sat on one side; the two children sat on the other."

The food on the table looked incredible. There was a good sized roast beef, sliced thinly, some boiled carrots and sliced roast potatoes. The children were drinking milk. Margaret had opened the wine I brought and had filled a glass for the three adults. With so much food it was overwhelming. I was glad when Margaret asked for my plate and served me. With the plate of food now in front of me I thought it would be easier to eat than to talk. I could not have been more wrong.

"Patrick," Gunter said, "would you mind leading us in grace?"

I did mind, and I had said grace most of my life, but the words weren't coming easily to me. I saw Jonathon and Emily giggle, but my mind finally worked and I recited the short prayer. I was grateful for the next sound of clinking forks and plates.

I may not have mentioned it earlier, but Gunter was a man who loved his food and the faster he put it in his mouth the better. He ate with abandon. With the distractions of his children and his beautiful wife eating with us it was much easier to watch him eat than to focus on the others. I couldn't bear to look at Margaret; her looks were intimidating. With the children it was different. They were probably close to the age that my children would have been had they lived. I found this unnerving. I ate quietly and efficiently, watching Gunter use his fork like a small shovel.

The food was excellent and the dinner progressed with little conversation. There seemed to be a coolness between Margaret and Gunter. They barely said two words between them. The children seemed to be aware of this. They ate quietly and were extremely well behaved and respectful. Not like all the children I had been around. When I finished my whiskey, Gunter would get the bottle and pour me some more. When my wine ran dry, Margaret would fill that glass. It wasn't long before I figured I would live longer, or at least be able to walk, if I didn't finish either glass.

For desert there was a pie that Margaret had made along with a very strong coffee. The two children ate their pie quickly. I think they wanted to get done so that they could play. When they were both finished they asked Gunter if they could be excused. He said yes and they both got up from their chairs. Little Emily pushed her chair in and looked at me. I smiled, but the look on her face was not happy.

"Mr. Moses," she said. "How come your kids got to go to heaven?"

Before I could say anything or even comprehend what I'd been asked, Gunter and Margaret were admonishing the poor girl and she looked close to tears. Finally Emily looked at me and apologized. "That's okay," I said. "God took my children early because it was their time to go. There is no other way I can answer you. Do you understand?"

She nodded politely and then was off to play with her brother near the tree. Gunter stood and excused himself to use the water closet. He looked a little unsteady on his feet, but he soon recovered and was off. When the door had closed I felt the grasp of Margaret's hand on my knee under the table cloth. She'd had a little wine and wore a suspicious smile.

"I'm very sorry about what Emily said and about your friend Father Luigi. If there is anything that I can do please don't be shy." She was staring very intently at me and I was very uncomfortable. Only the opening of the water closet door made me feel comfortable and, with that, Margaret's hand left my knee.

"Let's have one more drink," Gunter said.

"One more," I said. "Then I must be going."

"So early?" he pleaded.

"I've had a rough day," I said.

He nodded and we sat again in the two chairs and Gunter poured more whiskey for the both of us. He was much quicker drinking this round than I was. I was still suffering from the night before and my body was feeling the effects.

"This Isabella Rossini case, it seems to be spiraling out of control," he said.

"It is not a good situation when every person whose name comes up ends up dead."

"What does it mean?"

"Big Louie told me there were bigger names involved in this whole white slaving mess. What it means is they found out that the Harts and Mary Hastings knew too much. They had to be taken out."

"We need to find out those big names."

I laughed. "In the Levee it would be easier to find a virgin."

"At least with Kluge there were clues we could follow."

"Yes, there were," I said and took a sip of the whiskey. My throat was still so raw from my cold that the alcohol burned on the way down. "Speaking of Kluge, I've had a couple of visitors the last few days. They have left me presents."

A confused look crossed his face. "I don't understand."

"I wouldn't expect you to. A few nights ago someone left me a scarf that was identical, except for color, to the one Maria Scott was wearing when we found her body."

"That could be some crazy prankster."

"So I thought. Until last night. Last night someone left me the missing index finger of Estelle Perkins all gift wrapped in a box with a bow. It was from a right hand and bore the same light green finger polish. I'm convinced that this was her finger."

Gunter looked like I'd shown him a ghost. "But the only person who would have that would be the killer or an accomplice."

"Precisely."

"My goodness gracious," he said and took another drink. "What does this mean, Patrick?"

I finished my whiskey and stood up. "It means that Kluge was either the killer with an accomplice or that he was the accomplice."

"Which means?"

"The killer may still out there and he's decided to have a little fun with me."

I don't want to say that I left Gunter speechless, but that was about it. We finished our drinks and he didn't say another word as Margaret retrieved my coat, and I said goodbye to her and the two children. I could tell that my news had left Gunter in a sobering mood. I was, at least, relaxed. I had dreaded the dinner because I knew it would bring back memories of my own family and it had, but I had survived. I had even been able to deal with the indelicate question of a young child. The most disturbing part of the evening had been Margaret placing her hand on my knee under the table cloth. I couldn't get that squeeze out of my mind. I was glad when I was finally out in the cold, hailing a cab, and heading for home and the good night's sleep I needed.

## Saturday

I needed a good night's sleep but that was far from what I got. My flat was cold and even under the thick blanket on my bed I was unable to get warm. I blamed this for a good part of my night of tossing and turning, but in truth it was the dreams that plagued me. The first one was a repeat of my dinner with Gunter and his family, but instead of them it was Francis, Charlie and Bess, my family, that played host to a faceless guest. There was one thing about my family in the dream. They never smiled, especially as they looked at the blurred face of their guest. As I looked harder and harder at the face it went from no recognition to the face of Dr. Kluge. I awoke for the first time that night cold with a dry mouth and a pounding head. It was more than an hour before I could sleep again.

The second dream had me walking the streets of the Levee. All the many blocks of the district had become one long avenue. I walked it for miles and who did I see? I saw everyone. All of the madams were out, waving at me as I strolled on. Bathhouse John and Hinky Dink were there, smiling, but saying nothing. Big Jim Colosimo was there with Mary Hastings. She was pointing and yelling something at me that I couldn't hear; Colosimo wore a scowl on his face, only slightly nodding his head. Dr. Kluge was there, surrounded by the prostitutes he had murdered. They were all alive and well and the good doctor was laughing, at them or me? Isabella Rossini appeared, but only briefly, and many times. As I took a step towards her, she would disappear, only to show up farther down the street. Of course, Marshall Field, Jr. was present and resplendent in a grand suit. He was smiling and nodded briefly as I walked past. As I walked on, I became aware that the street was going to end, the last of the Levee. On the two steps that led into Freiberg's Dance Hall stood Jacob Fine, my father. With him was a beautiful woman I had never seen before. Fine wore a solemn look on his face; the lovely woman was crying. As I approached them he held up one hand to stop me and then pointed to the end of the street. I could see that the El tracks ran over this part of town and I could also see what looked to be a woman lying under them. When I looked back to Fine it was only him standing there with his head down. The woman was gone. I turned and ran the last fifty yards to the woman, expecting to find the beauty- my mother? - lying under the tracks. When I pulled up short and looked it wasn't her. It was Eleanor, slashed from throat to crotch and from ear to ear. My head was pounding and the only sound I heard in the whole dream emerged. It was Kluge and he was laughing. Then the pounding in my head became real and louder and I awoke. My head throbbed nastily, but the pounding I heard was someone beating on my door.

I dragged myself out of bed and again realized how cold my room was. With the blanket draped over my shoulders, I opened the door to find the gangly, ferret-faced, faro dealer Gussie Black. With the fading pictures of the dead Eleanor still in my mind, I think the shock of seeing Black at my door stunned me, but my head cleared quickly. I despised Gussie, but I did believe he would have nothing to do with harming Eleanor.

"Detective Moses," he said. He had a scratchy voice, one that seemed like it took effort to pull from his throat. "You don't look very well. Are you okay?"

"Black," I said. "I'm fine. I wasn't expecting you at this time."

"I don't think you ever expected me at your door, but it is not that early. It is after ten, sir. I must begin my rounds soon or the day will be lost," he said defiantly. "My employers, the Hustons, and our mutual friend, Eleanor Winter, have told me that you were looking for me. Actually, the Hustons said you were looking for me; Eleanor said you wanted my help in trying to find a young girl."

I knew I wasn't myself when I invited Black into my apartment. I offered him the chair by the desk while I sat on the edge of the bed. As soon as he sat down I saw the Maria Scott scarf and the closed gift box that held Estelle Perkin's finger. Thankfully, the lid was on the box.

"Thank you for coming to see me," I said dumbly.

He sat up straight in the chair, extending his long legs before him. He wore a cautious smile, an untrusting one. I'd seen him many times before, but up close I could not believe how tall and thin a man he was. I noticed that his finger nails seemed to glisten with clear polish; on his left index finger was a gold ring with a red jewel in it. He had a pencil thin mustache above his lip. "It is always a pleasure to help the police when I am given an opportunity."

It was this comment and the false smile that brought me to my senses. "Would you like a drink? I have whiskey."

"Not for me. I have many rounds today."

"The cocaine business must be keeping you a lot busier than dealing faro at Paris."

He smiled. "It is true that I am very busy these days."

"Eleanor tells me that you frequent just about every neighborhood in the city and have a great knowledge of the prostitutes who reside in our fair city."

Another smile and a shrug. "I travel quite a bit through the city and have many acquaintances."

He was playing me carefully, and I didn't blame him. We were not friends or even mutual trusted enemies. "What do you know of white slaving?"

His eyes narrowed, the obvious tell, and then they brightened. "I am not very familiar with that term."

"Forgive me. I thought in your travels that you may have become aware of the term and its practice."

He shrugged again. "I am sorry."

"Never mind that. What Eleanor said was true. I am looking for a girl, a very pretty, young Italian girl, about twenty. Her name is Isabella Rossini. She arrived in town over a week ago and some think she may have been taken against her will and is now working as a prostitute in the Levee. Her father is the brother of the Italian ambassador to the United States." I don't know why I mentioned that. Black would never be impressed by anything I said.

"There are so many young women in the Levee. One would be hard to find, but a young beautiful Italian girl that arrived only over a week ago? Maybe this won't be so difficult. Is there a fee?"

I wanted to tell him if he helped me I wouldn't shoot him and throw him to the pigs in the Yards, but what came to mind was the retainer Marshall Field had paid me to find out how his son had died. "Two hundred, but I want her alive."

He put his hands out to his side. "Why would she not be?"

"I have to bring her back to her father."

He thought on this for a second. "I can ask around and probably find her if she's down here, but a picture would help."

The only picture we had was with Gunter. "I'll have to get you that."

"Then I will have to start my search by asking around."

"You'll get your reward when you find her for me."

He nodded at this and was about to stand, but he sat back down. "You don't care for me much, do you, Detective Moses?"

"I can't say one way or another," I lied.

"Is your dislike for me based solely on my friendship with Eleanor because that is all we are?"

I wanted to measure what I said next and have it come out slowly. "It seems like she doesn't always go in the right direction when she is around you."

He laughed. "I see. If you are referring to the heroin incident of a few nights ago, I apologize. She seemed to have a poor reaction to it and got very sick. I did get her home to the

Queen's."

"That was awfully nice of you," I said. "When I got there she seemed barely alive. Getting a doctor for her might have been the reasonable thing to do."

"I am sorry," he said. "I would never want to hurt her."

This line I believed. I nodded my head. "Don't let anything bad happen to her. I made her a promise that I would never harm you, and I will honor that promise as long as she is alive, but if she were gone." Now it was my turn to shrug.

Gussie's Adam's apple bobbed once very hard. "I will do my best to make sure nothing bad happens to her. I will also start to look for Miss Rossini. That picture of her would be of great help."

"I will get it to you shortly."

With that he was up and gone. I was surprised that there was no noticeable smell in the unit after he left. When he'd left, I noticed that I still felt terrible and the pounding had returned between my eyes. I lay back down, closed my eyes again, and dozed off.

*****

I didn't think I'd fallen asleep when the pounding returned, but there it was again, first in my ears and then between my eyes. It seemed to get louder before I realized that there was someone at my door again. My first thought was that it was Gussie Black, returning to tell me something that he had forgotten or to tell me to go to hell. Neither would have surprised me. I got out of bed again, blanket still wrapped about me, and answered the door. It was not Black or anyone I'd ever seen before. There stood a short, husky man, a bit older than me, with a full, scraggly beard covering his face and thick spectacles over his eyes. My first impression was wealth, based on the cut of his overcoat and suit pants. The hat on his head, a bowler, was not from a cheap haberdasher.

"Detective Moses?" His voice was soft, quiet.

"That's me. Who are you?"

"I am Ernest Lehmann. My man, Oldfield, tells me that you have been inquiring about my whereabouts."

It took a moment for this to set in and then it came to me. This was the rich friend of Marshall Field Jr., the one who may or may not have been with him the night he was shot. "Oh, please come in and please excuse me and the state of my apartment."

Lehmann stepped by me into my unit and I could tell by the look on his face that he was nervous. "I called for you at the precinct and told them that I had an urgent matter to discuss with you. They told me you were not in, but they told me where you lived."

Since the Field matter was not an official case, I was, as first, alarmed, but then I relaxed and pointed Lehmann to the same chair that Gussie had sat in a while ago. He checked the chair first, I'm sure for dirt, unbuttoned his long coat, and sat down. It was then that I noticed for the first time the large belly that this rich man possessed. It looked like he had a peach basket stuffed under his vest and just above his waist.

"You wanted to discuss a matter with me?" he said. He spoke so quietly it was almost hard to hear him above the rattling of the struggling radiator in my room.

"I believe you told them at the precinct that you had something urgent to discuss with me."

He seemed to think this over a moment. "It depends upon what you first visited my home to ask me about."

The right answer, I assumed or maybe the smart one. "I ran into a neighbor of the Fields, I don't know his name, who told me that you and Marshall Jr. would make a habit of visiting the Levee together on Wednesday nights."

I thought I might shock him, but instead he sighed deeply and looked relieved. "I have thought of that night so much since it happened that I am almost bursting with guilt." He took off his glasses and wiped them with a handkerchief from his suit pocket.

The constant head pounding, and now this, had me wide awake. "Why would you be bursting with guilt? You didn't shoot Field, did you?"

His look went from relief to shock. "Oh, God no. I didn't mean that."

"What did you mean?"

He took a deep breath and I could see small beads of sweat lining his forehead, just below the rim of the bowler. "I was there the night that Marshall was shot. I was in the Levee with him."

This was far too easy. "Do you know who shot Mr. Field?"

"It's not like that, Detective Moses. I saw a few things and heard a few things, but there is quite a bit that I'm not sure of." Now, he seemed scared. "Do you have anything to drink?"

Unlike Gussie, I knew my guest wanted whiskey. I got up from my bed and poured him a double in a glass. He drank half of it with the first sip. "Relax, Mr. Lehmann. I am trying to help all of those concerned and that would include you."

He nodded slowly. "We were there that night in the Levee, the night Marshall got shot. It was Wednesday the twenty-second. We always went down there on Wednesday nights. You see we both enjoyed the roulette wheel and the good whiskey."

"What about the women?" I said, and I'm sure I was smiling.

He returned the smile, but it was one that was guarded. "Myself, yes, but not Marshall. He was madly in love with Albertine, his wife, and he was a wonderful father. He would never do anything to compromise what he had."

"Of course," I said, and I was not being glib.

"I mean it," Lehmann blurted. "Marshall was a good man. His vices were a short list. He loved roulette and he liked good whiskey. He never so much as flirted with a woman that I saw."

I could see he was deeply affected by what had happened.

"I am sorry. I meant no harm."

He drank the rest of the whiskey and said no when I offered another. He put the glass on my desk. "It seems surreal that something like this could have happened. With all of the filth and evil that lives in that district, how did someone as good as Marshall become a victim?"

I had no answer. "Why don't you tell me about what happened that night? Tell me what you heard and saw."

He seemed more relaxed, at least composed, but the sweat appeared more evenly across his forehead. He wiped it with the handkerchief. "It was like every other week, nothing special about it. We would play roulette and have a few drinks. If Marshall was doing well he would stay late. If he was losing he would go home. That night he did rather well and stayed until about one-thirty in the morning."

"Excuse me, but where were you playing?"

"Well, I thought you knew that. We were playing at the Everleigh Club."

For some reason that name stuck me in the gut like a knife. I heard it mentioned so often and back when the shooting occurred, but all of that had been dismissed as drivel. Now a participant in the matter confirmed it. "I had heard that rumor," I said. "Please go on."

"Like I said, it had to be close to one-thirty in the morning, if not after. Marshall had done well at the wheel and was in good spirits. I headed up to the Oriental Room on the second floor with a young lass named Cat. Marshall left by the front door and was going to hail a cab back to his house."

"You say this was around one-thirty?"

"Right about then. I remember looking at my watch twice that night. The first time was when we were finished playing roulette. The second time was after the shooting."

"So you were upstairs on the second floor with this young lady. What happened next?"

"I was standing by the window, the shades were drawn,

and I removed my suit coat. I had just laid it across a chair when I heard this commotion out in front of the building."

"A commotion? You mean like a fight?"

He shook his head. "No, nothing physical. It was just words, heated words."

"Do you remember what was said?"

"I'm sure, almost exactly. The first thing I heard was an accusation from the first party, a male, who said something to the effect that "you are embarrassing your whole family"."

"You couldn't see this person?"

"I didn't open the shades yet. They were still closed. Then I heard Marshall's voice say, "Who in the hell are you"? It was then that I pulled back the shade, but I pulled it from right to left. I could see Marshall clearly enough, but I could not see the person he was talking to who was on my left."

"Where was Mr. Field?"

"In front of the second building the Everleighs owned. He was just standing on the sidewalk. It was at this point that the person he was talking to said, "I am the savior of your poor family". Marshall raised a hand to wave at him, you know, to brush him off as a lunatic when I heard the shot go off. It was so loud, and it was just below my window, it sounded like a cannon. At first, I saw Marshall grab his right side and then he collapsed on the sidewalk. Obviously in great pain, he cried out for help."

"What of the other person, his attacker?"

"I am not sure, but I'm certain he ran in the opposite direction."

"Going south on Dearborn?"

He thought for a moment. "That would be correct."

"Did anyone come to Mr. Field's aid?"

"Yes, almost immediately. I saw several of the ladies who had been inside the resort and, of course, the two Everleigh sisters. They were milling about Marshall, and I could hear him calling out in pain. Someone must have suggested that he go to Mercy Hospital because I clearly heard him say, "Not Mercy". The two Everleighs looked to be conversing and then a brougham pulled up and Marshall was helped into it by the driver. The Everleighs talked to the driver and the cab proceeded down Dearborn, toward the north, in a hasty fashion."

"You have no idea where?"

"None. I closed the shade and was so rattled I forgot about young Cat. I waited about a half an hour and just went home."

I mulled this over for a second. Lehmann was as good as an eyewitness except he had not seen the shooter. He had witnessed Field being shot and then hustled off somewhere after he refused to go to Mercy.

"You have never spoken to anyone about what you saw and heard?"

He blushed. "Only this morning."

I found this incredulous. "Mr. Field was a friend of yours or at least a regular acquaintance. What you have described is a murder by some sort of crazy person. Why would you keep all of this so quiet when the killer is undoubtedly still roaming about the city?"

He hung his head. "You would never understand if I tried to explain it to you."

"You can try me."

He stared hard at me for a moment. "What do you know of my background, Detective Moses?"

"Not that much, really. I understand you to be the heir to the late E.J. Lehmann who opened up Fair on State Street."

"That much is true. The estate is managed by an executor, my manager, Henry Korr. One of the provisions of the estate states that I will do nothing to embarrass the Lehmann family name. This is at the discretion of Mr. Korr. I'm not sure that being in the Levee doesn't push that point on its own. Being in the Levee on the night Marshall Field Jr. was murdered might clinch the deal. Admitting this at all is suicide."

"I see," I said. I felt sorry for him.

"When I heard that Marshall's father had quieted the papers and wanted the official version to read that Marshall had shot himself while cleaning his gun, I went along with that as well. This was the story the old man wanted to accept. Who was I to stand up and say that Marshall Field was a liar and that his son was murdered on the doorsteps of one of Chicago's most famous brothels?"

That part, I understood, I thought.

"Lastly, and probably most selfishly, I liked those nights at the Everleigh Club. I liked the roulette, the whiskey and the girls. I particularly liked Ada and Minna. I didn't want to do anything to upset them or my standing at the club. I decided, wrong or right, that I'd done the best thing I could when I closed that drape and went about my own business."

"Until when?"

"When I got to thinking that Marshall had died. With these thoughts, I was overwhelmed with guilt. I was his friend. I should have stepped in. I should have told him that going to Mercy might have been the right thing. I should have acted like a man. If I had, he might still be alive."

I could see the hurt on his face. It was not hard to believe him. "I understand."

He shrugged. "I had hoped someone would. Ultimately it was Marshall who didn't want to go to the hospital. Where he went, I have no idea, but eventually he ended up back on Prairie and later that afternoon the whole charade began. I only hope he didn't suffer much and is now in peace."

I felt myself nodding. This wasn't like one of the games that Coughlin and Kenna played when they got the police to look in the other direction, but it was a different crime of the Levee. It was amazing how this slimy district controlled so many lives.

"You'll catch whoever did this to Marshall?"

I wanted to believe that I would, but first I needed to find out why someone wanted to shoot him. "I will," I said and Ernest Lehmann relaxed his shoulders and nodded.

*****

Based on the lingering cold that I had, mixed with the raging headache, I had no intention of showing up at the precinct that day, but that idea changed when I made the first of my required daily calls for status updates. That call led to my being told that I was required to attend a meeting at one o'clock in Captain Morgan's office. Other than lying and saying I was sick and unable to attend, I had no choice, but to be there.

Until then, I was able to contemplate the help and information that I had received from Gussie and Ernest Lehmann. There were days that I would put in a solid fourteen hours and not turn up as much as today had. There was no doubt that with Gussie checking his sources and looking for Isabella Rossini that our chances of finding her were greatly improved. With the information received from Lehmann, it was clear that Marshall Field Jr. had not shot himself. That had been debated from the date of the shooting. Now there was a clear answer. What was not clear was who had shot him and why. The story that the shooter had said that Junior was embarrassing the whole Field clan sounded farfetched, but it was what Lehmann heard. Now I had to find this person.

I remembered when we had met in Morgan's office with Lieutenant Shipley that I thought the space was rather small. That had been when there were only four of us crammed in there. When I got to the Captain's office, I could see that a fourth wooden chair had been added and that the first three were occupied. Gunter had taken the spot by the wall and he looked as if he'd planned on staying in bed the entire day. I envisioned him finishing the whiskey from the night before all by himself. Sam Walker was next to him, and I found this amusing because Gunter was responsible for the swelling and bruising on the left side of Sam's face that had caused his eye to shut. The best looking of the three was Horace Langley who, even while doing his plough horse impersonation, looked the most normal. Captain Morgan smiled when I entered the office.

"Close the door behind you Patrick," he said. "We're glad you could join us this afternoon."

Of the three other detectives, only Langley smiled at this joke and I found no amusement in it. It was just now a few minutes before one o'clock. I was going to say something in response, something laced with sarcasm, but I thought better of it. I took my place next to Horace.

"I'm glad we're all together," Morgan said. "We've had a number of developments recently that bring a couple of the cases were handling into a better light."

I heard Gunter groan. I didn't know if it was Morgan's comment or just the way he felt. I only shifted a bit in my chair.

"We have an odd bit of circumstances that lead us to believe the Rossini case and the deaths of the Harts may be connected," Morgan said.

He didn't mention Mary Hastings, but I held my tongue. Morgan seemed to have a path he wanted to follow along.

"Your source, according to your report, led you to The Ranch in Blue Island. He also told you that Mike Hart might be involved in white slaving and owned a piece of this property." Morgan was staring at me as he made these comments.

"That sounds about right," I said.

"About right?" Morgan said.

"My source gave us Hart and The Ranch. That is true."

Morgan nodded. "You also mentioned that this one girl that you rescued, her name was..." Morgan stopped to check come papers on his desk.

"Sally Crowe," I said.

"Yes. Sally Crowe. You said she stated that one of the men that held her captive was named Mike."

"This was also confirmed by Chester Gallanty, a shop owner in Blue Island, although he gave us James as the last name."

"So you are convinced it was Mike Hart who was running that prison in Blue Island?"

I felt Morgan was going the route of the Inquisition, but so far nothing had been damning. "I have no reason to doubt this."

Morgan sat back in his chair and put his hands together, interlacing the fingers, and wiggled them. "Does it bother you that the day after you visit The Ranch, that Mike Hart and his wife Mollie were murdered in their bed?"

"Surprised a bit, but not bothered. I think Hart and his group were depraved, running a disgusting operation."

I heard the scraping on the floor as Sam Walker pushed his chair back and stood up. His face was red as he looked in my direction. "Discovering a few whores in Blue Island does not mean you were onto some grand operation."

"Those few girls don't, Sam, but a few people I have spoken to believe this white slaving is a real concerning matter. I'd also like to be able to interview all of the prostitutes along Bed Bug Row. The women I saw at Sappho looked to be in a horrible way. I'd like to get the true story out of them as to how they got started."

"They got started because they needed work. Most of them are just ignorant foreigners who lost their way," Sam said sharply.

"Wait just a minute there, Sam," Morgan said before I could respond. "Let's not get away from the reason we got together today in the first place."

Sam Walker sat down hard, the wooden chair bouncing off the wall behind him; I was starting to get confused and blamed my cold and my headache.

"Your source, this blind bookie that runs the newspaper

stand, he told you Mike Hart was involved in this white slaving?"

I'd already answered this. "Yes," I said.

"Did he give you any other names?"

"I told you he also gave us Mary Hastings."

"Another homicide victim," Sam said.

"Any other names, Moses?"

Now I was Moses. "No. He stopped short of any other names."

"I see," said Morgan. "The girl in Blue Island, Sally Crowe, she mentioned that the Mike Hart was assisted by a big, mute man?"

"She did."

"It's got to be the same man," Sam said.

"Same man as what?" I asked.

"Just before they were murdered, a housekeeper at the Marlborough saw this big, mute fellow go up the stairs to the second floor of the hotel. He had been seen in the past with Hart. We think he may have been dispatched to do the killings," Sam said.

"Whether large scale or not," Morgan said, "your source's information seems to have disrupted whatever Mike Hart, his wife Mollie, and maybe Mary Hastings were up to. Whoever else is involved didn't care for this leak of information and sent someone, we think this mute, to do away with the three of them. He is our prime suspect in the case. A case that has now become a priority."

The word priority punched me right in the nose, not making my head feel any better. "One second, Captain. How did the murder of these three, people that we suspect to be behind some of this white slaving we've heard about, become a priority? No disrespect to the dead, but if they were involved in the slave practice, I would think that the city and the police would be glad to have them on the deceased roll."

A thin smile crossed Morgan's face. "When we assigned you

this case, Patrick, we asked you to try and find Isabella Rossini. How are you proceeding in that matter?"

I shrugged. "So far it has been tough. We've followed the few leads that we have. They have turned up little with respect to Miss Rossini." I intentionally left out my new agreement with Gussie Black.

"That's right," the captain said. "What has happened is three people have been murdered since you began your investigation and this has several people upset."

"Who are we talking about?"

"Sam?" Morgan said.

Walker managed to get his puffy, mangled face to smile. "The Hart's were citizens and respected business operators in the First Ward. They bought most, if not all, of their liquor from Solly Freidman and Jacob Fine. These two, if you don't know, handle most of the liquor operations for Bathhouse John and Hinky Dink."

There it was out in the open. Coughlin and Kenna ran the liquor sales in the ward. The Harts had been big customers and probably political supporters. Their murders, two upstanding citizens murdered in their bed, had led to an outcry from the two aldermen. "Coughlin and Kenna now tell us which cases are priorities?"

Captain Morgan spread his arms wide. "They are the ward bosses, Patrick. They want us to track down the killer of the Harts."

I nodded. "Fair enough. Did they have any knowledge of or advice on how to control or stop this white slaving that appears to have found a strong home in their ward?"

Now Morgan's face wore a scowl. "Surely you are not suggesting that the two aldermen in this ward would be involved in something as awful as that?"

I was suggesting that, but again held my tongue. "Of course not," I said.

*****

When I had collected Gunter, or what was left of him, and we stood outside the precinct in the cold and fading light, I could see up close how badly he looked. "Maybe you should take it a little easy on the bottle," I said.

He weakly waved a hand at me. 'I'm fine."

"Are you?" I said. "You don't look so good and things looked a little tense between you and Margaret last night."

"A little spat is all."

"Okay," I said. "I suggest you go home and get some rest."

"And what about you? Your eyes have deeper circles each day I see you. Do you get any sleep? That would help with that cold?"

"We've got to find this Rossini girl," I said as if that provided all the answers.

"And maybe the bastard that left the scarf and the finger. That has me sleeping with one eye open now."

"And that, too."

A cab pulled up. "I'm off now, Patrick. You should be, too."

"I will," I said, but I had one stop first. The Everleigh Club was not far from the precinct building.

*****

Anyone in town, who had just a touch of evil in them, and even some that had none, knew where the Everleigh Club was. The two, three story buildings on the twenty-one hundred block of south Dearborn were famous. This was the top of the line as far as brothels were concerned. I was pretty sure that after my visits to Sappho on Bed Bug Row, and now my visit to see the Everleigh sisters, I had covered the entire spectrum of houses of ill repute. I think I have been clear in saying that I'm not an angel. For God's sake, I cavort with a prostitute. I don't know if this explains why I have never been inside the Everleigh Club.

Knowing my background, some may ask how it's possible.

As I stared up at the two brownstones, I wondered what secrets were retained within their walls. I wondered if I would be able to pry any of those secrets loose. I only cared about secrets concerning the shooting of Marshall Field, Jr. If I could learn anything to help my case, it would be worth the visit. I didn't know what to expect.

When I rang the bell to the club, I expected the door to be answered by a maid or a servant. I never expected that one of the sisters would answer, so I was roundly surprised when the door opened and I was faced by Minna, the younger sister, and in my opinion, the prettier of the two. I am not sure exactly how I looked at that moment, but the look on her face told me that she was sure I couldn't afford what they were peddling and she didn't want to give me too much of her time.

"Yes," she said, and even in that one syllable there was coldness.

What I usually did in these situations where I wanted someone to understand that I was not just some common oaf, I would pull my badge and that would mostly put me on the same level as the other person. This didn't work this time because I was transfixed by the woman in the doorway. Not only was she young, maybe mid-twenties, and beautiful, but it was the elegant manor in which she was dressed. That alone may have caused the lapse of my brain's function. It was the middle of the afternoon and the club seemed quiet, but Minna was dressed in a silk gown, pink in color and blazing with jewels. She wore a diamond dog collar at her throat, a half dozen diamond bracelets and a ring on each finger. I had never seen this combination of beauty and wealth all in one.

"Yes," she repeated. Her mood wasn't getting any warmer.

I finally fumbled with my badge and got it out. "Detective Patrick Moses," I said.

She smiled weakly. "It's early in the day, detective. I wouldn't mind helping you out, but you'll have to come by a little later, maybe after seven."

"No, it's not that Miss Everleigh. I am on in investigation."

This brought about a bit of a smirk where the smile had been. "We have made our regular payments to Mr. Colosimo and I am not aware that we are not in violation with any of our operations."

I shook my head, still trying to compose myself. Again, payments to Big Jim or Mr. Colosimo were getting in the way of my investigations. "It has nothing to do with your operations. It's a follow up to the Marshall Field shooting investigation. We're just trying to revisit the story to make sure all of the facts check out." I knew this weak little lie wouldn't last, but I didn't think I would need that much time.

She still wasn't projecting happiness, but at least she let me into the lobby. She must have been able to see the look in my eyes. "Is this your first visit?" Now she wore a better grin.

"It is," I said.

"Then I will give you a short tour before you ask your questions."

I said nothing and soon we were on the tour of the brothel that made me think I was in Baum's Land of Oz. The two buildings housed fifty rooms for the courtesans to perform their trade. These rooms carried names such as Gold, Moorish, Silver, Copper, Red, Rose, Green, Blue, Oriental and Chinese. That was the easy part. There was a large library housing a large number of expensive volumes, an art gallery, a big dining room where the lavish Pullman Buffet was served, a ballroom and a music room that held a gold gilded piano that I was told was valued at fifteen thousand dollars.

I saw eighteen karat gold cuspidors, golden silk curtains, silk damask easy chairs, mahogany tables covered with imported marble, gold bathtubs, gold rimmed china and silver dinner wear. There were paintings and tapestries covering every space of wall. Some of the rooms had mirrors on the ceilings and I wondered how I would act in such a place with a woman.

Minna told me that the club employed between fifteen and twenty-five of the best chefs and maids the city had. She told me the dinners they served were opulent. After dinner, I was not surprised to hear, three orchestras would play music all night long.

At the end of the tour, Minna's face now wore a full, genuine smile. I am sure this was due to the look on my own face, probably the same as a young child when they go see Santa. "I'm sure my sister, Ada, will now be able to meet with us. I'm sure there are a few questions you wish to ask us."

"Your club is absolutely beautiful," I said.

Now the smirk was back. "I can see how you made the detective grade."

We returned to the library where I was still amazed by the number of volumes the shelves held. Minna summoned a servant and requested that tea be brought for three. She pointed me to an overstuffed arm chair and I sat down. She took a seat across from me. As she did, Ada entered the room and walked immediately to me where she shook my hand as I stood.

"Ada," Minna said. "This is Detective Patrick Moses. He is here as a police department follow up to the night that Mr. Field shot himself."

Still shaking Ada's hand, I turned toward Minna. The look on her face was calm after she had made that comment. I wondered how easy this interview would be.

"A very sorry situation," Ada said. She wasn't as pretty as her younger sister, but she wouldn't be last in many contests. She wore a lovely light blue gown, but did not wear any of the jewels or rings that her sister did. After she shook my hand the maid brought in the tea and Ada took a seat by Minna.

I took a sip of my tea which was very hot and flavored nicely with a slice of fresh lemon. "Mr. Field was here the night of the shooting?" I said.

"The night before," Minna said quickly; Ada said nothing. "From what I recall he was here, played a little roulette and then went home. This was probably the night of the twenty-second since the shooting took place the afternoon of the twenty-third."

This was not going in the direction I had hoped; I was not totally surprised. "He was a regular visitor here at the club?"

Both sisters looked at each other, said nothing, and returned their looks to me. "I would say he was a semi-regular visitor," Minna said.

"Interested in what?" I know I was smiling.

Minna returned my smile; Ada wore a serious, maybe a worried look. "The little that I knew of Mr. Field, he seemed to be a man that just wanted to get away from the family for a bit. He would have a drink or two, play the wheel, smoke a good cigar. Isn't that what you saw in him, Ada?"

"He was not interested in the services offered by our girls, if that's what you mean, Detective," Ada said.

Another sip of the still too hot tea. "Let's go to the night before he was shot. What do either of you recall about that night?"

"Well," Minna said, "it was hard not to forget that we saw him before the night of the shooting, but he was here. I don't remember anything specific. I'm sure I greeted him, shared a few words, but that would have been it. He played roulette and then left the club. Ada?"

"I barely recall him being here. That night was very busy if I remember accurately."

In my opinion, either Ernest Lehmann had completely lied to me or the two sisters were having a tremendous memory lapse. "Do either of you recall what time Mr. Field left the club that night or early morning?"

Again the two sisters took a quiet moment to look at each other. "No," Minna said.

I wanted to make sure that I phrased my next few

comments slowly and cautiously. "During this follow up investigation, we have run into a person or two that have stated that Mr. Field was here the night of the shooting and that, in fact, he was shot right out in front of your club. They have also said that a number of your girls went outside upon either hearing the shot or Mr. Field's cries for help. These people have stated that both of you also went outside to see if you could assist Mr. Field in any way. What do you have to say to that?"

The two sisters looked at me as if I had just told them that is was a fairly cold winter afternoon. There were no telltale sign of any nerves, one way or the other. "You have to understand a few things about the way this city works," Minna said. "Since our arrival here in Chicago we have been extremely successful. This has bred a tremendous amount of jealously. That was the reason for the initial comments that Mr. Field was shot inside of our club. That is undoubtedly the source of these comments, these new assertions that the shooting took place outside of our building and that some of our girls and Ada and myself went to Mr. Field's assistance. Like the original comments, these are preposterous."

Minna's comments were so strong and straight forward, I couldn't tell if I was being lied to. "What if I told you that there was an eyewitness to the shooting?"

There was a momentary hesitation, the slightest, and then both sisters laughed. It couldn't have been better timed if they were stage actors reacting on cue. Unless, of course, their laughter was genuine.

"If you did tell us that you had an eyewitness, we would probably have to tell you that this person is a liar," Minna said.

I felt a smile crossing my face. "So you believe that the story of Mr. Field shooting himself while cleaning his gun at his residence is the accurate one."

"What can we believe?" Minna asked. "That is what the papers said. Originally, that is what your department concluded. Any stories that are going around about Mr. Field being shot here at the Everleigh Club are lies. They are only being started by people who are jealous of our accomplishments and want to see harm come to us. There is really nothing more that we can say on this topic."

It was the first hint of annoyance that I detected in either sister. It was also my first clue that the interview was over. I took another short sip of the tea, which was still undrinkable, and stood. I thanked both sisters for their time. Neither was smiling. Then I thanked Minna for the tour of the resort. I had honestly been taken aback by what I had seen. Now she smiled.

"Please do visit us at another time, Detective Moses. There are some things that you have yet to see here at the club." She smiled demurely.

*****

It was while I walked from the Everleigh Club that I realized how tired I was and how stiff and sore my body felt. I knew my lingering cold was the cause of some of this, but I also knew my Friday of heavy drinking, opium and lack of sleep contributed mightily. I needed rest and sleep. This night and tomorrow, Sunday, I would catch up on both. It would also give me time to think about whether Marshall Field, Jr. shot himself at his home or was murdered in front of the Everleigh Club. I had almost forgotten. I would need a little time to determine our next move in trying to find the missing Isabella Rossini.

## Sunday

If I had one day that I said I cherished it would have to be Sunday. This seemed to be the one day where the whole world took a rest, where even the crime in the Levee was gone. Since I had been on the force, this had always been the day when the pace of the district slowed tremendously. This had always provided for some peace and quiet. This Sunday, I had hoped for rest, peace and quiet. What I got was conflict, and this took away from everything else.

It should have been easy for me to place my grief for Luigi's death at the head of things. His funeral was Monday and most of my thoughts should have been focused in that direction, but other situations kept pressing themselves to the front of my brain. My day of sleep and rest became a day of sleeplessness and aggravation.

Don't get me wrong. Thoughts of Luigi were prominent. How could they not be? I was only a few weeks old when he'd found me in the basket while pissing in the back of the orphanage. He had been my guiding light until early Friday morning. Who would be there for me now?

It might have been a great Sunday if I could have lay in my bed and only thought of all of the good times there had been with Luigi, but each time I got to thinking, these thoughts were overwhelmed by glimpses at the three cases I was involved in.

The official police department case I was handling was the disappearance of Isabella Rossini. As I tossed and turned on my bed, I knew that we had almost nothing. The two possible leads that Big Louie had given me, Mary Hastings and Mike Hart, had both ended up with their brains blown out. Someone much bigger than them was controlling the white slaving in the Levee. I had no idea who. Other than my offer from Gussie

Black, we had no control of this case. In one of my wakeful moments, I thought we might need some kind of miracle to find Isabella. I wondered if we'd even get a minor break.

The case I had taken for Marshall Field was just as perplexing but for different reasons. Did I believe that Junior had shot himself in his home while cleaning his gun? I didn't believe that at all. It's nice that Emily Penfield and Robert Lowe told me that same story but it didn't seem remotely logical. In all of the gunshot cases I'd been involved in there was blood everywhere. Miraculously, in this case, no blood seems evident. Probable? That did not seem likely. What seems more likely is what the nameless neighbor and Ernest Lehmann told me. Field Jr. was a regular visitor to the Levee, playing roulette, drinking a little whiskey and smoking expensive cigars. After one of these trips, in the early morning, some nut had plugged Marshall in an attempt to help save the Field name. This seemed crazy in itself, but no crazier than the Everleigh sisters denying that any of this had happened. Either Ernest Lehmann or the Everleigh sisters were lying. I reasoned that I could understand the Everleigh's motive for lying. I saw no reason why Lehmann would lie to me.

It occurred to me that rather than looking for a quick solution to this case I would be better off going back and interviewing some of the people and reviewing some of the evidence from the original investigation. From this thought, I hoped to find one, or maybe more, bits of information to lead me in the proper direction.

I mentioned that there were now three cases that I was involved in. I would be remiss, or even stupid, if I failed to mention the reemergence of Dr. Kluge. This was the man who had smiled at me from atop the gallows. We had executed him for his involvement in the murders. End of case? I had thought so, but I was wrong. If the case was solved who had delivered the scarf and index finger to my door? The scarf might have been from a lucky souvenir procurer, but the finger? This had to be from the killer himself or someone who was there when the murder occurred. I was bothered with both the Isabella Rossini and Marshall Field, Jr. cases, but more than once I got out of bed to feel the scarf and to look upon the severed finger. As the moments passed, it became clear that this case might need to move to the head of the line in my thought process. What I knew now was that we had erred. There was a good chance that Kluge had an accomplice, or maybe Kluge was the helper, and the killer was still out there. In any event it appeared that the women of the Levee might still be in grave danger.

# Monday

It seemed logical to me that the weather matched my mood as the hansom trudged through the streets on its way to Holy Trinity for Luigi's funeral mass. The air was cold and damp, and the city was covered in thick, dark clouds. There would be no chance of sunlight today. I also saw little signs of a break in my gloomy mood. At least, my night visitor had left no new gifts near my door. I also felt that my lingering cold had abated somewhat. My ravaged throat felt a lot better.

For some reason, I found it amazing that I had only been to two funerals in my life before today. Both of these had been for police officers who had been killed in the line of duty. I hadn't known either of these officers very well, so I wasn't moved emotionally by their deaths. We were told to attend the funerals and I had. It wasn't hard to pick out the immediate families at these events. They were the ones who had lost control of their emotions. I had no real family to speak of so I had yet to attend an emotionally taxing funeral. Today, I thought, might be my chance. Luigi was the closest thing I had to a real family and he was gone.

Holy Trinity's chapel was overcrowded for the funeral mass. I wondered if the mass would be said in Italian or English and also wondered if it would be nearly as dramatic as the last mass Luigi had said for himself while lying at Mercy.

From what I could tell, most of the people that crowded the church were from Holy Trinity. There were priests, nuns, students and orphans. The cooks and attendants also showed up. I also saw several faces that I recognized from the neighborhood. I knew many of these people and a few stopped by to touch my shoulder, shake my hand or give me a hug as we waited for the mass to begin. Very few words were spoken.

I felt relief when Father Allegretti began in Luigi's native Italian tongue; Luigi would have liked that.

During the duration of the mass, the gospel, homily, readings and hymns, I heard very little. All I could do was stare at the casket in front of the altar and know my good friend was in there and never coming out. At one point, about midway through the mass, I felt I was suffocating. I wanted to scream out. I took a few deep breaths and the feeling passed. I listened to Father Seamus, Luigi's closest friend, deliver the eulogy and I did pay attention to that. Seamus was kind and fair to Luigi, but he did seem to miss the point, at least, as far as I was concerned. He didn't seem to know the real Luigi. I was sure this was because I had to have much more personal feelings than any of these other people had. I didn't know if I could express exactly how I felt if I was asked to speak. I wasn't.

When the mass ended the six pallbearers, all priests, carried the casket to the small graveyard that lay within yards of the chapel's back door. This was where the church's clergy members found their final resting place. A grave had been dug near the northern corner of the yard and this is where the pallbearers rested Luigi. More prayers were said, the wind turned nasty, and snow began to drift out of the dark clouds. Finally, the service ended and the crowd began to go back inside the building or go home. Other than the two gravediggers, who waited patiently and politely while I said a final prayer, the graveyard was empty, I thought.

As I finished my prayer and turned back towards the chapel, I saw Gunter and Eleanor waiting for me by the rear entrance. Gunter wore a look someone would have after eating bad fish; Eleanor looked so sad it was sweet.

"I'm sorry," I said. "I didn't see the two of you earlier."

Gunter took my hand. I wanted him to breathe to make sure he was alright. "It's okay, Patrick. We know how much Luigi meant to you. I'm very sorry." I didn't know if it was him struggling with getting the words out or the large tear that rolled out of his eye, but I felt my first hint at any emotion.

Eleanor stepped forward and hugged me. I hoped that none of the good sisters, the older ones, saw a prostitute hug me. "You should have called me, Patrick," she said. I sensed a scolding in her tone. "I feel awful that I wasn't here for you sooner than this."

I looked into the softness of her eyes and wished I had called her, too. Instead I had tried alcohol and opium to try and reach oblivion and that hadn't worked that well. "I just," I started. "I just didn't want to bring anyone else down."

Her eyes narrowed. "That's ridiculous, Patrick," she said, and I knew she meant this was another instance of keeping her on the outside.

"I'm sorry," I said again, but I knew my comment hadn't done anything to change the way she felt.

Gunter could probably sense the awkwardness as he shuffled his feet in the new snow. "I'm going into the precinct now, after I drop Eleanor at the Queen's. Will you be coming along soon?"

I could sense the urgency in his voice. "Has something come up?"

He nodded. "When I called in they said they had a message for either one of us from Tommy Flynn at the *Tribune*."

Flynn was a reporter who covered politics. "Any ideas?"

"Not one," he said.

I told him I'd be along shortly and he nodded and backed away. I took Eleanor in my arms and she didn't resist me. "May I see you later?"

She looked up into my face. I could see she was sad for me, but mad that I hadn't called her. "Before nine, Patrick. You know how Miss Keesher gets."

I bade them both farewell and entered the back of the church. I could hear the clanging of the gravedigger's shovels before I closed the door behind me. The warmth of the chapel hit me and I'd only walked a few steps when I saw Seamus sitting in the sacristy, not far from where Luigi had fallen after his heart attack. I entered the small room.

He looked up at me as I walked in. "Are you okay, Patrick?"

He was seated at a small table with two chairs. On the table was a bottle of whiskey, two glasses and a worn, white envelope. "I feel better," I said, not lying.

"Have a seat," he said.

I took a seat across from him and he poured whiskey, evenly, into the two small glasses. He gave me one and grabbed the other. He raised his glass. "To our good friend, Luigi. May he rest in peace?" We clicked our glasses together and swallowed the brown liquid; its warmth felt good against my throat.

"Is this your plan for the day," I said, "to sit in the sacristy and drink that bottle of whiskey?"

He smiled. "I might, but I wanted to speak to you privately before you set out."

I was thinking I might get a lecture about watching myself and not drinking too much. "Don't concern yourself with me," I said.

"I'm not too concerned about you, Patrick." He stopped and refilled the glasses. "I am concerned, but that's not why I wanted to speak with you. I was going through some of the things in Luigi's room when I found this." He put one finger on the envelope and slid it towards me.

"What is it?"

"Have a look."

I sipped some of the whiskey and then took the envelope in my hand. It was thin, including whatever contents it held. I slowly opened it and removed two photographs from the inside. The one on top was clearly my father; he'd been much younger when the picture had been taken. I looked at it only briefly and put it aside. The second picture was of a woman, a young woman, maybe less than twenty years old. Her face was angular with sharp features, but there was beauty there. Her hair was full, light colored, with soft curls. Her eyes looked awake and bright. She wore a warm smile, no teeth showing. She looked happy. I turned the picture over and in Luigi's recognizable script was written, "Rose". I turned the photograph over and stared again at her face. I was haunted.

"Patrick," Seamus said softly, "I believe that is your mother."

\*\*\*\*\*

With Luigi in the process of being planted in the ground, and with my new possessions in my pocket, I took a cab to the precinct to catch up with Gunter. I had to deal first with several detectives and officers offering condolences before I found Gunter on the second floor. He looked hurried and not nearly as sad as he had in the past half hour.

"What's wrong?" I asked.

"We've got to hurry. I spoke with Tommy Flynn and he said he would only be at the *Tribune* offices until one. After that he would be on his way to catch a train for New York."

I looked at my watch. It was twelve-twenty. "We have to hurry."

In the coach on the way to the Tribune Building on Michigan Avenue, I could sense that there was something bothering Gunter. I thought it might be the situation at home with Margaret, but I didn't want to ask about that. "Are you okay? It seems that you are bothered by something."

He glared at me. "How can you always be so cold?"

I was stunned for a moment. "I don't understand."

"Of course you don't. It's your makeup. You never change. You never show your feelings. Whether it was the death of your closest friend, finding those girls out in Blue Island, the Harts, or this goddamned scarf and finger that have shown up. Doesn't any of that bother you?"

I looked off to the side as we crossed the Chicago River. It was nothing but ice. "Of course it bothers me," I said. "It all bothers me. I just don't show it like some people. I don't know why."

Gunter's glare softened. "He's back, isn't he?"

"Who?"

"Kluge. He has come back from the dead."

Gunter turned from me. I knew his comment was ludicrous, but I knew what he meant. The problem we had with Kluge had returned. "We'll have to try and deal with that," I said, but I had no idea where to begin. Gunter grunted something as the cab pulled up in front of the *Tribune* and he stepped out on the curb.

The air was cold and the skies cloudy, but the snow had stopped falling. This hadn't slowed down the number of holiday shoppers that milled about on the great avenue. With Christmas coming, I'm sure they would be there until the holiday was over.

I followed Gunter into the *Tribune* where we were told that the reporter's pool was located up on the fifth floor. We took a slow, rambling elevator- the damn things scare me to death- and we were dropped off amidst a number of desks, frantic looking people and the endless sounds of typewriters being pounded on. It wasn't that late in the day, but the only thing I could think of was deadlines.

We asked a couple of people and they pointed us in the direction of where Tommy Flynn had his desk. When we found him he was stuffing papers into a leather valise and smoking endlessly on a cigarette. His face was flushed and his nose was creased with the veins of a heavy drinker. He was a short man, skinny and you could count the hairs on his head. It looked like the last people he wanted to talk to were the police.

"Tommy Flynn," Gunter said as we stood in front of his desk.

Flynn looked over at us, clearly annoyed. "I'm a little busy now, fellas. I've got to catch a train in a bit for New York."

"You called us," Gunter said. He flipped his badge quickly. "We're with the Twenty-Second Precinct."

"Oh, the police. Why didn't you say so?" Now he had a broad smile. "You came over here because of the note the prostitute threw at me."

"What note?" I said.

Flynn looked around his desk for a moment and found what he was looking for. It was a crumpled piece of dirty paper. He gave it to Gunter who, after reading it, gave it to me.

*My name is Clara Hunter. I am being held as a prisoner here at The Palace. Please help me.*

"How did you get this?" I said.

"Like I said. I was walking by The Palace when this girl yells out to me from the second floor. I look up and I see her. She looked real pretty. Before I can even get a word in she throws the note out the window. I bent down to pick it up and by the time I look back up at the window, the girl is gone and the window is closed. I thought it was very odd and I called down to headquarters. They gave me a guy named Shipley, a lieutenant, and he told me to call your precinct and ask for you two."

"That's the whole story?" Gunter asked.

Flynn shrugged. "That's all there is. She called out to me, tossed me the note and was gone. I called and they pointed me to you two."

Gunter looked to me. "To The Palace?"

"We have a choice?"

"Are you done with me?" Flynn said. "Supposedly Teddy is going to say something very important in New York and the *Tribune* needs me there. God forbid I miss the earth shattering comments."

It was obvious Flynn was not a fan of Roosevelt. We turned and left him gathering things for his trip.

*****

Compared to Sappho, The Palace was just that. Compared to The Everleigh Club it was a dump. All the contrasts that thrust themselves at you in the Levee. It was a shame most of them had to do with whorehouses. The Palace was a two story, frame white building, crammed between a tavern and a pawn shop on State Street. The paint on the building needed a fresh coat. It was badly chipped and dirty, streaked from the latest storm.

The doorbell was answered almost immediately by a rather plain looking woman in a dark blue dress. She wore little makeup and smiled with a lot of effort. A serious woman, this one.

"May I help you two gentlemen?" she asked.

We each showed our badges and the woman took one step backwards. She hadn't been expecting the police.

"Do you still want to help us? Gunter said.

"Of course," she said. "We always want to try and help the police whenever we can."

Ah, I thought, the brothels always trying to help the police. "We are looking for a young woman who may be in your employ here. Her name is Clara Hunter."

She didn't blink at all. "Clara, yes. She is one of our newest girls. Has she done something wrong?"

"I don't believe so," I said, trying not to alarm her. "We just want to talk to her about one of the cases we are involved in, a missing persons case." No lie there.

"If you will wait here for one minute, I will go and get Clara." She turned and walked down a short corridor that led to a staircase to the second floor. The vestibule we were in was not dirty, but the carpet on the floor showed a lot of wear. There were dirt and mud prints from the sloppy outside, but most of these were from the days before and dried. There were several pictures on the wall, mostly of royals from foreign countries.

"This seems too easy. She doesn't seem concerned," Gunter said.

"Unless she's sneaking out of a window on the second floor."

'She didn't look that type."

CRIMES OF THE LEVEE

"She barely looked like any type."

Gunter smiled and was going to say more when we heard conversation coming from the direction that the woman went. She stepped into the lobby again and behind her was a young woman, not more than twenty, slim, had brown hair and wearing a pale green dress. The girl showed no sign of alarm or danger.

"This is Clara Hunter," the woman said.

"Miss Hunter," I said, and the woman looked right at me. "We were told that you had a conversation with a man on the street a day ago, a reporter from the *Tribune*. Do you recall that conversation?"

Clara Hunter seemed to be thinking. "I don't recall that. I haven't been outside the last few days."

"You said you wanted to question Clara about a case that you were involved in," the woman said.

"We do," I said, "but not here. She will have to come down to the precinct with us. Will that be a problem?"

"Of course not," the woman said too quickly.

"Do you have an overcoat?"

"I can get her an overcoat," the woman said to me. "Clara, please come with me."

They went back in the direction they had come, but stayed on the first floor. If there was any discussion we didn't hear it. When they reappeared, Clara wore a heavy wool coat, a hat and a pair of fine gloves. She almost looked like she could be going to church.

"She won't be gone long?" the woman asked. "She is working this evening."

"Only as long as our questioning takes," I said.

The woman nodded and we opened the door and stepped out into the frigid air. The hansom we had taken from the *Tribune* had waited for us as instructed and the three of us piled in. Clara sat between Gunter and me. I told the driver to run us to the precinct building. Clara Hunter had not muttered a word.

"Would you like to explain to us what is going on?" I asked her as the cab moved from the curb in the direction of the precinct.

She looked at me and the first hint of terror crossed her eyes. She pointed at the driver and then put a finger to her lips. Whatever conversation that we would have with Clara Hunter would not take place until we were safely behind the precinct walls.

She acted perfectly normal and remained quiet when we entered the precinct and headed upstairs to the detective division. Many of the cops in the place stared at us as we led the pretty woman through the halls. We found a small available room with a table and two chairs and we led Clara into it. She took off her gloves and coat, putting the gloves on the table and coat over the back of the chair. The hat sat on her head. She sat down and Gunter sat near her. I closed the door and remained standing. Once I closed the door, Clara Hunter burst into tears, sobbing as loudly as I'd heard anyone cry.

"Get her some water," I said to Gunter. He was out the door quickly, closing it behind him. I knelt by her and took her hand. "It's going to be okay. You're in a safe place."

She had barely calmed by the time Gunter returned and she took a long drink of the water. This helped settle her and she dabbed at her eyes with a handkerchief I'd given her. Make-up that had been around her eyes now streaked her pretty face; she looked a bit like a ghoul.

"Are you better?" I asked.

"Better," she said, "but far from good."

"May I call you Clara?"

"Yes, please," she said politely.

I saw Gunter smile and turn his head. I pulled the crumpled note from my pocket that Tommy Flynn had given to us. "A reporter from the *Tribune*, Tommy Flynn, told us that you tossed him this note the other day as he walked past the Palace.

He said you called out to him from the second floor, tossed him the note and then you were gone."

She looked over the note and then into my eyes. Was she seeking trust? She was looking for something.

"Clara," I said. "We are looking for a woman named Isabella Rossini. From what we know, she was abducted from the IC station and is being held captive by a resort down here in the Levee. We are told she is a victim of white slaving. Do you know anyone or have you seen anyone by that name?"

She shook her head no.

"The city seems to think this white slaving is becoming a plague, especially down here in the Levee. They seem to think a lot of young women are falling victim to this scourge. Do you know anything about this?"

She looked over at Gunter. He wore a serious, concerned look. She came back to me. No verbal response.

"We can only help you if you let us; you have to trust us," I said.

She nodded ever so lightly.

"Clara, do you believe you are a victim of white slaving?"

She lowered her head to her chin and closed her eyes. We needed her to talk, but she had yet to say anything. We waited a few moments and then she began to sob again, her whole body shuddering. I offered her more water, but she shook her head no. She lifted her make-up streaked face to me. She was a very pretty young woman.

"Did you write this note and toss it out the window to Tommy Flynn."

Once more she looked at the note. "I didn't know his name or who he was," she said slowly, the words measured. "I wrote the note and threw it out to him, calling to him. I thought it might be my only chance. I had a pencil, paper and the window was right there. I wrote it quickly and tossed it to the first passerby I saw. I was so scared that I closed the window before the paper hit the ground. If they had seen me, I might be dead now."

"Slow down one minute," Gunter said, but I raised my hand to quiet him. His temper seemed to be rising.

"If who had seen you?" I asked.

"Mrs. Sloan or one of the other girls. If they had seen me toss that note out the window, I would have been in serious trouble."

"Mrs. Sloan was the woman who let us in and went and got you?"

"That was her, but please don't be fooled. She is normally loud and demanding. She tells us the rules and we follow them. I have heard a number of stories about the girls that don't follow the rules."

I looked at Gunter. He shrugged and lit a cigarette. "Can we start from the beginning? Can you tell us how you ended up at The Palace in the first place?"

"It's my fault," she said. "I trusted all of those people."

"Who?"

She wiped tears away from her eyes; she was still having a tough time looking right at us. "At first it was the man in Milwaukee where I'm from. His name was William. He promised me that if I went to Chicago that his friends would find me work and a great place to live. I had been working in a shoe factory in Milwaukee and I wanted something better." Now she looked at me to see if I understood.

"Go ahead," I said.

"This man, William, bought me a ticket for Chicago that took me into Union Station. He told me I'd be met there by a man named Mike who could get me taken care of with the job and the place to live."

I swallowed hard. "This Mike met you at Union Station?"

"He did, along with this big guy who said very little."

Maybe nothing, I thought. "Can you describe Mike?"

"Sure he was a good looking man, tall, but he walked with a bad limp."

"What happened after they met you at Union?"

"They had a very nice carriage and they took me along the downtown area to see the shops and stores. I was awed by the big buildings. The big, quiet guy got out somewhere and it was just Mike and I. He spent the whole day with me and then he took me to dinner. It was one of the nicest restaurants I'd ever been in. He let me order a steak and then we had some wine. After that, I don't remember very much."

This story was sounding all too familiar. "What happened to you next?"

"When I did wake up I was in a room at The Palace and Mrs. Sloan was there with me. She told me that I worked for her now and that I must do whatever she told me to do. She told me I would not be any trouble or I would be punished. I was scared to death and in a new, big city. I did what I was told."

"You couldn't just walk out of the place?" Gunter said.

She shook her head. "I don't know what it was, something in the food or the drinks, but it made all of the women that worked there so unwilling to do something that would get them in trouble. If I made one false move any of those women would have made so much noise I would have been caught in a minute."

"How did you figure out how to write the note?"

"I thought they were poisoning me. I didn't want to eat what they gave me or drink anything. If they gave me anything I threw it away. That was tough enough. I got the idea to write the note and toss it out the window, but my opportunities were very slim. When I saw my chance I had to take it. Without food or drink, I was getting weaker as it was, and I was getting so down. I never thought I would ever come to this city and be pressed into the business of servicing men. It was awful."

The poor woman broke down again, sobbing heavily. I couldn't imagine what she had gone through, but she had been lucky. She had caught them in their misdeeds and done something about it. The girls in Blue Island hadn't been so lucky.

"Does this Mrs. Sloan own The Palace?" I asked.

She shivered at the mention of the name. "She is evil. I am convinced that she is the devil. If a girl acts up she will call the men and they will come over and beat the girls or rape them. It is awful. That is why the girls don't act up. The big, quiet man is the one who comes over. He is an animal."

"I am sorry to hear all of that, but I wanted to know if this Mrs. Sloan is the owner."

She shook her head. "I don't think so. I think she was working with that man named Mike and the quiet guy. They seemed to be running things, but more than once I heard a name, and it was usually in reference to a man who wasn't going to like that something had happened or he wasn't going to like the way things were going."

"What name was that?" I said.

"The name I always heard was Mr. Von Bever. I heard it more than once."

I knew that name as well. I had heard it from Eleanor's mouth more than a few times. Maurice Von Bever and his wife Julia owned several resorts in the city. I know they owned Paris where Gussie Black dealt faro. I was now certain that he owned The Palace and might me behind some of this white slaving that was taking place. I was also convinced that the Mike Clara mentioned was the now deceased Mike Hart; the quiet man could only be the mute from Blue Island. None of this meant we were anywhere closer to finding Isabella Rossini, but we were getting a better understanding of the white slaving trade.

"I won't have to go back there, will I?"

"Absolutely not," I said. "Do you still have people back in Milwaukee?"

She teared up. "My mother, father and two little sisters. They are probably worried sick about me."

I patted her on the shoulder. "We'll make sure you can

contact them, and then we'll have an officer take you back to Union and you can catch a train home. We'll need all of your home information so that we can contact you when we catch all those responsible for what happened to you and can bring them to trial."

She was crying again. "I just want to go home now, but I will do anything that you need me to do to punish those people, especially Mrs. Sloan. She is a witch."

*****

When we got Clara settled down, we placed her with a pair of junior officers and told them their entire responsibility was her. They were told to make sure she was allowed to call her home and then to get her on the next train for Milwaukee. When we had that settled we stopped for a moment by our desks.

"We have to go back there right now," Gunter said. "There has to be other women there that are being held captive."

I could tell his blood was running hot; I'd seen it before. "We will go right now, but you have to promise to hold your temper. The law will take care of these people."

He nodded. "I am fine, Patrick. I just don't believe how cool and convincing our friend Mrs. Sloan was."

I couldn't believe it either. Everything seemed so normal. "There appears to be more and more of that going around."

"Speaking of strange behavior, what are we going to do about Kluge?" he asked quietly.

I looked at him for a long time before commenting. "Gunter, Kluge is dead."

He got very close to me; I could smell his smoke laced breath. "You know what I mean. Don't be coy with me. Some bastard left you that scarf and finger. What are we going to do?"

In his eyes, I could see both fear and frustration. We could lose our jobs over such a large blunder. Potentially, we had a killer still loose in our district. I wondered what part was bothering him more. What bothered me was that I didn't have any idea what to do. "Gunter, I have the scarf and the finger, nothing more. I have no idea what to do or where to go from here. I suggest we stick to The Palace for now and let something develop before we get too excited."

"When you say develop, do you mean allow him to kill someone?"

I swallowed hard and Gunter saw this. "We don't have anything else to go on."

He nodded and I could see his resolve. There was nothing more we could do at that point with what we had. "Let's get over to The Palace. Maybe this is one problem we can put an end to."

I agreed and we headed out the door, prepared to make an arrest. How wrong we were to think that.

Back at The Palace, we were once again greeted by Mrs. Sloan. It may have been some kind of foreboding, but I found the brothel to be darker on the inside than I remembered. I told Gunter to watch himself before we entered the place, but I could feel his anxiety as he stood next to me. Mrs. Sloan maintained the same professional, businesslike manner she had showed us before.

"You did not return with Miss Hunter," she said dryly.

"We did not," I said. "There is a reason for this."

She didn't reply, implying that it was up to me to state my reasons for our return. "Miss Hunter made some startling accusations."

If there was any indication that she might crack under our questioning it was minor, maybe a flicker of her eyes. "Miss Hunter is a bit delusional. She seems to think that she can do a better job of running The Palace than I do. She is a silly, confused girl."

I heard some animal like growl starting to emit from

Gunter, but he kept it in check. I hoped he didn't punch her in the face. "She wrote a note to a reporter from the *Tribune* that said she was being held here against her will. What do you think about that?"

She smiled and then emitted a short laugh. "Detective, do you see any locks on the windows or the doors? This is not a prison. The girls that work here are free to go as they wish. I can assure you that no one, including Miss Hunter, has ever been held captive here."

It was the way she said it, the inflection of her voice. It was convincing. I believed her.

"She told us," Gunter said loudly, taking me out of my moment of reflection, "that she had been taken from Union Station, possibly drugged and brought here. She told us she had been threatened with her life if she said anything or tried to leave."

"Preposterous lies," she said.

"Did you know a man named Mike Hart?" I asked.

"I know Mike," she said. "He owned a good part of the Marlborough. He and his wife were nice people. It was a shame what happened to them. Have you caught the killer?" The last question brought forth a change in tone, an accusation of the police force.

"Not yet," I said, "but we're not here about that. Miss Hunter described the person that picked her up at Union and brought her here. It was an accurate description of Mike Hart."

She shook her head. "Not even close to the truth. Miss Hunter came here on her own in search of work, another lost soul from the Godforsaken city of Milwaukee, thinking that Chicago is the Promised Land. She was attractive so we hired her. End of story."

I checked on Gunter. His breathing seemed normal. Maybe he believed this story, too. "So everything that Miss Hunter told us is a lie?"

"You haven't told me one thing that she has said that is

true? Like I said, a young, ambitious, foolish girl, trying to climb the ladder to success. Just going about it the wrong way."

"Who owns The Palace?" I said.

"Mr. Von Bever." She didn't appear to be hiding anything.

"Do you mind if we talk to the girls that are here? We want to ask them what they think of staying here at the Palace."

"I don't see any problem with that. Give me a few minutes and let me round them all up and bring them down here."

When she walked away, I looked again at Gunter and he only shrugged. "This is the most amazing situation," I said.

"Another mystery," he said. There was bitterness.

It was crazy, I thought. Clara Hunter telling us a wild, emotional tale, and then Mrs. Sloan calmly denying it and acting like everything was normal, that is, for a brothel. At least she hadn't told us, like Mary Hastings, that they were protected from police intrusion because they had made payments.

She returned shortly, in less than five minutes, and trailing behind her were eight women. These women all looked to be within the age of twenty and twenty-five. Unlike Sappho, where the women had looked sickly and putrid, the women of Palace looked reasonably healthy and alert. They were also cleaner and better dressed. That didn't mean they weren't in trouble or under some threat.

"Here you are, detectives," Mrs. Sloan said. "These are the women that we now employ here at Palace, minus Miss Hunter."

I looked at their faces. Some looked at me, a couple smiled, but more looked down at the floor. They didn't look particularly scared or nervous. I was beginning to think we had been taken by Clara Hunter.

"Did you want to ask them some questions?"

"Are you all happy to be working here at The Palace and for Mrs. Sloan?" Gunter said, catching me a bit off guard.

There was a bit of quiet murmuring and we heard a few of the women mention that they were happy where they were.

One mentioned that The Palace was a lot better than some places. My knowledge of the resorts in the area proved that to be true.

"And you can come and go as you please?" Gunter persisted.

"Of course," one woman, a busty brunette stated. "This ain't no prison."

When she spoke up I looked at her. She was loud and clearly spoke, but for that short sentence, I thought I detected a weary, forlorn tone.

"Do you have anything else that you'd like to ask the girls?" Mrs. Sloan asked. "They have to get some rest before tonight."

"Did any of you know Clara Hunter very well?" Gunter said.

There was quiet for a moment; a few of the women looked at each other. "She was somewhat new, maybe only here a few weeks," a dark haired woman, younger looking than the others said. "She seemed out of place, like she'd made a mistake coming here. She complained a lot. She didn't like Mrs. Sloan."

I was looking at Mrs. Sloan as the woman spoke. There was no sign on her face of what she thought of these comments.

"Why didn't she just leave?" Gunter said.

"I told you," Mrs. Sloan said. For the first time there was a hint at anger. "She didn't like me, didn't like the way I ran things here. If she wrote this note, as you say, she was only trying to get me into some trouble with the police."

Whether this was the truth or some intricate plan to throw us off balance, I felt we had all that we were going to get from the meeting. We were certainly no further along in finding Isabella Rossini. If anything we were more confused. I knew the white slaving was going on, but at The Palace, I wasn't sure. Some things were not making any sense.

"I placed a call to Mr. Von Bever before returning with the girls," Mrs. Sloan said. "He believes there is a gross misunderstanding here. He'd like to see you two at Paris tomorrow morning, first thing, if that's possible."

Gunter and I looked at each other, more frustrated, and knowing less and less. We shrugged, told Mrs. Sloan to tell Von Bever we'd be there and returned to the precinct.

*****

There were two detectives who were prominent in the investigation into the shooting of Marshall Field, Jr. Riley O'Donnell was a hardnosed, tight lipped, Irishman who was known to not drink and attend church on a regular basis. He had been married twenty five years and had five kids. The other detective, George Loftus, was a regular drinker and had no problem talking about cases he was involved in, particularly any part of the case that featured his role in solving the crimes.

I found Loftus, a fortyish bachelor, near his desk on the second floor. He was wearing a pin-striped gray suit; his thin hair was combed straight back. He was leaning back in his chair, reading a copy of the *Transocean*. A cigarette dangled from his lips, smoldering slowly.

"Tough day, Loftus?" I said.

He looked up at me and took the cigarette from his mouth, exhaling a ring of smoke into the detective's room. "Sorry about your priest friend, Moses."

I nodded. "Yeah, that was tough. Got time for a drink, George?"

He gave me a look that suggested I wanted something, but nodded. "There's nothing going on here."

We went down to The Lantern, a small pub around the corner on Twenty-Third that was usually a place where you could find a number of patrolmen or detectives. Today, maybe because it was a Monday, it was fairly quiet. We found a table near the back of the pub, away from the cold that the door let in. Loftus ordered a whiskey; I stuck with beer.

"How long have I known you, Moses?" he asked when our

drinks were brought to us.

"Since I've been on the force, maybe ten years."

He took a sip of the whiskey, wincing a bit as the whiskey torched his tongue. "Ten years. That's a long time. It seems longer now that you have asked me to have a drink with you."

"You didn't seem very reluctant when I offered."

He smiled. "I usually don't mind who I share a drink with."

"I have that same problem at times."

"But you didn't just ask me along today so that you could buy me a drink?"

"I was just curious," I said. I took a drink of the beer. It was bitter. "I got to wondering about the Field case. It seemed to happen, and there was all of that mystery around it, and then it just got shut down, almost like it never happened."

He laughed. "Why are you so curious? Mysteries happen all the time in this job. They are only magnified in this city, especially down here in the Levee."

"So the shooting is a mystery?"

"What do you think, Moses? The kid shoots himself and dies, end of story."

"Is it?"

"Not even close to the truth, but let me clarify that for you." He finished his first whiskey and raised his hand for the bartender to see. "It wasn't like Riley and I had any proof that Junior didn't shoot himself. It was just all of the stuff that we ran into the indicated that he hadn't."

The barkeep brought over the new drink. "Care to elaborate?"

He drank half the second whiskey; it seemed to be going down a lot easier than the first. "You've got to understand that our investigation didn't get underway until a couple of days after the shooting. If there had been a crime scene it was gone, cleaned up by the Field staff."

"If he was shot at home."

He lit a cigarette and pointed it in my direction. "Exactly.

No proof to that."

"What did you find?"

"The staff that was there when Junior shot himself, that pompous butler and mousey nurse told the story we all heard. Field shot himself in his room and they came to his aide. His brother in law and several doctors were called. Field was rushed to Mercy, surgery was performed and he died a few days later. A bunch of rumors and theories hit the papers, but Mr. Field, Sr. made sure those went away."

"Like the Everleigh Club rumors?"

"Like those. Those two sisters were tighter than a virgin when it came to their side of the story. Field was there the night before the shooting, but no one heard or saw him get shot. The last they saw was him going out their door."

I thought of Ernest Lehmann, but kept quiet. "After the staff's story, what did you have?"

"Little or nothing. We talked to the coroner, Hoffman, but he had little to add. An inquest was necessary because of the mysterious cause of death, but it was half- hearted. Again the father had called the mayor and the police chief. His son had died because of an accident. Was all of this probing really needed? Busse and the Chief agreed. No autopsy was done."

"What did Hoffman think about that?"

"I could tell he was agitated, but he said very little. I could tell he thought the whole story had not been told."

I thought about this and then wondered why Marshall Field had shut down an earlier investigation, but then had hired me. "Anybody else tell you anything that stuck out?"

"It's not what anyone told us. It was what wasn't said." He tipped back the glass and downed the remaining whiskey. He threw his hand into the air, signaling another round. "Like the gun shop owner who sold Field the gun he shot himself with. Guy's name was Steven Hirth. Has a small shop on the west side. He wouldn't talk to us at all. Said he was too upset that Mr. Field shot himself with a gun he had sold him. To Riley and me it sounded like hogwash, but we respected what he said and didn't pester him for a comment. The only thing we got out of that discussion was the Field had bought the gun there."

The third whiskey came and Loftus took another sip; I was still on my first beer. That didn't bother George. "Another thing, the wife, Albertine Huck, a real beauty."

"What about her?"

"We never got to talk to her. We were told to leave her alone in her time of bereavement. We understood that, but the time for a talk never came. The department wanted the case closed and it was. It was called an accident and the case file was shut."

"What do you think, George?"

He picked his glass up and finished the whiskey. Some sloshed on his lips and he wiped it away with his sleeve. "We heard the young Field liked to go into the Levee to play. What I think is that he got into a fight or an argument down there-these rich people think they know everything- and somebody plunked him. Somehow he got home, someone fixed him up a bit, but he was injured too badly. They called in the brother in law and the doctors and he was rushed to Mercy, but the damage had been done and it was too great. That was why he died. There had been a cover up and his wound wasn't dealt with properly. It's a damned shame, but I think if the truth is told and he goes right to the hospital, he's still alive today. You want another beer."

I was only halfway through my first. My head was swimming with what George Loftus had told me. "Sure, I'll have another," I said, but I ended up barely finishing the first one.

*****

Eleanor and I made love later that night. For me, I thought it was wonderful. I felt very close to her. It wasn't until we were finished and lying there in her bed did I realize how far away she was from me.

"How is your search going for that young woman?" she said.

"Isabella Rossini?"

"I couldn't remember her name."

"It's not going all that well. Anyone who might have had an idea where she went ended up getting murdered. After that, we have no clues at all."

A look of worry crossed her face. "Has Gussie gotten a hold of you?"

"He did, actually. He came by my apartment and told me he would put the word out and keep an eye out for her."

"I told him to try and help you."

I knew he hadn't come to me voluntarily. "I appreciate that."

"I wish you had come to me sooner about Luigi. I would have wanted to be there for you."

This caught me off guard. "I told you I was sorry about that. When Father Seamus got a hold of me and when Luigi died, I went into a shell. I just couldn't believe he was gone. I didn't know how to react."

"I thought I would have been one of the people you would have called first or at least personally. I didn't think I'd have to hear that from Gunter."

"I said I was sorry."

She crossed her arm across her chest and looked the other way.

"I am sorry, Eleanor. This just hasn't been the best of weeks. We're trying to find this young Rossini woman, and that has provided nothing but frustration and people dying, and now, Luigi's death. It hasn't been easy."

She looked back at me; she wore a saddened look. "Poking around all of these people who are dabbling in this white slave business is dangerous. I hope you know what you are doing."

I had told her about the mystery of Clara Hunter and the apparent charade at The Palace. "These are just common thugs that are involved and we are the police. It is our duty to find out what's going on and put a stop to it."

She laughed at my comment which probably sounded staged. "These are dangerous types behind this. I have heard enough talk. I don't think it is a small time operation; I don't think you should take it lightly."

"I don't," I said, but maybe I had. "What do you know of Maurice Von Bever?"

Now the look she gave me showed either fear or disdain or both. "He is nothing more than a pimp. He owns a couple of brothels here in the Levee."

"I was told he owns The Palace. I don't know much about him."

She took my hand and gave it a tight squeeze. "I hear he is partners with Big Jim Colosimo, a very dangerous man. Some of these people feign at being tough. Colosimo is a tough one. You should stay away from him."

To me, Colosimo was a precinct captain for Coughlin and Kenna, another in a long line of their bagmen. "He doesn't seem all that big to me."

"Maybe not Von Bever, but Colosimo, for sure," she said. Her grip was making my fingers hurt. "It's been said that Colosimo has ties to the Black Hand."

I nodded. This was an organized crime unit out of New York. There was word they were moving into Chicago. "I'll take that into consideration."

At that Eleanor practically jumped out of bed, pulling a gown around her naked body as she rose. "You really aren't hearing me, are you, Patrick?"

I smiled a bit. "I heard you fine," I said.

"Yes, you hear me, but you don't take me seriously and this is nothing to smile about. I am telling you that this man, Colosimo, is dangerous, and you have pushed my comments aside."

"I haven't done anything like that. I hear what you're saying."

"You might hear me Patrick, but I don't think you understand. It's like when you tell me that you love me, but it's only when you are drunk. It's the same feeling I get now. It's how I felt when you didn't tell me that Luigi had died. Everything I mean to you, words, feeling, thoughts, they are all secondary. I don't think I can go on like this."

It was the first time she'd actually raised her voice to me; I was concerned everyone at Queen's would hear her. I didn't know what to say.

"I wish you would just go right now," she said. I understood that clearly.

"I am sorry that I hurt you, but I do listen and I do understand."

She looked down at me, lying on her bed, giving me the same look you'd give a bad puppy. "I have to get ready for tonight," she said finally. "You need to be going."

Sensing that anything further that I said would only get me in more trouble, I gathered my things and got dressed. I left her room without a kiss or a word. I said goodbye to no one as I left the brothel.

She was right, of course, I thought as the cab made its way through the cold night back to my flat. I had kept her on the outside and I probably hadn't been totally honest with her. Maybe she would never replace my lost wife. Maybe I didn't want her to. I tried to promise that I would be better to her, but immediately wondered if I could. There was so much wrong with the world that I lived in, and I felt frustrated that I couldn't figure much of it out. With the Marshall Field, Jr. case, I would have to ask more questions. Maybe the answers I got would lead me in some direction. With Isabella, we were close to a door to door check with everyone in the Levee, but that would be ridiculous. We would go see Von Bever. He seemed to have something to do with the white slaving. I would try and enlist his help in finding Isabella. It was only one girl. Finding her would upset no one's empire.

When I left my apartment to meet Gunter for our appointment with Maurice Von Bever, I was glad to see that there were no gifts left on my doorstep. This was much easier that dealing with some of the earlier findings, but I didn't know what it meant. Had someone managed to fall into the two souvenirs that had been presented to me? Was that all they possessed or was the person who'd left them planning something new? I supposed I'd have to wait to find out.

Gunter was not as patient as our cab left the precinct. "I assume that our new friend has left you no new presents?"

"You have assumed correctly." This conversation sounded too much like a Conan Doyle story; I almost laughed.

Paris was another middle of the road brothel. When we entered the lobby we were greeted by a polite woman who told us that she would let Mr. Von Bever know we were there. As we looked around the parts of the resort that we could see, it was easy to see that it was at least clean and neat. When we met Von Bever we could tell where this came from.

Maurice Von Bever was only average in height and looks. Everything else about his person and office were first class. The suit he wore was from the finest wool. His shirt and tie were expensive silk. The cufflinks and chain to his watch, solid gold. His office, on the second floor of Paris, smelled of cleaning solvents. There was a lemon hint in the air. The furniture, a mixture of mahogany and leather, looked new.

"Mrs. Sloan tells me that you gentlemen visited The Palace yesterday," Von Bever said. He had piercing, dark eyes. "It seems you have been very busy."

"We have," I said. "We are looking for a young woman by the name of Isabella Rossini. We think she might have been abducted over a week ago from the IC Station and that she is being held against her will and possibly being forced to work as a prostitute. We believe she may be held in one of the brothels down here in the Levee."

Von Bever laughed. "One of the brothels down here in the Levee? It might be easier to find the old proverbial needle in the haystack. There are more than a few brothels in the Levee. Why would you settle on one that I own?"

"Mr. Von Bever," Gunter said slowly. I could hear the tension, or anger, in his voice, "one of the girls that used to work for you at The Palace tossed a note to a *Tribune* reporter that said she was being held against her will."

"Ah, yes. I am familiar with this young woman. Her name is," Von Bever shuffled a few papers on his desk, "Clara Hunter."

"That would be the young woman," I said.

"A trouble maker from the first day she came into our employ, according to Mrs. Sloan. Apparently, she thought she could run things better than the way we were running them."

"That is the story that Mrs. Sloan gave us," I said. "So if this woman, Clara Hunter, was so unhappy with the operations at The Palace, why didn't she just leave?"

Von Bever's eyes settled on me. "A good question, Detective Moses. Why didn't she just leave? I would say she had some further motivations and they weren't working out so she decided to hatch this scheme of hers." His answers, like Mrs. Sloan's, came with conviction. It was hard not to believe him.

"Do you know anything of the practice of white slaving down here in the Levee? It has to do with women being abducted and then forced into prostitution. Raping and drugging these young women may be part of the process."

There was no hint of surprise on his face. "I have never heard of such a vial practice in my entire life. I certainly would never condone that practice. The women that work at Paris or The Palace come voluntarily."

"I see. Did you know Mike Hart or Mary Hastings?"

"Of course. Mike owned the Marlborough Hotel and Mary, Sappho. It's an absolute shame what happened to them."

"It is," I said. "Why would you think that someone would kill them?"

He looked surprised at that. "I haven't the vaguest idea. You're with the police. Don't you have theories?"

I smiled. "Of course we do. It has come to our attention that Mike Hart might have had a second business, trying to procure young women to sell to brothels. We know he owned a house out in Blue Island where he held the girls, drugged and raped them, until they were ready for the Levee."

Von Bever's eyes didn't flinch. "Obviously, that is disturbing, if it is true. I knew nothing like that about Mike."

"We also think that Mike Hart might have been selling girls to Sappho."

"Both Mike and Mary Hastings are gone. That might be hard to prove."

"Some say it is a much larger operation that Mike Hart or Sappho."

"I am unaware of this operation." Again, the response calm.

"Do you know of a big, mute man that used to work with or for Mike?"

"I do not?"

"Do you know Big Jim Colosimo?"

Von Bever laughed again. "Who doesn't know Big Jim? He's a precinct captain down here and is involved in a lot of businesses."

I nodded and took out the picture of Isabella Rossini and placed it in front of Von Bever. "Have you ever seen this girl?"

For the first time, I could see some unsteadiness in his eyes. "This is a very pretty woman."

"That's obvious from the photograph. I asked if you had ever seen her."

"I would remember a woman this beautiful. I am sorry that

I have not seen her nor can I help you locate her."

I wanted to believe him, but it was hard. Like Mrs. Sloan, his story was unwavering and direct, but it was in such great contrast to what Clara Hunter told us, but why didn't Clara Hunter just leave if she was free to do so. Nothing was adding up.

"We may just have to begin a door to door search for Isabella," Gunter said. We were back in the coach, returning to the precinct.

"Like trying to find a virgin in the Levee."

"They're lying," Gunter said. "Both Von Bever and Mrs. Sloan."

"Do we have enough proof or witnesses beside Clara Hunter who could help with a conviction?"

Gunter slapped his hand on the seat of the cab. "We have no one?"

This was becoming the central issue in the Isabella Rossini case. We had no one and the ones we had ended up dead.

*****

We barely got inside the precinct doors before Mike Sweeney, the big desk sergeant on duty, told us there had been a murder in the Austin District. My heart leapt at the thought that this had something to do with Kluge. My stomach plunged when he gave me the next bit of news.

"It's that little guy that owned the newsstand on Adams, Big Louie. Somebody killed him. Sam Walker called in a little bit ago. Langley and he are at the site. They said to notify you if you came in."

We left the precinct as fast as we had entered and found a cab. We told the driver to get to the address on west Jackson that Sweeney had given us. We told him to get there fast.

As the cab sped along, the poor horse churning as fast as

traffic and conditions would allow her, Gunter grabbed my arm. "We may be closer on Isabella Rossini than we think."

I was in no mood for light talk that made little sense. "I'm not sure what you mean."

"Think about it, Patrick," he said. "Louie gave you Mike Hart and Mary Hastings. He also told you about Blue Island. Not less than ten days later, all three of those people are dead and the stockade out in Blue Island was abandoned. Hart and Hastings had to be connected and we're pretty sure it was the girls he was providing to Sappho. Clara Hunter mentioned a Mike at Palace. It's got to be the same Mike. Hart had to be working for someone, helping to run this white slaving ring. And this big mute guy shows up too much. There's got to be a connection to all of this and when we find it, we might be able to find Isabella Rossini."

I patted Gunter's arm and smiled. He was connecting the dots. It all made sense. The question that remained was who did Mike Hart work for? What was the name Louie wouldn't give me? What big person scared Eleanor so much that she had twice warned me of danger, big danger? "You might make half a detective one day, Krause," I said.

"Just half?" he said, but he laughed.

The address that Sweeney had given us was for a three story, six flat on Jackson Boulevard in the west part of the city known as Austin. These were all working class people that lived out here, and I found the neighborhood to be neat and tidy. I was surprised Louie lived in such a nice spot, but then I remembered hearing he had stashed a lot of his jockey winnings and that was how he had purchased his newsstand. That was probably how he afforded the rent.

Like the scene at the Marlborough, the morning of the Hart's murder, there were a lot of cops and some of the public milling about outside the building. It wasn't nearly as crowded as the Marlborough, but it was a good sized crowd. A patrolman I knew told me that Louie's apartment was on the first floor.

There were two apartments on the first floor. The one on the west side of the building had its door open and a large cop was standing watch. We showed our badges and were let into the unit. I wish we hadn't been.

Big Louie Pagano was lying on his back in the middle of the main room. His throat had been slashed deeply from ear to ear. In his mouth was stuffed what looked like a white towel. Unlike what I'd heard about Marshall Field, Jr's gunshot site, there was blood all around the head, neck and back of Louie.

"Oh my God," Gunter said behind me.

I began to think that I was responsible for all of this death from the Harts to Mary Hastings to Louie when I saw Sam Walker come out of a room to my right; Horace Langley followed behind like a puppy. "Well, if it isn't the great detective, Gunter Krause."

"Shut it, Walker," Gunter said behind me, and I put out my arm to hold him back.

"Hold your dog, Moses," Walker said. His hand was near his gun, and I didn't doubt for a minute that he wouldn't use it.

"What happened here, Sam?"

It still looked like the bruising from Gunter's punch hadn't totally receded. "Same thing as with the Harts, I think," he said. "Someone didn't like what was being said about them and sent a messenger to make sure Pagano said nothing else."

It occurred to me to me that the only people I'd ever told about Louie being my source were Gunter, Captain Morgan, Sam Walker and Horace Langley. Now Louie was dead. I calmed myself. "Who found him?"

"Mrs. Jessup, the landlord. She lives across the hall and used to help Pagano with some of his needs due to his faulty sight. She let herself into the unit as usual and found Pagano like this. She called it in right away."

I nodded. "Where's Little Louie, his dog?"

"The shepherd? Here, have a look." Walker crooked a finger

and we followed him as he went back into the room he'd just come out of.

In this room, Big Louie's bedroom, there was a light burning on the table by the bed. The bed had not been slept in; night clothes were at the foot of it. On the floor, near the bed, lay Little Louie. Like his master, his throat had been cut and a similar white towel had been stuffed in his mouth. Blood lay all around the massive dog.

"Somebody didn't care for the dog either," Sam said. "Maybe they thought he talked too much, as well."

Horace Langley found this funny; he started to laugh.

"No clues, I assume?" I asked.

"None. The landlady found them and called us. We called to make sure you'd find out. We knew this guy Pagano was a friend of yours and we also know our two cases are connected. You keep looking for this Rossini girl and people keep ending up dead."

I could hear Gunter by me, simmering, almost growling. "You'll let us know what you find, Sam?"

"Sure, Moses," he said, "and you let us know who you are going to question next. Maybe we can watch them and stop a murder."

"Come on," I said to Gunter, tugging on his sleeve to pull him out of the room.

Outside, he lit a cigarette as we hurried back to our waiting cab. "That guy, Walker, he's going to get it one day."

"He will," I said, "but not today." It occurred to me that I was within walking distance of the gun seller who had supposedly sold the gun to Marshall Field, Jr. so he could shoot himself with it. "Why don't you go back to the precinct and cool down a bit? Put together a list of brothels we can have searched and we'll submit it to Morgan to try and get help from the foot patrol. There's a friend of Louie's who lives close to here. I want to ask him a few questions and let him know what happened to Louie."

Gunter detected nothing of my lie nor did he question why he couldn't come along with me. He nodded quickly and soon was on his way back to the precinct. I started walking over to Madison Street.

*****

There was nothing mysterious about the gun shop that Steven Hirth owned. It was located almost at the western tip of the city, as far as Madison Avenue went. The sign over the door said GUN SHOP in big, red block letters. The door had the only window to the shop. I peeked in before opening and saw an older man, with mostly white, thinning hair behind the counter. When I opened the door he looked up at me with half spectacles, the type you used for reading.

"Mr. Hirth," I said. Behind him, on the wall, were handguns, shotguns and a number of rifles. On the counter, he seemed to be working on a small derringer.

"That's me," he said in a friendly tone. "How can I help you?"

I showed him my badge and let him read it clearly before placing it back in my suit jacket. "I'm Detective Patrick Moses. I was asked to do a little follow up on the Marshall Field case and since I was in the neighborhood on another matter, I thought I'd stop by and see you."

"Moses?" he said his face lighting up. "Aren't you the detective who solved the Dr. Kluge case?"

"My partner and I were the ones given credit for closing the case." I hadn't lied yet.

"A nasty case," he said, as if he knew. "Brilliant police work."

"Thank you," I said modestly.

"And now the department has you doing follow up work on the Field case?"

"Well, it was an important case, too. We just want to make

sure that nothing at all was missed."

"Nothing missed? If you ask me about it, everything was missed."

His directness caught me off guard. "How so?"

"The thought that Marshall Field, Jr. shot himself is about as preposterous as the thought of his father being destitute."

"Are you telling me, Mr. Hirth, that the cause of his death wasn't accidental?"

He pointed an oil- stained finger at me. "I am telling you, Detective Moses, that I would bet my house on that not being what happened."

"Do you mind telling me why you think that?"

He wiped his hands with a rag that was nearby. "Over the years, maybe ten or so, I had sold Mr. Field a number of guns. He would visit my shop and use my range on a regular basis. With some of my not so regular customers, I could see some of them being stupid enough to shoot themselves in the ribs, but not Mr. Field. He was very accustomed to handling many guns, an accomplished marksman and hunter. I would call him an expert in the handling of handguns if asked to testify. There is no way that Mr. Field was either stupid enough or inexperienced enough to have shot himself. I refuse to believe it. It didn't happen."

"You seem very convinced of your belief."

"I won't ever waiver."

"Home come you didn't tell this to Detectives Loftus and O'Donnell when they visited you?"

He got a look of worry on his face and I could see some of the bravado leave his expression. "When the story first went around about Mr. Field shooting himself with one of my guns, I was heartbroken. He was a good friend from a good family. I knew he had left behind a beautiful, sweet wife and three children. I was devastated. I told those officers I had sold him the gun in question, but also said I couldn't talk about it at the time. They told me they would come back in a few days and we would discuss it then. When Mr. Field died and all that nonsense was going around about it being an accident I was appalled. I expected those detectives to return, but they never did."

"What do you think happened?"

"Marshall Field told the papers and everyone else, cops included, that his son died cleaning his weapon for a hunting trip. Everyone bought what his father said and the case was closed."

"You must have some thoughts on what really happened?"

He smiled. "What do I think really happened? I think Mr. Field got himself into some kind of trouble down in the Levee. I don't have any idea what kind, but that's what I think. He got into trouble and somebody shot him. That was a lot worse for the family business than shooting yourself in your house, so daddy covered all that up. But that is what I think happened, if my opinion matters."

*****

It has been my experience that losing your temper is never in your best interest. I have only known it to cause problems for me. As I rode in a much slower carriage back to the precinct, I knew I had gotten Big Louie murdered. Five people in all knew he was the one who had given me the names of Mike Hart and Mary Hastings. I knew Gunter had nothing to do with the murders, but what about Captain Morgan or Walker? I ruled out Horace Langley because he was too stupid. Morgan was a Coughlin and Kenna loyalist, but what was their interest in the white slaving, if anything? They were involved in everything in the ward that made money, most of it on the fringe with being legal. Would they get involved in slaving? Maybe if it made them a few dollars.

Sam Walker was another story. We'd come onto the force at the same time and risen through the ranks to detective at a similar pace. I'd always felt that from Sam's side of things there had always been a little competition and maybe some jealously. I didn't know him that well. I probably knew a little about the cases he was involved in, but that was about it. After that, I knew nothing.

\*\*\*\*\*

I found Gunter at his desk on the second floor of the precinct building. He didn't look too happy with things, but he had prepared a list of twenty-seven brothels in the area that would require a man to man search for Isabella Rossini. These were all brothels of lesser quality that might resort to getting their girls from the white slavers.

"What do you propose?" I asked.

"We go in and ask Morgan for permission to make the searches and to see if we can get a few beat patrolmen to help us out."

I nodded approval and the two of us went down the hall to Morgan's office; he looked like he was asleep at his desk when we knocked on the door. He jumped in his chair. "Oh, Moses, Krause, come right in."

We entered the office, closing the door behind us. We each took one of the uncomfortable, wooden chairs in front of his desk.

"Sorry about your friend, Louie Pagano, Moses. That's a sad ending for a man."

"It is," I said. I would get to that in a minute.

"What have you got for me?" Morgan said.

"Captain," Gunter began, "we only had limited resources to begin with in this case. Louie Pagano gave us a couple of leads which we followed up on. We do believe the people he gave us were involved in the white slave trade. Unfortunately, those leads, including Pagano, have all been murdered, but we're not even sure if those people could have helped us find Isabella

Rossini. This white slaving has gotten a bit out of control."

Morgan leaned back in his chair and rubbed at his chin. "What do you propose?"

Gunter placed the list of brothels in front of Morgan. "This is a list of resorts that we feel might use the services of the white slave traders. We feel that Isabella Rossini, if she is acting as a consort, might possibly be in one of these resorts. What we are proposing is a man to man search of the brothels on this list. In order to be effective, we feel we'll need at least one other two man team, maybe two. We thought we could get some patrolmen to help facilitate the search."

"You have nothing further on your search, other than the names Pagano gave you?" Morgan's tone was terse.

Gunter looked over to me; his face had reddened. "This is a very difficult task, Captain, looking for one girl in all of these resorts."

"Shipley just called me yesterday. The Italian Ambassador's people are constantly harassing him. They can't imagine why we have not been able to find the ambassador's niece."

I laughed out loud. "They can't imagine why we haven't been able to find anything?"

"Is something funny here, Moses?"

"Funny? Not really funny, but more like ridiculous. The first task you gave us, finding Isabella, was nearly impossible. We had no leads to the girl's whereabouts. If Shipley doesn't put us on the white slaving angle, we would have had no place to even start. With what he told us, I went to Louie Pagano who gave us Hart and Hastings. Now all three of those people are dead. We can't even get our treading before our source and possible suspects are murdered. And every time we talk with someone we get the runaround or are told that they made payments to Big Jim Colosimo, like that stops our investigation."

"What are you saying, Moses?"

"I'm saying there are too many leaks around here. Only a

few people knew about Big Louie and now he's dead."

His eyes narrowed. "Careful what you insinuate."

"I'm not insinuating anything. It's just that every time we get a little lead it gets snuffed out before we can even begin to investigate it. Someone knows we're onto them and they're one step ahead of us."

He took a deep breath. "I think you are getting emotional, perhaps over Pagano's death, and I think you are getting out of line."

I could tell by the look on his face that I had pushed it too much about a snitch on the force. "May we have the permission to do the door to door and can we get some patrolmen to help us out?"

"I've already gotten a call from Alderman Coughlin about your aggressive behavior in this case. You talked to that Hastings woman and she ended up murdered. Coughlin tells me you went by The Palace and Paris and bothered Maurice Von Bever, a respected businessman. I got another call from Jacob Fine on the same matter. It seems your disrupting business down here in the Levee."

The mention of my father's name and even Coughlin made me ill. "I thought Shipley, an aide to the Chief, was asking you for answers."

"He is," Morgan stated.

"Gunter and I feel that the only way to find this girl is to begin an aggressive search for her, with more than just the two of us. We need additional manpower with this case being their only assignment. That is the only chance we have of finding Isabella Rossini."

Morgan gave this some thought at he stared at the two of us intently; most of his hateful looks were centered on me. "Let me talk to the powers that be and see if that authorization is acceptable. I see your point, but don't want the aldermen talking to the chief about the way we're handling things."

When we were outside Morgan's office, Gunter turned to

me. "Do the powers that be include Shipley and downtown or are we talking about Coughlin and Kenna?"

My stomach knotted. "I'm sure we will find out soon enough."

*****

I spent a lonely dinner, eating a dry beef stew, and drinking what turned out to be a warm beer when I got around to putting the glass to my lips. At first, I felt a bit sorry for myself, alone in a quiet restaurant on a Tuesday night. Gunter had to be somewhere with his wife and children; I think he told me there was a Christmas play at their school. Eleanor had told me she didn't want to see me for a while and that brought forth a good part of my gloom. I knew I needed to mend my differences with her or I would lose her forever. Lastly, I couldn't get the last two deaths out of my life, three if you counted Little Louie. I couldn't do anything about Luigi dying; his time had come, and I could rationalize his passing. With Big Louie, my friend and confidant, it was totally different. I knew that I was partially, if not fully responsible, for his death. If I don't ask him about white slaving, he's probably still alive.

Again, my three cases, wore heavily on my thoughts. I didn't think we were ever going to find Isabella Rossini. She was somewhere out there, supposedly lost in the Levee, and I wasn't sure the people who ran the precinct, from the aldermen to the police, wanted her found. The investigation was causing too much of a disturbance to the loyal, paying businesses of the ward. Also, any person we were told to question ended up dead. This was not very good for the department's record.

With the death of Marshall Field, Jr. I felt differently. I wanted to solve this crime and I did believe it was a crime. There was too much pointing to the fact that he didn't shoot himself. The thing that got me there was his father. If he doesn't come along and have the first investigation shut down, because of the possible embarrassment to the Field name, the killer might have been caught a month ago. Now he comes to me and wants to find out what really happened. At first, I felt sorry for the old man and wanted to help him. Now, I realized I was just digging up facts that he had helped to cover up. Upset and confused was what I was, but I wanted to get to the bottom of it.

With Kluge, admittedly the most perplexing of the three, and the most dangerous, I didn't know what we had and what to think. Someone had placed two pieces of evidence on my doorstep, the scarf and the gruesome finger. Was it a sick lark or did it mean there was someone out there who was prepared to carry on the killings? I didn't know, but I was very nervous, heart pounding quickly, as I took the stairs to my unit, but no other presents had been left for me. Maybe the game was over.

*****

I had barely entered my cold unit, taken off my coat and hat, put on the lights and turned the radiator up when there was a knock on my door. It was just past nine and I was expecting no visitors. I usually don't react this way, but with what happened to the Harts, and now Big Louie, I grabbed my gun and held it in my right hand as I opened the door with my left.

In my door stood a tall woman, blonde hair and blue eyes, wearing a brown overcoat and brown hat. Both were moderately expensive. "Detective Moses," she said with a smile that could melt most men.

I slipped my gun in my suit pocket. "I am Patrick Moses," I said.

She smiled again. "I am Charlotte LeFreur. I work at the Everleigh Club and I would like to talk to you for a moment. I believe I have some important information for you."

I quickly let Miss LeFreur into my apartment, taking her hat and coat from her. Underneath the coat she wore a dark green dress, with a nice plunging neckline that helped showcase her ample bosom. She was a most beautiful creature. "Would you like something to drink? I have whiskey."

She sat down on my desk chair, smiling. "I don't drink, Mr. Moses, but thank you anyway."

"You said you work for the Everleigh sisters?"

"I do. I am off Monday and Tuesdays nights."

"I see," I said. I suddenly wondered if the two sisters had sent this lovely courtesan to me as a gift to keep me quiet. "You said you had some important news to give me."

"Yes," she said, a most serious expression crossing her lovely face. "It is in regards to the shooting of Marshall Field, Jr."

I nodded. "I want you to know that I have visited the Everleigh sisters and have gotten their story on this matter."

"I know. I heard you were at the club and interviewed Minna and Ada."

"And you can add something to their story?" I was dubious as to what tale Miss LeFreur intended to tell.

She lowered her eyes from mine. "I believe they may have lied to you."

I won't say surprised was my reaction, but I was interested. "In what fashion?"

She cleared her throat, clearly nervous at the situation. "They can never know that I was here to see you. It would cost me my position."

"I understand that. What you tell me will be held in the strictest confidence."

"The night that Mr. Field was shot he was at the club."

She looked up at me for my reaction. I simply nodded again, indicating she should go on.

"He was there playing roulette and having a few drinks. It was all he ever did when he was at the club. Anyway, it was after one, and he was done playing, when he decided to leave the club. The two sisters both said goodnight to him; this was their practice with such important guests. The door had only been closed for a moment; we were there in the main lobby, when we heard a gunshot ring out. It sounded like a bomb going off. We opened the doors and rushed outside. Mr. Field was down on the walk, moaning in pain, and requesting that we get him help."

"Did you see anyone else on the street, cabs or people?"

"I don't think so. It was very late on a Wednesday night, actually early Thursday morning."

'What happened?"

"Minna suggested we get him a cab and get him right over to Mercy, but it was Mr. Field who suggested he just be taken home. The sisters conferred for a bit and suggested they knew a doctor on Wabash Street who would treat Mr. Field and hold everything in confidence. They told Mr. Field they would call ahead and that he should get there at once. He agreed and they got him a taxi, a rather cheap, open air hansom and he was helped into it and was soon on his way. Minna and Ada rushed back inside to call ahead to this doctor."

I had heard a close version of this story from Ernest Lehmann. At least, I was now certain where Field had been shot. I also had a good idea who the doctor was that Minna and Ada sent Field to.

"There's something more that I should tell you," she said. Her face showed she was scared.

"What is it?"

"I had a visitor to the club several weeks before the shooting. He was a very short, intense looking man with a closely cropped black beard and he wore a monocle over one eye. The patches of his cheeks that you could see were flaming red. He scared me."

"Did you get his name?"

"He went by the name of Mr. Jones. I thought that was a fake. Anyway, we went up to the Gold Room and I asked him what he was interested in. That's our custom at the Everleigh Club. I was astounded because he told me that all he wanted to do was to talk with me."

I smiled. "All he wanted to do was to talk?"

"Yes. He had paid for my services and he had specifically asked for me. I have no idea how he got my name and thought I'd be willing to discuss this topic with him, but I can only assume it came from the fact that I'd had several fights with the sisters regarding my employment with them. Somehow, word of these disagreements must have gotten to him and he must have thought I'd be willing to entertain his business proposition."

"What kind of proposition?"

"He told me that very soon someone who was rather rich and famous was going to be shot in or around the Everleigh Club. He didn't give me a name of this person, but he did tell me that if I told anyone of this plot that harm would come to me. He told me this story in such a calm way that I became frightened. I told him I would say nothing. My heart was beating so hard I thought it would leap out of my chest."

"What was this plot?" I was so intrigued, I couldn't wait to hear this.

"He told me again that an important person was going to be shot in or around the Everleigh Club. After the shooting we were to meet and go thru the intricate details to indicate that Minna Everleigh had shot this person while he was at the club. It was to have been over a dispute about roulette."

"That sounds fanciful," I said. "There were always so many witnesses inside the club."

"He did tell me he was hoping the shooting could take place outside. He was hoping to get Minna out there with the person who was going to be shot. I didn't think much about it at the time, but now I think it sounds very convoluted."

"What was to be your part in the shooting?"

"Nothing to do with the shooting, but I was to be a witness, and I was to go to the police and tell them that I saw Minna shoot the victim."

This story sounded too amazing to believe, but up until now, not much made sense with this crime. "What did you tell him?"

"At first, I said no right away. Then he told me it would be worth twenty thousand dollars if I helped him. I told him no again. I told him I was very fond of Minna and Ada. I wouldn't be involved in such a plot, regardless of the price."

"What did he do?"

"He got up from where he was sitting and came over to me. I was sitting on the edge of the bed. I was trembling. He put one of his fingers to his lips and then took both of his hands and placed them near my throat. I thought he was going to choke me. I couldn't move; I froze. He took his hands away and told me he was sorry we couldn't work things out and that I should remember what he said. Our little discussion never took place."

"I assume you have never told anyone of this meeting and story?"

"Not until tonight. It bothered me tremendously when Mr. Field was shot and then when I heard you came to talk with Minna and Ada, I thought you were looking into this rumor that Minna had been behind the shooting. I finally knew I had to tell someone."

"You have done the right thing. This will help me tremendously. The man, the one who came to you, you have no idea who he was?"

"Only that he was referred to the sisters by a wealthy client and that he went by the name of Mr. Jones."

I agreed that the name Jones was probably fictitious. "Nothing more you can tell me about this man."

"There is one more thing, Detective Moses. The man was missing half of his right ear. At first he saw me looking at it and he was so nice about it. He told me was sorry if his severed ear had scared me. He told me he lost it in Cuba. Then he went into his story."

## Wednesday

I would like to say that I went into the next day with a bit of a plan about how we were supposed to find the missing ambassador's niece, Isabella Rossini, but I had no plan. I didn't know how long it would take Captain Morgan to check with his contacts to see if an aggressive search of the Levee's brothels was an acceptable practice for members of the police department or if it was thought to ruffle too many feathers. That seemed to me, even though it was unlikely to succeed, to be the only method I could think of that gave us a shot at finding the missing girl. All other ideas had ended up with numerous people, and a dog, being murdered. Without Morgan's approval to proceed with the search, and some manpower help, we had nothing and could do nothing more on the case.

It was mid-morning when Morgan approached Gunter and me as we worked on reports at our various desks. "We will be leaving in a few moments for a meeting," he said authoritatively.

"A meeting with whom?" I asked.

"Downstairs in five minutes and ready to go. We will be leaving the building."

Not really having any idea what this all meant, we had little to do but cooperate. We were both standing by the lower level exit when Morgan came limping down the stairs in some obvious discomfort from his back pain. There was a police cab in front of the building waiting for us. We quickly piled into it as a windy, cold rain began to fall.

"Goddamn weather," Morgan said. "Makes every joint in my body hurt."

"Mind telling us where we are heading, Captain?" Gunter asked. He had not been in the best of moods this morning.

"We are going to see the heads of the First Ward," Morgan said. "We have a meeting with Mr. Coughlin and Mr. Kenna."

As much as I detested the two aldermen and wanted to jump from the moving carriage, I stayed put. Out of curiosity, more than anything, I wanted to hear their theories on running an investigation on finding a missing girl. The more I thought about it as I leaned back against the hard bench, it made sense. Who knew more about the operations and the people of the Levee than Bathhouse John and Hinky Dink?

It was true that Coughlin and Kenna ran the ward as aldermen, but they maintained several acquaintances with potential ties to the case. The whole thing with the First Ward was who held the power. Coughlin and Kenna held that power. If you wanted to operate a saloon, resort or gambling parlor you paid the two aldermen their weekly fee depending on exactly what you ran. These fees were often paid to Big Jim Colosimo, a precinct captain, or Jacob Fine, my father and a link to the regular people of the Levee. My father owned a percentage of Freiberg's Dance Hall with Solly Friedman. If you wanted to buy liquor in the Levee you dealt with father and Solly. Coughlin and Kenna got a cut of these sales.

Colosimo provided a different service for the two aldermen. It was said that Colosimo owned from four to twenty brothels. He was an elegant looking Italian, a big man, often dressed in all white suits and sporting rings on each finger. He seemed to exude class. What he did provide was muscle. It was known that he had ties to the crime ring, the Black Hand. There was no proof that he used his contacts there, but it was known that he carried out some of the tougher collections for the ward. If Colosimo came to collect the money that was due you paid up.

Coughlin often made the rounds of the Levee each morning, accompanied by two uniformed policemen. The people in the ward loved him. You paid him and he made sure you operated without interruption from the police. Actually, the two aldermen were loved by most in the ward. Kenna operated the Workingman's Exchange on Clark Street, a grand establishment with a one hundred foot long bar. The saloon boasted of serving, "The Largest and Coolest Schooner of Beer in the City". This schooner would cost you a nickel and a free lunch was included. The Workingman's also included on its top floor, the Alaska Hotel, a flophouse for the down and outs. Kenna would allow anyone to stay there for free. When election time would roll around these bums and vagrants would be gathered up and taken to the polls to vote, for our two favorite aldermen or their designees. In return the new voters were given at least a half a dollar, if not more. This was a practice they used for a long time to make sure they were always reelected.

So it did not surprise me on this cold, damp morning that we were on our way to talk to Coughlin and Kenna at the Workingman's. If we were about to embark on a grand tour of a good number of brothels and clubs in the Levee it might upset more than a few of the proprietors. These were the same people that were paying the aldermen weekly fees so that their businesses were not disrupted, especially by the police. Getting a lot of complaints from the constituents would upset the aldermen. Hearing that some of them were ending up dead would probably push them over the top. So when Morgan called for permission for a search of the brothels, Coughlin and Kenna wanted to meet about it. Gunter looked upset about having to go to the meeting. I was not very happy myself. Morgan look mortified.

The two Lords of the Levee were seated at a round table in front of the long bar. At this time of day, the place was mostly deserted except for a couple of railroad workers who looked like they had been drinking since their shift ended. Coughlin and Kenna stood and shook hands all around. Coughlin had on a green suit with a red vest. The tie he wore was yellow. His grayish, white hair was bushy and looked as if a brush hadn't seen it in days. He eyes were bright and shining. Kenna, always the serious one, dressed in a black suit, not smiling and glum as ever, shook our hands weakly. He looked like a mortician.

"Well, it's an honor to have the two heroes of the Dr. Kluge case in a meetin with us," Coughlin said, his smile never diminishing.

Gunter looked over to me, but I avoided his glance. Neither one of us knew how long our hero status would last.

"Captain Morgan here, he tells us that you have now been given another tough case, one that involves the Levee to some degree."

"I would probably say, Aldermen Coughlin, that it involves the Levee in a great degree," I said.

"Well, yes, yes, that's what I mean, but that's only someone's guess." Coughlin looked perplexed; Kenna looked like he wanted us dragged out in back and shot.

"The order came from Lieutenant Shipley from headquarters. He was placed in charge of the investigation by the mayor's office." That probably should have come from Morgan, but he still appeared to be in some sort of muted trance.

"I can't imagine someone tellin you, down there at the Twenty-Second, that somethin like five hundred girls are disappearin in Chicago each year, taken in as slavery prostitutes, and many of those girls are endin up down here in the Levee."

"Five thousand girls," I said.

"What?" Coughlin said.

"The number of suspected missing women taken into this white slavery trade is suspected to be around five thousand each year."

"Five thousand?" Coughlin blurted. He looked at Captain Morgan who kept his eyes down.

"That is the most ridiculous comment I have ever heard, both from the police or that foolish mayor of ours," Kenna said, his face and eyes showing the annoyance he felt.

"That's the number we have been given," I said.

"And what is your mission, detective?" Kenna asked, spitting out the question.

"We are just looking for one girl, Aldermen Kenna. Her name is Isabella Rossini." I took out the picture we had of her and placed it on the table. "She is the niece of the Italian Ambassador to the United States."

Both aldermen thought on this for a minute. "You're lookin for one girl down here in the Levee?" Coughlin said.

"A difficult task," I said. "That's why we want to try an extensive house to house search or, in this case, brothel to brothel. That may be the only way we can find her."

"It seems your other methods have failed," Kenna said. "Four murders so far."

"Mike Hart was a good fellow and his wife, Molly, was a dear," Coughlin said. "I can't believe they killed that poor Mary Hastings as well."

I didn't agree with Coughlin's character references. "Who killed them?" I said.

There was an odd silence for a moment. "It's justa figure of speech," Coughlin said. "It seems somebody killed those people because of the investgatin you were doin. That's all I'm sayin."

"Captain Morgan," I said.

Morgan lifted his eyes to the two aldermen. "The boys would like to conduct this house to house to see if they can turn up anything on the missing girl."

Coughlin looked over at Kenna, and I could see Hinky Dink shake his head ever so slightly. "That's goin to be tough to do because of all the disruptin it does to the businesses down here. We don't think that's such a good idea."

Morgan said nothing in return; I felt my breakfast burning in my belly. "How would you propose we go about finding this young girl?" I asked.

"You'll never find her," Kenna said. "There's probably a good chance, a very good chance, she's not even down here in the Levee."

"Aldermen," I said as politely as I could, "it is our job to try and find her until we are convinced we have exhausted all means. Until that time, we have to keep looking."

Kenna's face darkened a red color that made it look like his head might explode at any minute.

"Maybe there's another way," Coughlin said. "Big Jim Colosimo does most of the tough collections with the brothels. He knows most of these people and he has a way to speak to them that brings about results. Maybe he can talk with them and find out what they know about this missin Italian girl."

"I think that's a great idea," Morgan said, before I could respond. "I think that's a splendid alternative."

"Great," Coughlin said. "Let me talk with Big Jim and see what I can find out. It shouldn't take very long."

"That will be fine," Morgan said and, after thanking the two aldermen, we were outside piling back into our carriage.

"Captain," Gunter said, once we were all seated. "Why is it that we have to ask the aldermen for permission to search these brothels?"

I smiled as I waited for Morgan's response. Finally, he cleared his throat. "Those two men, Coughlin and Kenna, control this ward. Make no mistake of that. Cross them or make life difficult for someone they protect and you could end up walking the beat by the Yards on the graveyard shift."

As absurd as the comment was, it rang with the truth and was easy to understand. Gunter grunted, but there was no other sound the remainder of the ride back to the precinct. Our search for Isabella Rossini had met another road block.

*****

I got a little lucky later on in the day when I heard that the Cook County Coroner Peter Hoffman was going to release his autopsy results on Louie Pagano. It seemed to everyone who had been at the murder scene that Big Louie had his throat slashed so that would be the cause of death, but in the case of a murder, Hoffman had to make it official. He was to do so at three o'clock and I would be in attendance. I knew that Walker and Horace Langley would also be there, but my reason for being there was different than theirs. I wanted to see Peter Hoffman about Marshall Field, Jr.

Hoffman had a reputation for fairness and for being a good coroner. He also had a reputation for taking a bribe in certain situations. I didn't know much about the bribes, but Hoffman's locale for reporting the autopsy results was a little daunting. He addressed the small group of men, three detectives and two reporters, in front of a room with a window where a cadaver could clearly be seen. Most were focused directly on Hoffman, avoiding contact with the body beyond the glass.

"You may be surprised to know that Mr. Pagano did not die directly from the wound to his neck," Hoffman said. He was a short, round man with a bushy beard that covered most of his face. His voice showed both confidence and arrogance. "It is my opinion that Mr. Pagano's cause of death was actually the towel that was lodged in his throat. This caused an insufficient amount of oxygen to reach his lungs which proved to be fatal. The wound to his neck was secondary, and would have been fatal, if Mr. Pagano had not suffocated."

This was all very interesting, but the end result was that Louie was dead. I was sad about this, but at this point, there was nothing I could do for Louie. Others didn't seem to agree with me.

"I hope you're not planning on sticking your nose into our investigation," Walker said. His face was still a little purple from Gunter slugging him.

"I wasn't planning on it, Sam, unless, of course, your investigating calls for me to get involved."

Horace Langley laughed at this; Walker turned and walked away with Langley not far behind him.

I followed Coroner Hoffman into a small office and he seemed startled that I was there. "Can I help you?"

"I'm Detective Moses from the Twentieth Precinct."

He didn't look impressed. "I know who you are. I thought Walker and Langley were handling this case."

"They are. I wanted to ask you a couple of questions about a different matter."

The look he gave me showed concern. "What matter would that be, Detective?"

"I wanted to ask you a couple of questions about the Marshall Field, Jr. shooting."

He eyed me momentarily and let out a deep breath. "That case was closed as an accidental shooting."

I laughed. "Humor me for one second. The case was closed and was called an accident. Is that what you believe?"

Hoffman's look went from concern to anger. I took two hundred from the initial money that Marshall Field had given me and slipped it across the desk to Hoffman. He looked down at the bills and then grasped them with his hand. His look softened. He calmly put the money in his pocket.

"The case bothered me from the moment I got involved with it," he said. "The doctors who performed the surgery at Mercy Hospital called the shooting an accident. Marshall Field, Sr., in his effort to quiet all of the rumors, called all of the papers and the shooting became an accident. The case needed to be closed out as quickly as possible. Because it was called an accident, and everyone was happy with that, no autopsy was needed. The family requested that none be done. There was no autopsy."

I could hear it in his voice, the concern that the truth hadn't been reached. "What do you think happened?"

He took another deep breath and exhaled. "I got a very good look at the wound. As you know, I spend a good amount of my day looking at gunshot wounds. Some of these wounds are from close range; others are from a bit of a distance."

"What were your findings with Mr. Field's wound?"

"There was no doubt in my mind that Marshall Field, Jr. was shot from some distance; I'd say thirty to fifty feet. There was no powder burn evidence or other signs that the wound occurred from close range. That should have been present from Field shooting himself from a few feet away. That was the one thing that garnished my interest initially, but what could I do. The police and the doctors called it an accidental shooting. The family was happy with that explanation. There was no autopsy or further inquiry."

"So you're convinced that Field was shot from a distance of at least thirty feet."

He gave me a wry smile. "At least thirty, Detective. If that is the case than Mr. Field would be the first individual to shoot himself from that distance. If you follow what I'm saying, Mr. Field did not shoot himself."

I followed as clearly as Hoffman spoke it. Now the only thing that occurred to me was to find the man who had challenged Field in front of the Everleigh Club on the night of the shooting. Could it be the mysterious man who was missing half of his ear as Miss LeFreur had said? If it was someone who was so concerned about what Marshall, Jr. was doing to the Field name, perhaps it was a person who was close to the family. Maybe the only one who knew who this might be would be Field's wife, Albertine Huck. She would be the next person I would talk to and it would be soon.

*****

As the day came near its end, I felt that I had to see Eleanor. I knew it had to be frustrating for her as she assumed I was unable to commit myself to her fully. I knew she thought I couldn't do this because I didn't love her. That couldn't be farther from the truth, but I couldn't give you the reason why I couldn't commit. My wife and children were only gone two years and maybe that was it. Maybe it was still too soon. I felt in my heart that I did love Eleanor, but something was not right about our relationship, and it had to do with me.

I arrived at The Queen's House after nine when I knew all of the girls would be in attendance. As I walked up the stairs to the brothel, I could hear the merriment of the season emanating from behind the walls. There seemed to be a lively crowd in attendance and it was early. I rang the door, hoping that Eleanor would be free to see me.

One of the girls I had seen on a number of my visits answered the door. I couldn't remember her name if I knew it. She smiled wickedly at me, but then seemed to recognize me. "Ah, you're Eleanor's friend," she said.

"Is she available?" I asked.

"If she's not, I am." The smile was still there.

"I just want to see Eleanor for a bit if she is available."

The smile dimmed. "Stay here for one moment and I will find Miss Keesher."

I took my hat off and held it in my hands in the lobby of the building. They had done a nice job of decorating the front parlor for the holidays; there were a number of colorful lights twinkling away. Christmas was getting closer and I felt none of the holiday spirit."

"Detective Moses," a stern voice said behind me.

I turned and Miss Keesher was there without the girl who had greeted me. "If you are here to see Eleanor I am afraid she is not here this evening."

I wondered if this was some kind of bluff. "Miss Keesher, I know she is mad at me, but I just want to talk with her for a moment or so."

"Do you think I am kidding," she said? "She came to me

earlier in the day and told me she didn't feel well. She said she was going to a friend's for the day. You know nothing about this?"

I was bewildered. "No. I had no idea. I wouldn't have come here."

"Of course," she said. "I should have figured."

"Figured what?"

"I am afraid, Detective Moses, that Eleanor is having a relapse and has sunken back to the drugs. I think she might be with that evil looking man, Gus Black. You know what I said about her drug use. I can't tolerate this much longer. I am trying to run a business."

I put my hand up to stop her. "I know, Miss Keesher, and I am sorry. I will do what I can to find Eleanor and to bring her back here. What makes you think she's with Black?"

She lowered her eyes and spoke softly. "I know you despise that man. I can't blame you, but several of the girls saw Eleanor get into a cab with him."

I thanked Miss Keesher for her time and stepped back out into the cold night. The dampness had never left the day and it made my misery even worse. At least the cool air made my hot cheeks feel better. Eleanor had been upset when I saw her, mostly at me, and now she was absent from Queen's and probably with Gussie Black. My sour mood only got worse.

I wandered through the damp, cold air, trudging through sloppy old snow up to Twentieth Street and then two blocks down to the apartment building that the Hustons owned. I stood across from the building and could see that there were no lights on either the first or second floors. These residents were either asleep or not at home. On the third floor, where Gussie Black lived, his lights were on. Someone was up there. I had no proof because no one walked past the windows or gave me other notice that they were home, but I knew. I knew Gussie and Eleanor, my Eleanor, were up there.

At first, I was going to walk up those flights of stairs and knock on the door and get her out of there, but was that what she wanted? I knew at this time that it wasn't. I also knew that if I found them using heroin or perhaps caught them in a private moment, I might kill Black. So I stood there, looking upward and shivering. Finally, knowing I would do nothing this night, realizing it was for the better, I headed back towards Dearborn and the night life. I wasn't looking for a woman. A bottle of whiskey would do fine.

*****

I didn't make it through the entire bottle, but it was close. I didn't feel as drunk as I thought I should feel and that was probably a good thing. I managed to wobble along the streets and found myself on Wabash, near Seventeenth, in front of the small house owned by Doctor Albert Mitchell. Doc Mitchell had been the one who had cared for Eleanor after her last bout with heroin. It seemed, from talking with Charlotte LeFreur, that Doc Mitchell was also the doctor who cared for Marshall Field, Jr. on the night he was shot in front of the Everleigh Club.

It was almost eleven-thirty when I rang the door to the house. For most houses, this would not be a proper time to come calling, but I knew, based on the clientele that Mitchell kept, that he would be awake. In his trade, he never knew when one of the girls of the Levee would need his services.

Mitchell answered the door himself, still wearing a suit, minus the coat, but his hair was still a mess, similar to the way it looked the night he helped Eleanor. I decided that must be the way he kept it.

"Moses," he said. "A problem with Eleanor?"

I stepped into the small house as he kept the door open for me. On my second or third step into the small parlor, I almost knocked over a lamp. I took a seat very close to it.

"Have you been drinking, sir," he asked. He didn't look too happy.

"Just a bit," I answered.

"Is this late visit about Eleanor?"

"It's not that late, Doc, and, no, this time it's not about Eleanor."

"That's good," he said, taking a seat across from me. The parlor was decorated neatly with newer furniture. I knew the room to my left, closed off by a solid oak door was where Doc examined patients. He kept his residence rooms on the second floor. "I do worry about that girl."

I worried about her too and my knowledge that she was with Gussie Black did nothing to help my doldrums. "I have to ask you about another matter."

Doc appeared calm; he knew that I knew that he dealt with a lot of dregs of the Levee. "What matter would that be, Moses?"

"Marshall Field, Jr."

His face showed alarm. "What on earth are you talking about?"

For some reason, I took my pistol out of its holster and rested it across my thigh in clear view. Maybe I thought this would speed up some of Doc's answers. "I've been doing some checking for the family," I said. Doc Mitchell had secrets that I had kept for him; he would be discreet. "I have talked to two people now who have verified for me that Marshall, Jr. was shot in front of the Everleigh Club. One of the people, a courtesan at the club, said that Minna Everleigh wanted Field rushed over to see you." I said this even though I knew Minna had not mentioned Doc's name.

Doc relaxed his shoulders. "I knew that this would eventually come out. I knew someone was going to find out."

"Find out what, Doc?"

"For Heaven's sake, Moses. Find out about Junior, his trips down to the Everleigh Club, how he got shot. All that including that he came to see me that night."

"It's only the two sisters and a few girls at the Everleigh and you that know for sure," I said, trying to calm him. "I figured it out."

"What do you want to know?"

"I know he came here after the shooting and I know you fixed him up. That was why there was little blood in his room at the mansion. Obviously, you could not do the surgery on him so you fixed him up as well as you could and you sent him home."

"I cleaned the wound and stopped the bleeding as well as I could. I told him that bullet needed to come out. I told him there might be infection or damage to organs. I'm not capable or equipped to handle that type of injury."

"Did he go right home?"

"No. That's just it. He spent a long time trying to reach his family physician, Doctor Frank Billings. He called his residence three times and three times he was told the doctor was not at home. I think he was partially delirious by then. Finally, I convinced him to go straight to Mercy or go home. He went home. You know the rest."

"Most of the rest. At least from the stories I have been told and what the papers said."

"Mostly lies," Doc Mitchell said, "to protect what? The great Field family name? The man liked to gamble a little and have a drink or two. I understood he never touched a woman down there. What damage was there to be done to the family name? Instead the father kills the investigation and calls the whole thing an accident so everything just goes away. What sense is there in that, Moses?"

I had to admit, I saw little sense in the whole matter. "You, too, have kept quiet in the affair?"

"I had to. I can't have the Everleighs upset with me, and I was not about to take on the Fields. Neither sounded like a good idea for maintaining business."

"So who shot him?"

"I don't know that. He didn't tell me that?"

"What did he tell you?"

Doc took out a handkerchief and wiped away sweat beads that had appeared on his brow. "He told me a lunatic had shot him. He said he couldn't believe the son of a bitch had shot him. He said he would have never done anything to hurt his father or the family name, but his shooter had thought that was going to happen. He was mumbling crazily about this."

"But no name or indication of whom the shooter was?"

"No name was given. I am sorry for the whole matter and sorry I can't tell you more now. Will I get into any trouble?"

"What have you done wrong, Doc? You treated a man with a serious injury, doing everything in your power to take care of him. Then you sent him on his way. He chose to go home instead of Mercy, probably costing him his life. The fact that no detectives came to talk to you is of no fault of yours. You didn't lie to anyone. I can't see that you did anything wrong."

He looked relaxed; a small smile crossed his lips. "You won't be telling anyone."

"This is a private investigation, not a police one. I'm supposed to find out what happened to Junior, but I'm sure no one will be prosecuted, unless, of course, I find the actual killer."

"Thank you, Moses."

I put the gun back into the holster. Maybe the effect had worked. "Once again, Doc, it is I who owe you the thanks."

He smiled again, this time a bit broader. "And your friend, Eleanor, is she managing to stay away from problems?"

I know I didn't smile, but I truly didn't know the answer. "We can only hope so," I said.

### Thursday

When I returned to my apartment, head spinning from both the alcohol and the information that I had received from Doc Mitchell, I wasn't even concerned about another present from the Kluge loyalist, but I did jump when I saw the piece of paper wedged between my doorknob and the door. I pushed quickly into my flat to read the note, fumbling for the lights. For an instant, I was upset when I recognized Gunter's big, loopy handwriting, but the content of the note erased my displeasure. I had left the precinct early to visit the coroner and had not been back. A meeting had been set up. Gunter's note read:

*Will pick you up at eight. Meeting with Colosimo.*

Everywhere that I went now, I heard Colosimo's name and it was not sitting well with me. Mixed in with the booze and Doc Mitchell's confession, it gave me plenty of reason to toss and turn and miss out on sleep. When Gunter arrived at five minutes before eight, I was still groggy, half dressed and completely hung over.

"You look like hell, Patrick," he said, eyeing me closely as I climbed up in the hansom.

"Feel close to it."

"You're always telling me I should watch my liquor."

"And you should," I said, "but today I need you to take the lead with this bastard."

He smiled widely. "It will be my pleasure."

Colosimo's office was located on the third floor of a brothel he operated by the name of The Lucky Lady. The building was a three story gray stone with a black wrought iron fence around it. It wasn't nearly as classy as the Everleigh Club, but since it was Colosimo's base, it was by far one of his nicer places. A black servant offered us coffee and then led us up to the second floor to meet Big Jim.

There was nothing in between about Colosimo's office. It was a mixture of mahogany, polished floors, leather, gold, satin curtains and two large, gaudy chandeliers. Colosimo, a big, broad shouldered man, with a dark, olive complexion, did not rise to greet us. He was not dressed in white, as I assumed, but instead wore a black and white plaid suit. His bushy mustache had been professionally trimmed. He did not smile, only pointing to two leather chairs in front of his overly large desk. In the corner of the room, near the windows, sat a large man who stared at us from the moment we entered the office. He wore a suit, but no neck tie. His hair was blonde and parted right in the center. He also did not smile. Gunter and I took our seats.

Colosimo was writing something into a leather bound notebook. "Alderman Coughlin tells me you have a problem down here in the Levee and that I might be able to help you."

My head hurt; I nodded towards Gunter.

"That is correct," Gunter said. "We are looking for a missing girl, an Italian girl, named Isabella Rossini. She is the niece of the Italian Ambassador."

Colosimo seemed to consider this. Maybe the fact that she was Italian would help us. "Where you from?" Colosimo lifted his eyes and stared at Gunter.

"Near west side," Gunter said, smiling.

Colosimo laughed. "That's funny." He turned to look at me. "You sick."

"Not as good as I normally feel," I said.

"Want a drink?"

The thought of more booze made my stomach lurch. "No," I said. "I'll be all right."

"You don't look all right," he said and he went back to making notes in his book. We were patient.

"This speech you gave to the two aldermen about white slaves down here in the Levee, that's all nonsense. Nothing like that exists and you should stop running around and saying they do. It's upsetting to some people."

"What's that big ape keep looking at us for?" Gunter asked and before I knew what was happening the big ape was out of his chair and approaching us. Gunter drew his revolver and aimed at the coming beast.

"Gentlemen!" Colosimo said loudly. "This is a business meeting."

"Well, what the hell's he looking at?" Gunter countered.

"He doesn't speak," Colosimo said, "and he is as loyal to me as a good dog. He is probably looking at you two because he feels threatened. Does he have any reason to feel threatened?"

This had to be the big mute who we had heard about first in Blue Island and then at the Marlborough Hotel. He was tied in with Colosimo and now appeared to be his guard dog.

"Please call off your man, Mr. Colosimo," I said, headache raging. "We're just here to ask some questions and hopefully see if we can find this girl."

Colosimo waved his hand and the big mute left the office, Gunter never taking his eyes off of him.

I continued. "I got a tip that there was some white slaving going on down here in the Levee. That led us to Mary Hastings who used to run Sappho and a beat up old house in Blue Island where girls were being held called The Ranch. We heard that Mike Hart was involved as well. In no time at all, Mary Hastings, Mike and Mollie Hart and my source all ended up murdered. Any idea why?"

"Dealing with whores is a dangerous business," Colosimo said calmly.

"You have no idea about any of this?" I asked.

"Murder? None at all. I am a businessman. All I can tell you is that there is no prolific problem down in the Levee concerning white slaving. That is a fairy tale and your superiors downtown have sent you on a wild goose chase."

I was willing to give up on that if that was what Colosimo believed. It wasn't really what we were after. "What about Isabella Rossini? Do you think you can help us find her?"

Again, he pondered my question. "One girl, down here in the Levee? That would be a tough task."

"But you can try and help us find her?"

Colosimo spread his hand wide. "I can try, but make no promises. Her name again?"

"Isabella Rossini."

"Do you have a picture?"

I placed our one and only photo in front of him. It was wearing badly. "You can keep it." I sensed we were ending our search soon and got the feeling I'd never need it for Gussie Black.

"A very pretty girl," he said, picking up the picture and looking intently at it. "Why do you care so much, Moses?"

"About what? Finding Isabella Rossini?"

"All of it. Finding this little Italian girl or these missing women that you say are entering white slaving, why do you give a shit?"

He had me for a second. "Because it is the job that I gave my word that I would do, you know, Serve and Protect?"

He laughed. "That does surprise me, since I know your father. That is someone that never cared about the well being of anyone else, particularly a woman. Just surprises me that you didn't follow closer in his footsteps."

I stood up. "Just see if you can find her," I said.

He gave me a little mock salute. "Yes, sir."

I couldn't get out of the office or the brothel fast enough, taking two stairs at a time. Gunter followed quickly behind me. "What the hell was all that about at the end?" he said. "You were an orphan. How can he know your father?"

I looked my big German friend in the eyes. "Kind of an orphan, Gunter. I'm not sure who my mother is, but I'm getting close. My father dumped me at Holy Trinity to let them raise me."

"You know who your father is?"

"The person you told me at the First Ward Ball who you trusted the least."

Gunter thought for a moment with no reply, no memory of our short discussion.

"My father," I said, "is Jacob Fine."

The look of total bewilderment that crossed Gunter's face was priceless, but a cab pulled up for me before he could say anything. I hopped into it quickly and turned to him. "I have a couple of places I need to be. I will catch up with you at the precinct later. We can talk then." Before he could answer the cab was racing down State Street.

*****

Marshall Field, Jr's wife, the former Albertine Huck, greeted me in the vast library on the first floor of the Field mansion. I was told by one of her staff members that she was extremely busy this date, but when I explained that I had important news about Mr. Field's death, and that it was paramount that I see Mrs. Field; I was allowed an audience. She was due at a charity luncheon very soon. She was dressed in a lovely red dress, fitting for the season, but her mood was anything but joyous. This was the only thing that diminished her natural beauty. She had pure skin, dark hair and dark eyes, but the sadness that rimmed her eyes and tested her face was obvious. It had only been a month since her husband's death.

"You have important news for me about my husband's death, Detective Moses"? She sat across from me in a Queen's Ann chair; I was seated in a wooden backed chair that wasn't all that comfortable.

"What has your father in law told you?"

"Only that he hired you to review the facts of Marshall's

death, to look for accuracy, and that we should all cooperate with any questions or needs that you had."

"And how do you feel about all of this?"

She looked to the ceiling for a moment, perhaps looking to the divine for help. "This whole thing, Marshall's death, the rush to judgment, losing my husband and having to tell my children that their father won't be here any longer, has been incredibly tough to deal with. Other than that, I am fine." She gave me a forced, weak smile.

"Do you believe that your husband's death was an accident?"

She laughed and covered her mouth to suppress it. "You are supposed to be one of the top detectives on the force. You don't believe it, do you?"

"No, I don't."

"Then we are on similar ground. Marshall was a hunter and he knew how to handle guns. The whole story that he shot himself while cleaning his gun was preposterous."

"Then how was he shot?"

"I thought you were supposed to figure that out."

"I think I have. I just want to hear what you have to say about it."

She spoke quietly. "I am not naïve or stupid, detective. I know that Marshall went down to the Levee on Wednesday nights to play roulette and have a few drinks. He told me he never touched another woman and I believed him. For some reason, someone down there shot him. For another reason, before the investigation could even get under way, his father chose to have it covered up and called an accident. The mighty Field name could not deal with the truth."

"Someone down in the Levee did shoot your husband, Mrs. Field. I have two people who were there the night it happened outside of the Everleigh Club. I'm trying now to figure out who it was."

Suddenly there seemed to be more light in her eyes. "You

have witnesses?"

"No one that saw the actual shooting, but two people I've talked to who either heard the shooting take place or saw your husband after he was shot."

"Who would shoot Marshall?"

"That's what I came here to ask you. Who was upset with Mr. Field?"

She sighed loudly. "That has bothered me since the shooting. You had to know my husband, Detective Moses. Everyone liked Marshall. He was a good, fair man. He had few enemies, but there was one person."

I sat up stiff on the hard chair. "Do you know who it was?"

She shook her head quickly from side to side. "Marshall was arguing with someone about his behavior. Someone didn't like the fact that he made his weekly trips down to the Levee. Like Marshall's father, this person believed that what Marshall was doing was damaging the Field family name."

"What did your husband think of that?"

"He thought nothing of it because I told him that what he was doing was not hurting anyone. I believed that he needed to relax a bit, among other men. I saw no harm in the little diversions. Marshall continued to go to the Levee and that's what ultimately killed him."

I felt bad for her. I now knew that her sadness was partly brought on by her complicity in the matter. "Did Mr. Field ever tell you who this person was who questioning him?"

Sadly, she shook her head again. "I thought it might be a family friend. Marshall seemed so upset by it, that made the most sense, but I don't know. The person would reach him on the telephone and they would argue. I'm not sure Marshall knew who it was. I wish I had pressed him more about it."

I wanted to ask her if she knew a man with half of his ear missing, but I'd keep that for Marshall Field, Sr.

"It's such a shame that Doctor Billings was out of town hunting when Marshall was shot. Marshall made several attempts to get a hold of him, but Doctor Billings was in Downers Grove hunting, a trip arranged by my father-in-law's staff. I know Doctor Billings feels terrible; he thinks if he were in town that he might have been able to get Marshall to Mercy sooner and operated before the infection and internal bleeding did all that damage.

I nodded. "We'll never know that, will we?"

"You will find him, won't you, Detective?"

I knew she meant the killer. "Did you say that the hunting trip for Doctor Billings had been arranged by your father- in-law's staff?"

"Yes. That was why Doctor Billings was not in town."

"I will find your husband's killer, Mrs. Field."

For the first time there was a bit of a crack in the sadness that covered her face and she smiled.

*****

When I returned to the precinct, I meant to track down Gunter down and have a talk with him about my father. I'm sure it surprised him that I knew who my father was. It must have come as a shock to him to find out that my father was someone he despised. I also wanted to apologize to Gunter for not telling him sooner and to make sure he knew I was not upset with him in any way. Gunter made it no secret, his dislike for Jacob Fine, and his comments were raw and nasty. They didn't bother me and I wanted him to know that.

Gunter was nowhere in sight. I was told that he had said he had an appointment to attend to and might not be back for the day. He hadn't said anything to me about any appointment, but I had not told him I was going to run away from him to go see Mrs. Field. I fixed myself at my desk and began the usual and mundane work of detectives, completing reports. It was late afternoon, with Gunter not returning, when a messenger came from downstairs to tell me that I had a visitor. When I inquired who it was I got a shrug of the shoulders. "Some squirmy fellow," was the answer I got.

The visitor, a truly squirmy one, especially in a police precinct building, was Gussie Black. Even as I approached him, I saw his eyes darting about. He didn't look at all comfortable that he was there.

"There's nothing wrong with Eleanor, is there, Black?" I asked.

His eyes jumped to me and he actually looked calmer, as if he could trust me, and not the others. "No, Moses, it's not Eleanor."

"But you have seen her?"

"The other night, but not since." Now, he looked more concerned. "Can we step outside?"

I abided and we stepped outside in front of the building. There were a few officers congregating out in the cold, smoking cigarettes. Gussie motioned to me and I followed him up the street a bit. I was not wearing an overcoat and it was very cold.

"I have news for you about the missing girl, Isabella Rossini," he said.

I thought this a bit coincidental especially after our meeting with Colosimo. Maybe someone wanted the Rossini mattered closed. "Have you found her?"

Gussie looked nervous again and tried to light a cigarette. A cold wind blew out the match, but his second attempt was successful. "I have. I do business with a house on the west side and they have an Italian girl, same age, who goes by that name. She hasn't been there that long. It has to be her."

"West side, you say? Not in the Levee?"

"West on Congress, but I can say no more. The owners agreed to turn her over, but they want no trouble. In other words, you get the girl and everything else is forgotten."

"How did you find her?"

He smiled, exhaling smoke. "I have dealings with a number of brothels. They are a customer."

I nodded. "Did they happen to tell you how they came to have Miss Rossini in their employ?"

He looked at me; I know that I was seeking information that he was reluctant to give. "They didn't say. I assumed that she came to work for them of her own free will."

I nodded again. "When can I get Miss Rossini back?"

He handed me a piece of white paper, folded into a square. "Here is the address. It is an old house on Congress Street, deserted. She will be there after midnight. Do not come before. The house is being watched. She will be in the back room. If any policemen or other detectives are seen near the house, at any time today, the whole deal is off. Otherwise, she will be there safe and sound."

I cocked my head to one side. "I have your word on that?"

"Don't get dramatic on me, Moses. The girl will be there."

A big gust of wind roared down Twenty-Second Street at the moment, and I ducked my head against it. When I looked up, Gussie Black was scurrying quickly across the street.

*****

Knowing the kind of people that Gussie associated with gave me a distinct advantage. I could assume they were as low as you could go. Taking this into account, I figured they had little regard for human life, particularly one of a prostitute. If Colosimo were involved, it might even be worse. I would take every precaution with the exchange. I would have to explain the details of the meeting to Gunter so nothing went wrong. Everyone else would find out about it after we secured Isabella Rossini, if we secured her. It was an odd feeling, but I trusted Gussie. If he lied to me, he knew there would be problems, for him.

The problem now was to let Gunter know about the meeting. I kept expecting him to plod up the stairs at any moment and resume working at his desk. This never occurred and as the afternoon got later I went down twice to the desk sergeant and asked if there had been any messages from him. There had not been.

When I left for the day, I stopped at two places that Gunter liked to frequent for a drink or two before going home. None of the people that worked there had seen Gunter all day. His whereabouts were still unknown. This had me worried. I went to dinner, watched my drinking, and made my way home. It was past seven. We still had plenty of time to meet up, but I got the feeling something was wrong. It was just past seven-thirty when a loud pounding came to my door. I quickly opened it, sensing the urgency behind the pounding. There stood the beautiful Margaret Krause.

"Patrick, it's Gunter, you have to come right away," she said, seeming to be nearly out of breath.

"What is it?" I asked.

The tears started to pour from her eyes before I could complete my question. "Someone beat him up. He is not in a good way."

I grabbed my coat and we were soon in the cab that she left waiting outside of my building. It whisked us along as quickly as it could to Gunter's apartment, the cold air slapping around us.

"What has happened?" I asked.

"He is very stubborn and would not say. He told me that it was important that I find you," she said. In a subtle way she had taken my hand; I had not refused her grip or shied away from the encounter.

It took less than ten minutes to get to their building and soon we were up the stairs to the unit. Both children were in a familiar spot, playing in front of the Christmas tree, but they didn't look half as happy as they had the last time I'd been there. Little Emily looked like she'd been crying.

Gunter was in their bedroom behind a closed door. Initially the light was off, but when Margaret turned the light on I could get an initial read on his condition. It was not good. Other than the fact that he smiled at me, his face was a mess. There were a number of bruises and welts covering any flesh that I could see. His face was a mixture of purples and blues. One eye was completely shut; the other had a nice black ring around it, but it was more than half open. His lips were covered with dried and caking blood. At least two teeth were missing from his smiling mouth.

I knew that under the suit of clothes he still wore his body was covered in bruises and possibly bone breaks. His hands, which rested on top of his slowly beating chest, were scratched and torn. I didn't think there was much of his body that had not been abused.

"Patrick," he said, slowly and painfully. "Thank you for coming."

"Jesus, Gunter, we've got to get you to a doctor."

"No doctors," he said. "These are all just minor scratches." When he said that I could smell the booze on him. I looked over at Margaret, but she offered nothing.

"Do you want to tell me what happened?"

"I had a few drinks," he said. As he talked his voice made a new whistling sound through the missing teeth. "Then I went looking."

"Looking for what?"

"Little Miss Rostini," he said. "Who the hell else?"

"Where did you look for her?"

"Bed Bug Row. I think she's there."

"What places on Bed Bug Row?"

He smiled, his teeth a crimson color from the bloody lips. "All of them. I knocked on every fucking door on the little strip and asked about Miss Rostini. Nobody'd seen her."

With me out of commission for a bit and despite what Morgan, Coughlin, Kenna and Colosimo had said, Gunter had started his own door to door search for Isabella. "I know where she is."

His one good eye looked at me and even through the bruises on his face I could detect a frown. "You do?"

I unfolded the piece of paper that Gussie Black had given to me. "She'll be at twenty-three- o-one Congress tonight after midnight. Whoever has her has agreed to turn her over at that time." I looked him over quickly. "They only want one cop to show up so I am going up there on my own."

Gunter tried to sit up, the pain in his movements crossing his face. "I'm going, too."

"No, Gunter. Not this time. Only one of us can go. If any more than that shows up they'll shut down the agreement. I'll go up there at midnight and get the girl and we'll be done with this whole charade."

He sat back down and nodded. "Charade," he said quietly.

"Where did you get jumped?"

"Bucket of Blood," he said. "Side alley where the hansoms wait for the clients. Three of em. They had clubs."

"See any of them?"

He shook his head. "First shot caught me in the head. I was mostly covering up. I never saw anyone."

"We need to get you a doctor."

'I'm fine, Patrick. No doctors. I'll be okay in a few days."

What he was really saying was that he didn't want any attention brought to his little investigation along Bed Bug Row. A doctor might spread the word to the wrong people. "You rest up," I said. "Take a couple of days off, call in sick. Things will be fine."

"I should be there tonight."

"You can't be, for the case and for yourself."

He nodded slowly. "You be careful."

"I am always careful."

I walked out with Margaret who locked my arm in hers as we waited for a cab for me. She had been crying a lot. "You need to keep an eye on him," I said.

"I know Patrick, but he never listens. Look at what

happened today. It's the same with our marriage. He doesn't listen to what I say and he never stops drinking. I don't know what to do any longer."

I wasn't sure how to respond to their domestic problems. A carriage soon came along and I hustled over to it. Margaret followed me and grabbed my arm before I could climb aboard; she turned me and gave me a kiss right on the lips. "Be careful tonight, Patrick," she said. "It's bad enough Gunter getting all beaten up. Don't let that happen to you."

"Why would anyone want to beat me up?" I said. She didn't smile.

*****

I want to be as honest as I can about my feelings as I approached the vacant, little house on Congress just past midnight. For a street that was known for being a lively one, with brothels and gambling houses, it appeared to be dead this night. Maybe it was just because I wanted more people about that it seemed quiet. It was a very clear, moonlit night as I walked along Congress to the front of the house, a small two story frame job, with a porch lining the front of it. Had I not known any better, I would have said this was just some little quiet house, like so many others in the city. Based on my arranged meeting and pickup, I felt this house had seen some dark moments. I also knew I was more than nervous as I walked up the front steps to the door of the place.

I paused before I pushed the front door open; looking both ways up the street. I was still amazed at how peaceful it was. Nothing seemed out of place as I gave the door a push. It opened with little sound.

I walked into a small vestibule with a staircase to the left of me leading to the second floor. On both my left and right there were small rooms that could be used for dining or entertainment. Directly in front of me was a small hallway that led to the back of the house. The house was totally unlit except for the moonlight that gave some of the rooms enough light to see in. The house had an old, musty smell to it. I had been told that Isabella Rossini would be in one of the back rooms so I drew my gun and headed slowly in that direction.

I was as cautious as I could be, moving with as little noise as possible. At the end of the short hall was a small room and I could make out a chair on the other side of it with what looked like a body slumped over in it. The light wasn't that good so I took one step into the room to get a better look at the person in the chair.

My eyes were focusing on the chair when the club flew from my right and caught me across the arms. My gun clattered to the floor and bounced away as the club smashed into my right knee, sending me to the floor. The pain was intense. A tall figure lurked over me. The figure wore a long black coat and had a cloth hood pulled over his face.

"You're so Goddamn stupid, Moses," the voice said. "Thinking you'd just walk in here and find that girl. So stupid."

I wanted to place the voice, but it wasn't coming to me. My first thought was Gussie Black, but he had that more distinctive, nasally tone. It wasn't Black.

"I'd like to say that things are going to get better for you," the man said, "but that would be a lie."

My leg was screaming with pain and my arms had a dull pain shooting through them. All I could do was look up at the figure. It was then that I saw long barreled gun looking down at me."

"You just had to keep poking your head in the wrong direction. Good bye, Moses."

I had no time to think; certainly there was no time to pray. I closed my eyes and heard the boom of a gun going off in the room. There was a thud as the bullet hit the head of my assailant and then there was a splashing of brain matter and blood that hit my face. I had a moment to open my eyes and watched at the body teetered and then fell in my direction. I was just able to get out of the way as the body fell. It slammed into the floor next to me, and I knew he was dead. My vision in the room was getting a bit better, and I was able to see a man leaning against the jam of the door across the room, smoking gun in hand. I was able to make out the large frame of my friend Gunter Krause.

"Bet you're glad I made the trip," Gunter said.

"Nice shot, Gunter," I said and reached across to pull the cloth hood over the dead man's head. It was still pretty dark in the room, but I could make out the horsey face of Horace Langley, Sam Walker's partner. I could also make out the large hole between Horace's eyes where the bullet had exited.

I got up from the floor, legs and arms still hurting, and moved to the body on the chair. It wasn't a person. From what I could tell it was just a large burlap sack that had been filled with cloth. Langley had been right. I had been stupid. "The girl's not here, Gunter." There was no reply from Gunter, and when I looked over at him he had passed out and fallen to the floor.

With my knee throbbing, I was able to limp out of the house and down the stairs. Luckily there was a call box on the corner, less than a half a block away. I called in the shooting and asked for a coroner's carriage and an ambulance for Gunter. My knee hurt so bad that I sat down by the box until the police showed up. I looked up Congress and suddenly the street was lit up and there were a number of people out in front of the buildings. There is nothing like a good shooting to wake up a neighborhood.

*****

There is no doubt that Gunter saved my life in that vacant house. If he hadn't been there Horace Langley would have finished the task and blown my brains out. There was also no doubt that Gunter had endangered his own life by not going to Mercy Hospital as Margaret and I suggested. Beneath his clothes there was a severely bruised body that had sustained a number of whacks from wooden clubs. Gunter had suffered several cracked ribs and some organ damage, mostly internal bleeding. The doctors who I had talked to told me that it was a miracle that he could even make it to the house, much less, fire a shot of such perfection.

I won't say that Gunter was going to be treated with a hero's worship when he got out of the hospital. The department, specifically Captain Morgan, had a number of questions to ask and to follow up on. Morgan had already gotten a number of calls, Coughlin included, asking why Gunter had begun a search of the brothels along Bed Bug Row, in search of Isabella Rossini, when it had been decided that such a search should not be conducted. Morgan made it clear that Gunter, although he had saved my life, had stepped over some lines and would answer for it when he was healthy. He was put on indefinite sick leave.

I didn't escape Morgan's wrath myself. He understood that we were going into the house to try and find Isabella. What he didn't understand was how I could undertake such an action without proper back-up. I told him that I was told to show up with no support or the operation would be called off. Morgan seemed to understand, but when I explained my own physical problems, a broken left arm and a severely swollen knee, he also told me to take some time off until I felt better.

The biggest mystery of the night, the one that had Morgan scratching his head the most, was Horace Langley. I knew that Gussie Black had set me up. I also knew that Black and Horace were connected. Morgan was horrified that one of his detectives, Langley, was a bad cop. His own partner, Sam Walker, pled ignorance and asked for absolution. He felt awful that Langley was sour and had tried to kill me. He also had no idea who Horace was connected to. My guess might have been

Colosimo, but the list of possible candidates was long. It was all connected to the white slave trading, but as with our prior leads, this one also ended up dead. We would have to start fresh on that, I thought.

"Patrick," Morgan said to me on the steps of Mercy as I was about to leave. "One more thing."

"Captain?"

"This Isabella Rossini case. I know you're going to be out for a bit, but I'm going to tell Lieutenant Shipley that we have done all that we could and that we can't find the girl. At the rate that witnesses and leads are being killed it's not worth it. I don't care who the Goddamn girl is."

I couldn't disagree with Morgan's assessment. Everyone who became involved in this case ended up dead, except for Gunter and I, and we came close. I didn't know if Shipley would agree or tell Morgan that headquarters wanted us to keep looking, but I was okay with Morgan's decision. "It might be safer for us all," I said.

*****

It was past four in the morning when I got to the Huston's building and painfully made my way up the stairs to Gussie's apartment. I pounded on his door and when there was no answer, I drew my gun, gained my balance, and kicked the door open with my good leg. I expected as much, but Gussie was nowhere in sight. I searched the entire flat. The place still looked lived in so he had made a hurried exit, taking little with him. He'd obviously heard of the debacle on Congress Street and didn't want to be around when I came calling. When I came back out into the hall Eugene and Lottie Huston were both there, looking frightened and wondering who was making this ruckus in their building.

"Aren't you that police detective?" Eugene asked.

"I'm not sure right now," I said.

"Is Gussie in some trouble?" Lottie asked.

"Let me put it to you this way. I think you might want to look for another errand boy because I don't think Gussie is going to be returning here very soon."

I left them both standing there in the cold hallway in their bed clothes, and I slowly made my way down the stairs and out of the building.

More out of curiosity than anything, I went by The Queen's House in search of Eleanor. My curiosity turned to wonder and fear when I was told that Eleanor hadn't been in that night or for a couple of days. "I don't know where she is," Miss Keesher said.

I wondered if she was with Gussie Black and they were on their way out of town. I wanted to go in search for her, but where. I only hoped that she was safe. The fact that she might be with Black did little to make me feel better.

On leave and with no official case, and a bum knee and arm, there was little for me to do but head home and try to get some sleep. I should have been exhausted, but I was strangely wide awake. It's funny the effect that almost getting murdered has on the body. I walked a bit, realizing how sore my knee was, and then grabbed the first hansom I saw to get me back to my apartment.

## Friday

I woke up and found myself sorer than I would have imagined. The arm that wasn't broken throbbed where it had been hit and my knee kept reminding me why I was on medical leave. It was a struggle to just get dressed, and when I finally was I made it to a small restaurant that served an adequate breakfast. Unfortunately, when your mind is elsewhere it can be hard to summon the sense of taste. I was hungry and ate the food, but don't remember anything about it, good or bad. The coffee, I remembered tasted sour. The edict to end the search for Isabella Rossini made sense, but still left me feeling like we had failed. The girl had disappeared and there was a strong belief that she was down in the Levee, but we might not ever know. That bothered me, but there wasn't much I could do unless I wanted to risk losing my badge. I left my last cup of coffee unfinished, paid my bill and caught a cab for the Loop. The only thing I could do now was figure out who had killed Marshall Field, Jr. I thought I knew who had done it, but I didn't know him by name or face. That was my challenge.

*****

Doctor Frank Billings, the regular Field family doctor, had been out of town, deer hunting in Downers Grove, when the shooting had occurred. His office was listed on Madison Avenue just west of State Street in the Loop. The downtown district was overloaded with holiday shoppers and it was a slow trudge through the streets crammed with carriages; the electric streetcars didn't make it any easier for travel. At least the weather was cooperating a bit; it was milder than it had been and clear. Billings' office was located on the sixth floor of the building. There were stairs, but in my condition climbing six flights might take all day. I was resolved to take the elevator.

I don't have many fears in life, but there is one thing I dread. That is the use of elevators. To make my life easier, I avoid high-rise structures. If I must enter one, I try and take the stairs. Some buildings, these days, are just too tall. When your knee is busted up, you have no choice.

After a nervous few minutes, while the elevator clanged and crawled up the six floors, I found myself in Billings' office. A pretty receptionist went to get him after I identified myself. It gave me time to consider walking down the stairs when I was done.

Billings took me back to his private office for our discussion. He was a white haired man, wore glasses, and walked with a bent over stoop. More than anything, he looked like a family doctor should.

"I have been the Field family doctor for over forty-years. I have been there when all of the children and grandchildren were born," he said proudly. "I have been around for any family member that has taken sick, except for when young Marshall was shot. I can't ever forgive myself for not being around when that terrible incident took place."

I felt badly for the old doctor. "You can't blame yourself for his death. You were out of town. How were you to know that something like that was going to happen?"

"What did you say your interest was in the case, detective?"

"We just do a follow up on all suspicious deaths, murders, and serious crimes."

He nodded but made no further comment. "He called my home so often that night looking for me. He needed help, but I was out of town. I let the whole family down."

"He was calling from a doctor's office, the man who initially treated the wound. The doctor wanted him to go to Mercy, but Marshall wanted to go home and tried to reach you."

He looked stunned. "I thought he shot himself in his home

accidentally?"

"A popular myth. Confidentially, I believe he was shot outside of the Everleigh Club and then made his way to the doctor who took care of him. Then he went home before going to Mercy."

Again a nod. "All of that accidental shooting sounded a little suspicious."

"Do you think if he would have made it to Mercy on time it would have saved his life?"

"There is no doubt. All of that trying to call me and then going back to his house is what really killed him. If he had gone right to the hospital, and the surgery had been rushed, he would be alive today. There would not have been as much internal bleeding or infection."

"But he tried to reach you. Do you know why?"

He shrugged. "I am the family doctor. Other than that, I have no idea why he didn't go to the hospital. Maybe he felt that if I helped him it would have been more private."

I nodded. "It seems Mr. Field was being dogged by someone who knew of his occasional trips to the Levee. This person claimed Mr. Field was damaging the family name by making these trips. He may be the person who shot Mr. Field."

"That's ridiculous," Billings blurted. "Marshall was as good a man and as nice a man as there is."

"Apparently not to the one who shot him."

"I know no one who would make such a claim against Marshall or would even dislike him in the least."

"Well," I said, "we can't fix what's happened in the past. All we can try and do is find what really happened and bring some justice."

"I hope you can," he said with sad eyes. "Do you know what is ironic, detective?"

I told him I didn't.

"The trip that took me to Downers Grove was arranged by Mr. Field Senior's Chief of Staff. He is a gruff sounding man who goes by the name of Major Thorsen. I have never met him, but he sounds like a tough one. Anyway, he is the one who called me and told me of the trip. He said it was a gift from Mr. Field. All I had to do was be dressed for the occasion. Mr. Field provided the carriage for transportation, lodging, food, guns and ammunition for the hunt. If his top aide had not arranged for this hunting trip for me I would have been in town and home when Marshall called for my help."

*****

I found a call box and placed a call to the private number that Marshall Field had given me and was glad when the woman who answered, an older woman, told me that Field was in his office and would see me as soon as I could get there. It was only a short walk and even with my sore knee it only took a few minutes to get there. The knee actually felt better as I moved it more.

The last time I had been in Marshall Field's State Street store was when I was with Francis, my wife, before we had children. I remembered how young we had been then and how giddy we acted walking amongst the fine wares that Field's sold. The feeling was vastly different today. There was still a magnificent display of items for sale and the store was resplendent in its holiday décor, but I felt no joy. I knew who Marshall Field Jr's killer was and now I was going to deliver what I had to the dead son's father. I hoped that he could name the killer for me.

When I had called Field's office I was told he was located on the seventh floor of the store. That meant another elevator trip for me. Any joy I did have was lost with that thought. Also the jostling through the shopping crowds bothered my knee more than the walk I had just made to get to the store. The store was packed.

This elevator smelled better and moved smoother and faster than the one at Doctor Billings' office. It felt like a quick launch and then we were at the seventh floor. The woman who greeted me could not have been less than seventy, but she was very spry and moved like a younger person. She led me into a vast office that looked more like a museum than a work place. There were paintings and book cases adorning every inch of every wall space. A few heads of wild beasts had been mounted throughout the room and I wondered if Field had shot them. The only light in the room was from a small lamp on Field's desk. The windows in the room had their curtains drawn. The room was in near darkness.

Field was seated behind an immense desk and was talking quietly on the phone. His voice seemed a whisper. The woman led me to a stuffed chair in front of Field and told me to be seated. She left the room quietly. I studied Field as he completed his call, a discussion about surplus and costs to ship. I had seen him in a badly lit carriage a couple of weeks before so I can't offer a perspective on how he looked. Today, in the dim light of his office, I could see that he looked old. The hair on his head and in his thick mustache was completely white. His skin had an unhealthy, gray pallor to it. His eyes, blue, were somehow cast in a dreary fog. Now, as my eyes adjusted to the poor light, I could see that he was old, not healthy and sad.

"Ah, Detective Moses," he said, hanging up the phone and rising slowly to shake my hand. "Miss Barnes tells me that you have some important news for me."

I knew he was busy and probably was the type who didn't care for small talk. "I hope you are doing well, sir?"

He looked over my right shoulder to a place somewhere not in this room. "It is the Christmas season, our best time of the year. If you can't be merry at Christmas, you never will be."

"Yes, sir," I said lamely, sorry that I had asked. "I do have some news for you."

He leaned forward in his chair and his stare was intense. "Have you discovered the truth behind Marshall's death?"

"I'll be honest with you, it is hard to discover the truth about anything these days," I said, but I failed to get a smile out of him. "What I have found is that your son was shot in the early morning hours of November twenty-third outside of the Everleigh Club in the Levee."

I let the comment sink in for a moment and watched for his reaction. There was just a twitch of his lips, nothing more. "Go on," he said.

"I have talked to three witnesses who have confirmed this story. I don't doubt that it happened."

He nodded. "Can you tell me who shot Marshall?"

I felt myself take a deep breath. "Apparently, he was shot by a man that made the claim that Marshall was damaging the Field family name by making his weekly trips down to the Levee to play roulette."

"There may be some truth to that."

"That he was shot by such a man?"

He smiled. "No, detective. There is some truth to the fact that Marshall may have been hurting our family name due to these trips down to the Levee. I knew he went down there. I asked him to stop on many occasions, but I can only guess that like many other men, he had a weakness."

I found it odd to hear this admission that he felt that Marshall was hurting the family name. "Your son's killer made some comment that Marshall was hurting the name and shot him on Dearborn Street right out in front of the club. The Everleigh sisters first saw to him and got him a carriage which got him to the first doctor he saw."

"But you don't know who this man is?"

"A prostitute at the Everleigh Club told me she was approached by a man who was willing to pay her twenty thousand dollars if she backed up a scheme that had her telling the police that Minna Everleigh shot Marshall."

Field shrugged his shoulders as if to lessen tension. "Do you have the man's name?"

"I was told that the man used the name Jones, but I think that is false. I was told by this prostitute that the man had a gruff voice and was missing a part of his ear; he had lost it in Cuba."

At this, Field's eyes widened and I could see the understanding registering.

"Do you know this man, Mr. Field? Marshall's wife said someone, unknown to her, had been badgering Marshall about damaging the family name. Do you know who this might be?"

Field did not answer me. Instead he picked up his phone and dialed only one number on it. "Miss Barnes, have Major Thorsen come into my office right away." He hung up the phone and looked past me again at that spot to my right. We sat there in stony silence until I heard the door behind me open and close. I didn't turn, but I watched Field's eyes track the new guest, and heard footsteps as the visitor strode up to the side of Field's desk.

The man was short and very stocky. His suit fit him snuggly and showed off thick arms and broad shoulders. He was lean in the middle. His hair was dark, but looked to be going gray in spots. He had a beard, covering most of his face, and the spots of skin I could see were flaming red. His eyes were dark, one covered by a monocle, and they moved continuously from Field to me. One ear that I could clearly see looked overly large on a smaller head; the other ear was missing half of it.

"Major, this is Detective Moses," Field said. "You met him briefly outside of his apartment on the night that I engaged his services."

Thorsen nodded in my direction; I shifted in my chair, making sure I could get to my gun in a hurry. I was nervous; I didn't notice any throb in my knee. I had met Thorsen, but only briefly on the morning Field hired me.

"Detective Moses tells me that there are witnesses who say that Marshall was shot in front of the Everleigh Club by a man who stated that Marshall was damaging our family name because of his trips to the Levee. They also say that this man had a gruff voice and was missing part of his ear from a mishap in Cuba while helping Roosevelt vanquish the Spaniards."

Thorsen's eyes kept moving, but he was still and did not speak.

"Major Thorsen," Field said, louder this time. "Will you please comment on what Detective Moses has told me?"

Thorsen's eyes went to the floor. I took this opportunity to draw my gun, holding it in my lap. "I asked Marshall discreetly a number of times to stop going to the Levee," Thorsen said. "I knew that you had asked him on many occasions. He wasn't going to stop and I feared greatly that he was going to hurt you or his wife and kids. I knew how much you cared about the Field name. I could see no other way to get him to stop," he paused. "I shot him just above his hip. I meant to scare him. I thought he would get treatment right away, but he delayed seeing a doctor that could help him for almost seventeen hours. I only meant to scare him, to get him to stop going down there. If he would have gone straight to the hospital he would be alive today."

I expected to see a greater sadness in Field's eyes or maybe even anger, but what I saw appeared to be relief.

"Mr. Thorsen," I said, standing, "I must arrest you for the murder of Marshall Field, Jr."

Thorsen nodded, but his eyes never left the floor.

"Wait, Detective Moses. That will not be necessary," Field said.

I was about to cuff Thorsen, but stepped back. "Excuse me, sir. This man murdered your son."

He shook his head slowly. "Not murder. An accident as he has described. Major Thorsen is a man of the highest honor, recommended to me by the President. He will not leave this building in hand cuffs. What he will do is clean out his office, tender his resignation and then turn himself into police headquarters to Chief Collins by tomorrow at noon. If he does not do that than you may tell your cohorts your story and a warrant can be put out for his arrest. Is that understood,

Major?"

Thorsen slowly lifted his eyes to Field. "Yes, sir," he said. "Am I dismissed?"

"You are," Field said.

I was shocked and reeling when Thorsen left the office. I couldn't understand the bizarre ending. I had to ask. "Do you really think he will just show up at headquarters tomorrow?"

"Detective, Major Thorsen is a man of honor. He tried to do what was right for me and the Field name. He made a mistake, a terrible mistake that cost my son his life, but he will do nothing to damage his own honor or name any further. He will turn himself in. If you were to arrest anyone it would have to be me. I asked Major Thorsen to try and get Marshall to stop going down to the Levee. I am as much at fault as anyone. For me, it is punishment enough that I ordered Thorsen to do the job. I will have to live with that forever."

After listening to Field's reasoning, I was stunned, to the point of being almost speechless. "Then I guess we are done, sir." I wanted to get away from this bizarre environment.

"Only a matter of payment," he said. He reached into his desk and removed some cash which he placed in an envelope. Then he scrawled a note on a piece of stationary. He handed both to me. "The balance of your fee and a personal note that will get you into Potter Palmer's fine restaurant at his hotel. Take as many guests as you like. It is my treat." I finally saw the warm Marshall Field smile that I had seen from pictures in the *Tribune* before his son had been killed. Between this smile and his odd behavior, there was just too much to understand.

I did not thank him or shake his hand before I left his office. I had been stunned by murder before, but I could never remember such a shocking resolution to a case. Before I'd left the office, Field was on the phone to Miss Barnes, asking her to get a Mr. Stone in New York. As I entered the elevator, I was still shaking my head.

*****

Suddenly I was a detective with no cases and on leave from the job. I felt a strange bit of satisfaction at solving the Field mystery, but at the same time I had a sense that the case would not come to its proper close. I was in an excellent position to arrest Major Thorsen, but deferred to my "employer" in this instance and let Thorsen walk right out of the room. I believed in honor and in trust, but in my business you dealt with mostly liars and distrustful types. I wondered if Thorsen would actually show up voluntarily and admit to shooting Marshall Junior or if he would disappear. I also couldn't figure Marshall Field's rationale with the matter; I would never understand that.

I was equally skeptical of the outcome of the Isabella Rossini matter. I couldn't blame Captain Morgan for his decision to suspend the search for her. It had proven incredibly difficult to find the girl and the bodies continued to pile up. With the involvement of Coughlin, Kenna and Colosimo, the case took an ugly political turn. These men all knew something, I thought, but what that was would be hard to find. I knew that the business of white slaving was real, but to what extent I could only guess. I had no idea if Isabella had actually fallen victim to this evil practice, but she was missing. I had no idea is she was down in the Levee or even in Chicago. I didn't know how hard Colosimo would press to find her or if Morgan had gotten word to him that the police had stopped looking. Maybe Colosimo had, too.

We might have learned a lot if Gunter hadn't shot Horace Langley, but if Gunter doesn't kill Langley, I couldn't record this story. Langley was working for someone crooked, no doubt. Somehow, the little son of a bitch, Gussie Black was tied in, but how? Now Langley was dead and Gussie was gone. It upset me that I thought Eleanor was with him, wherever they were, but that was my fault. I should have done a lot more to secure her love.

I also knew that Morgan had jumped to shut down the case because Langley was somehow involved. The murders that occurred because of us snooping around were one thing. Learning that a police detective was embroiled in the mess was another. Morgan wanted to shut things down, to let things cool off, and to protect him. Again, I couldn't blame him.

My knee was aching fiercely and there wasn't very much to do. The weather turned foul as the day rolled along, dark clouds and cold mist filling the air. I stopped by The Queen's House in the late afternoon. No one had seen or heard anything from Eleanor. Miss Keesher asked me, not in a nice tone, where she was and when she would return. I told her the truth and said I didn't know the answer to either question. She muttered something about the evils of drug use and left me alone in the brothel lobby.

It occurred to me in the cab on the way to my apartment that not only did I not have any cases, but I also had no one to talk with. When the hansom dropped me in front of my building I looked up the street. A good many buildings in either direction were adorned with twinkling Christmas lights. Tomorrow was Christmas Eve. Father Luigi was dead, Gunter was banged up and sedated, lying in Mercy, and Eleanor had disappeared. Those were my closest friends at that time and I couldn't talk with any of them. I was alone.

## Saturday-Christmas Eve

With nothing pressing to do, I managed to sleep a good part of the day away, not rising until one o'clock in the afternoon. The arm that was broken gave me little pain, stuck in the cast that bound it. My unbroken arm was still quite sore and my knee, although better, was still stiff as I got out of bed. I did my best to get dressed and made my way out of the apartment in search of something to eat. I settled on a small restaurant up the street called the South Side Inn. When I got there, after two, it was quiet and void of holiday revelers. In other words, it was perfect. I ate some roast chicken with potatoes and carrots while reading the *Tribune*. I felt a little like I was on vacation. When I was done with my meal I decided to go over to Mercy and see how Gunter was doing. I hadn't spoken with him since he saved my life. If he was awake, I might be able to cheer him up.

Again, it was a cold and damp afternoon as the cab sloshed through the Levee on the way to the hospital. It was too early in the day for the district to be in full swing, but there were signs of it. There were a lot of people milling about, and I knew in a few hours things would be in high spirits.

I found Gunter in his room, resting his head against two pillows, while looking out of the window. There was still a significant amount of bruising around his head and face, but he smiled at me when he saw me enter his room. "You're up and about," he said slowly.

"That's more than I can say for you. Another day of slumming?"

Gunter smiled again. "They told me your knee was swollen badly and that you broke your arm."

"All true, but nothing like what you have to put up with."

"It's all temporary. What happened with Isabella Rossini?"

"The case has been suspended for now. It's been tough to find her and the bodies keep piling up. Horace Langley being involved didn't help matters. I think this all spooked Morgan. He shut the case down."

"Horace Langley," Gunter muttered through gritted teeth. "He deserved nothing better than death."

"I'd be dead if you hadn't come along that night. I owe you a debt of gratitude."

Another weak smile. "I couldn't let you go up there alone. Things didn't smell right to me."

"I'm glad you came. Anyway, the case is suspended and you and I are on leave. I guess it's time to enjoy the holiday."

"Some Goddamn holiday."

I didn't get a chance to respond. There was a little noise behind me and when I turned Margaret entered the room. She wore a rather plain dress for her, which was a surprise, and she looked like she might have been crying.

"Hello Patrick," she said. She gave me a light peck on the cheek.

"Did you bring my books?" Gunter said rudely from his bed.

"I have them here," she said, raising a cloth bag.

This didn't look to be starting out to be a great meeting so I took it as a cue to leave. Before I left I had an idea. "Margaret, do you and the kids have anywhere to be for dinner?"

She looked at Gunter who didn't seem to mind my intended invitation. "Not at this time, we don't."

"I did someone a favor and they paid me back with a dinner," I lied. "Would you and the kids like to join me for dinner in the restaurant at the Palmer House? I'd like to return the favor for the dinner you made for me."

"Do you mind Gunter?" she asked.

"I don't mind," he said gruffly. "Someone should enjoy Christmas."

"Seven o'clock?" I said.

She smiled. "That would be fine."

I went to the side of his bed and took Gunter's hand. "Thank you again for what you did for me."

He blushed. "You'd have done it for me, Patrick."

I told Margaret I would see her at seven and left the room. I didn't like the tension that seemed to be mounting in the small space, and I was glad when I got outside, even into the damp cold.

*****

I had thought I had seen the height of grand design and decoration when I had visited the Field mansion and the Everleigh Club, but I was mistaken. These two palaces were at least matched by the effort that the late Potter Palmer had put into his rebuilt Palmer House at State and Monroe. The original structure, which had been completed in 1871, had burned down thirteen days after its opening in the Great Fire. The new structure, it had been rumored, cost Palmer almost two million dollars. It stood seven stories tall and was the nicest hotel in the city. Upon entering the great lobby one had to shield their eyes to absorb the glint from the lights and the gold. A massive Christmas tree took its place in the center of an atrium. The remainder of the lobby was decorated to its fullest with seasonal adornments.

The Palmer Room, named after the patriarch of the family, was equally as lavish and well decorated as the lobby. Mixed in with the Christmas decorations was Santa Claus, who was busy visiting any table that had children seated at it. I found myself at a large square table near the rear of the room after presenting Field's letter to the maitre'd. The man, probably not happy with working this night, gave the letter a cursory glance, gave me a weary look and took me to my table. I found myself to be oddly nervous about the whole encounter I was facing and ordered a whiskey to help my fraying nerves. I didn't realize why I was nervous until a waiter led Margaret and the two children up to the table.

I have said it before and will repeat it here. Margaret Krause was one of the most beautiful women that I have ever laid eyes on. She wore a purple dress with a single pearl at her throat. Her long dark hair was done up completely on top of her head, revealing the beauty of her face, the dark eyes and full lips. She was almost too good looking for any man. She didn't seem to fit with Gunter. Apparently, from what I'd witnessed recently, their match wasn't going that well.

I helped her get young Jonathon and Emily seated and then pushed her chair in for her. The two kids were dressed in their finest clothes; Jonathon wore a nice suit while Emily had on a light blue dress. I could tell the two children were uncomfortable in this setting. Counting myself, that made three of us that were nervous at the table. Margaret looked comfortable as she stared around the room, wearing a broad smile.

"Is this your first time here, Patrick?" she asked.

"It is," I said.

"It must have been a rather large favor that you did."

I guess when you solve the murder of someone's son, that is a large favor, but it was a little hard to tell with the way Field had treated the outcome. I had no word whether Major Thorsen had turned himself in.

Our waiter came and Margaret ordered a glass of wine. The two children got milk with some chocolate in it. I had my second whiskey. We were told that the special that night was turkey, goose and duck, served with boiled potatoes and a sweet and sour cabbage. I told the waiter to bring enough for all of us and he, too, gave me a sidelong glance.

Margaret's hand touched mine to gain my attention. "I can't thank you enough for what you did to get Gunter over to Mercy in time."

She left her hand there. "He saved my life and he is my friend," I said a bit too coldly.

"Sometimes he is careless and that scares me. Sometimes I think he forgets that he has a wife and children."

I was going to respond, but was saved by a visit from Santa to our table. This gave me the chance to slide my hand out from under hers. Jonathon and Emily stared up at him in wonderment as he talked to them of the gifts that would later be under the tree for them. He presented each of them with a large candy cane which brought about more smiles. They asked if they could eat them now, but Margaret told them to wait until dinner was over.

I was worried that when Santa left Margaret might want to resume discussing Gunter, but again I was saved. This time it was a stream of waiters, carrying trays of fowl, potatoes and cabbage. There was enough food for ten people. The head waiter did a nice job of placing generous helpings on all of our plates and, in unison, we begin to eat. I won't say that I was a slave to the fork, but I did like to eat. This meal, more than any I'd had recently, was delicious. Every bite seemed to be full of flavors. I watched as Margaret and the two children ate. Thankfully, Margaret had to help them at times, and our conversation was held to small talk.

When the waiter came to inquire about desert, triple layer chocolate cake for the adults and ice cream for the children, we couldn't say no even though we were as stuffed as the goose had been. When the desert arrived, and the children started in on their ice cream, Margaret grabbed my hand. This time it was a firm grip. "I wish things weren't so difficult with Gunter and me," she said. Her eyes had that haunting beauty to them. It was hard to look right at her.

I was going to say something to the effect that things would get better between them, but I noticed a couple of people two tables over from us. The man was tall with a full head of blonde hair and a neatly trimmed blonde beard. Even from where I sat

I could tell from his smile that he had perfect teeth. It wasn't him that concerned me so much. It was the woman he was with. She was young, pretty, dark haired and with an olive complexion. I had seen her before, but only in a picture. I couldn't believe I was seeing her here. "Excuse me for a moment," I said to Margaret and got up before she could say anything.

The young woman was laughing at something her handsome prince had said as I walked up to their table. They had only both been served a glass of wine. They both looked shocked as I pulled out one of the extra chairs and sat down.

The prince looked at me and a flash of anger crossed his face. "What is the meaning of this intrusion, sir?" he said.

With my good hand I took out my badge and laid it on the table. I turned my attention to the woman. "Good evening, Miss Rossini."

She looked at the badge and then at me. "Do I know you, sir?" There was a slight Italian tint to her voice; the crescent scar on her chin seemed to quiver.

"Not really," I said, "but I can tell you that the Chicago Police have been looking all over for you. Your father reported you missing a couple of weeks ago and my precinct was given the task to find you."

"Sir, I asked the meaning of this," the prince stammered.

I turned to him. "I'm afraid, sir, that you are harboring a runaway. Her father has requested that the police track her down, and I believe I have done so."

"My father is an oppressive ogre," Isabella said.

"This is ludicrous," the prince countered.

I could think of nothing else to do. "Sir, I am going to ask you to leave. It will probably save you and your family, whoever they are, some embarrassment. I am going to place Miss Rossini in my custody and transport her to police headquarters."

"You're not going to leave me here, Jeffrey?" Isabella

pleaded.

I wasn't sure what the prince knew of her history. "When this clears up, you know how to get in touch with me." With that, he stood and placed his napkin on the table. He did manage one more sip of his wine and then he was off quickly for the exit.

If I could tell a story by just looking into someone's eyes, I could tell that she wanted to kill me. "I will only leave my father again," she said.

I had made a mistake, I thought, with Major Thorsen. "You may do whatever you like, Isabella, as soon as you are out of my custody."

I had one of the waiters get another policeman to come in from the street and guard Isabella while I bade farewell to Margaret and the children. I could tell from the sad look that Margaret gave me that she might have expected more than dinner that night, but it wasn't to be, and I wasn't ready to engage in that kind of relationship with my partner's wife. I did kiss her lightly on the check and returned to Isabella at her table.

*****

Isabella did little, but cry and curse, as our carriage made the short drive from the Palmer House to police headquarters. I told the desk sergeant to find Lieutenant Shipley wherever he was and I sat in one of the holding rooms with Isabella until he showed up. He arrived within the hour.

"Your Captain Morgan told me the search had been abandoned," Shipley said, not at all bothered about having to show up on a holiday.

"I hadn't quite given up," I said slyly.

"Well, you have once again displayed excellent police work. We are contacting Miss Rossini's father as we sit here."

I laughed at this. "Am I free to go, Lieutenant?"

"You may go, Detective," Shipley said with a smile, "and have a merry Christmas."

I smiled in return. It was still a couple of hours before it was officially Christmas, but I had nothing else to do, but celebrate. I was alone again and I felt the only thing that could make me feel better was a little more whiskey. There was nowhere else I could think of to have that next drink than close to home. I wasn't unhappy when I told the carriage driver to take me to Cooper's, a small pub not far from my apartment, in the heart of the Levee, my home.

## Sunday-Christmas

My plans for Christmas Day had been simple. I was going to sleep as long as I could and rest my ailing knee with the idea that this would help me get back to work sooner than later. I did have an invitation for dinner at Holy Trinity from Father Seamus, but I didn't know if I could go there knowing that Luigi wouldn't be there. For now, the plan was a lot of sleep and rest. I had done enough drinking at Cooper's the night before to help me sleep, and I might have succeeded at my goal if the now somewhat constant pounding at my door didn't return. At first I pretended it wasn't there, but whoever was pounding started to call my name. I sat up in bed, pulled the covers to me and checked my watch. In the dim light of the room, I could see that it was just past seven-thirty.

I got out of bed a bit too quickly and received a good jolt to the center of my forehead, reminding me that too much whiskey can hurt. I opened the door and found a young patrolman about to pound again.

"What is it?" I said.

The young man looked scared and anxious. "I'm sorry to have to wake you up, Detective, but there's been a murder. Detective Walker sent me here to get you."

"A murder?"

"It's down at Bubbly Creek. Detective Walker told me not to return without you."

Bubbly Creek was a filthy arm of the Chicago River on the south end of the Union Stock Yards. It was here that the Yards pumped all of their waste from their disposed animals. It was a disgusting mixture of entrails, blood, fur and parts. The creek always smelled, worse in summer, and it had once caught on fire. I couldn't think of a fouler way to spend Christmas morning or a more gruesome spot for a murder to take place.

The carriage we were in took us as fast as it could go and we soon arrived at a gathering of cops and police vans near a turn in the creek. We got out into a biting cold and the young patrolman told me the body was just past a large growth of bushes on the left side of a trail. I followed the icy trail and heard voices. When I got close to the creek itself the wind shifted and I caught a whiff of the ghastly smell. It was the smell of death, but in this case it wasn't just the dead body.

Sam Walker was standing next to a large rock smoking a cigarette and talking to a cop I didn't know. When he saw me coming he left the cop and walked over to me.

"Sorry to have to wake you, Moses, but I thought you'd want to see this." He turned and started walking down the trail, and I followed along. The smell got worse with each step.

There were four or five cops surrounding the body which was lying close to the bank. The creek, which I could now see, was frozen. When the other cops saw Walker and me approaching they cleared the way for us. I could see the feet of the victim as Walker stopped. When I got up to Walker and saw the victim my heart jumped.

"Sorry, Moses," Walker said.

Eleanor was lying in the dirty snow and ice that had gathered on that bank and she had been there at least a couple of days. She was wearing a light green dress which had been ripped right down the middle, exposing a large gash from her Adam's apple down to her crotch. Her throat had also been cut from ear to ear. All the blood that had seeped from her body was frozen and had soaked the dress she wore and the ground around her. Her hair, which was normally full and lustrous, was plastered to her scalp. In contrast to all of this was her pretty face. Other than the dirt that had blown on it and the onset of rigor mortis, it looked peaceful. I was glad that her eyes were closed.

"Any ideas?" Walker said quietly.

I shook my head. "I haven't seen her in a few days. I thought she had run off with Gussie Black."

"I hate to say it, but this looks like the work of Dr. Kluge."

"He died two weeks ago."

"Then what?"

"Then he had someone helping him and he's still out there."

"Jesus have mercy on us."

"Jesus may not be able to help us," I said.

There was a bit of noise behind us and I turned to see that the coroner's van had arrived. They would soon be there to take Eleanor to the morgue. I knelt down close to her and said a silent prayer. It was then that I noticed something in her right hand. The stiff fingers were holding it tightly. I looked closer and saw a thin gold chain. At the end of the chain and dangling just above the dirty snow was a heart shaped locket.

*****

I would like to say that I dealt with Eleanor's death like a man, but that would be a lie. I was barely able to contain myself in the hansom back to my apartment. I definitely wanted to cry if not scream out loudly. Once I arrived at my apartment, the Wilder family, who lived upstairs, were leaving the building for an outing. They were all cheery and bright, wishing me happy holidays. I could barely speak.

Inside my apartment, I didn't bother to take off my coat. I slumped on my bed and immediately began to cry. It was my fault that Eleanor had died. If I had been there more for her she would not have run to Gussie Black. Perhaps, if I had shown her a little more truthful love she would still be alive. The other thing that punished me was Dr. Kluge, the case that Gunter and I had so famously solved. It now appeared the great headline case hadn't been solved at all. Someone, working with Kluge or doing a good job of copying him, was still out there. That someone had taken Eleanor from me.

When I was finally able to stop crying, I got up from my bed and found the whiskey that I had in the apartment. I began to drink and my plan was to drink until I could fall asleep. I just wanted to get away from all of this. All the death I had seen the past two weeks, from the people I loved to those who I thought deserved to be dead, had worn on me. I was breaking down.

I finished the whiskey and found a bottle of vodka. I remembered getting sloppy and crying some more. I lay my head back down on my bed and then I didn't remember much until I awoke. I was cold and had a terrific headache. I looked at my watch. It was past four o'clock. I had been asleep a long time, but not enough to erase the whole day or the memories. It was still Christmas. I stood up uneasily and splashed some cold water onto my face. I felt a little better, but then I had to throw up. I retched so hard that my ribs ached on both sides of my body. At least, I thought, much of the poison I had ingested was out of my body.

I was looking about my apartment, searching for a clue as to what I should do next. Saying that I was lost would be an understatement. It was then that I saw the envelope that Father Seamus had given me on the day of Luigi's funeral. It was the envelope that held the picture of my father and the picture of the woman with the name Rose on the back of it. That was the clue I needed. I was going to visit my father, Jacob Fine, and find out who this woman was. I wanted to know if this was my mother. I wanted to know who my mother was. It was the only Christmas gift I wanted.

By the time I cleaned up and changed my dirty, wrinkled clothes it was close to five-thirty by the time I got to Freiburg's Dance Hall. I had only been inside the place once before, but was not surprised to see it crowded, even on Christmas Day. The bar area, where the girls who worked the club would lure men to the dance floor and then maybe to the Marlborough Hotel, was busy with a number of men and a lot of very young looking women. I had to make sure of what I was seeing. The girls who were working in the club couldn't be more than fifteen or sixteen years old. All were dressed and made up to look like the prettiest courtesans you'd ever seen, but there was no mistaking their young age.

During my only visit to Freiburg's I had noted where my father's office was. I knew father would be in. He was Jewish. Christmas meant nothing to him, and if there was money to be made he would be working. I headed for his office in the back.

I found my father shuffling through a large stack of what looked liked invoices on an old, well used desk. His office was small and smelled of rotting cigars and smoke.

"Jesus Christ," he said when he saw me. "What in God's name brings you here, Patrick?"

I realized looking down at my father that I didn't like his face. I didn't like his beady, black eyes or his thin hair or his beak- like nose. My father disgusted me. "Merry Christmas," I said.

His look showed he didn't find me amusing. "I hear you had a little problem with Coughlin and Colosimo," he said. "It's not a very good idea to cross some of those people."

He made me sick. The girls that were working his club were underage. I wondered how they had all gotten here. I wondered if they had been products of the white slave trading. "We were looking for a missing girl," I said.

"Well, you caused a bit of a stink, and a number of people got killed over it."

"Those girls you've got working out in the bar, they look like they are no older than fifteen, maybe sixteen."

He smiled, his lips showing only a pencil thin line of his teeth. "They are all just whores, Patrick. What's the problem with that?"

"They are underage," I said. "Where did they come from?"

"Come from?" he said. "They come from everywhere. They come here looking for work. We give it to them. What's so wrong with that?"

I eased up a bit. Maybe the girls had come there voluntarily. Maybe father and Solly Freiburg hadn't paid for them. I took the envelope out of my pocket and took the picture of the woman named Rose out of it and placed it in front of him on the desk.

He looked down at the picture for some time, and I thought I saw a softening in his eyes. "Where did you get this?"

"It was given to me after Father Luigi died."

"This is a very pretty woman," he said, still not taking his eyes from the picture.

"Is that a picture of my mother?"

He looked up at me and there was a look of sadness on his face. "I guess I owe you that much," he said. "This is your mother. Her name was Rose McGovern. We used to call her the Irish Rose."

I took the picture out of his hand and put it back in the envelope. I returned that to the inside of my suit pocket. "Is she still alive?"

"She may be. When you were born, I made two very quick decisions. The first was to turn you over to Holy Trinity. The second was to give your mother money to leave town."

"I almost froze to death on those steps, I was told."

"You didn't."

"Where did my mother go?"

"I don't know, but she left. I heard maybe St. Louis or perhaps New York, but I don't know for sure."

"She never contacted you about me?"

"No. That was all part of the deal. I would turn you over to the orphanage and make sure you got proper care. She would leave town."

I felt a rage covering my body. "Did you ever think of how all of this might have affected me?"

"I didn't. I did a stupid thing by falling in love with her in the first place. Then when I found out she was pregnant, I almost went crazy. I wanted to be a success in this city, not a laughing stock. Fathering a child with a prostitute was not such a good idea, especially a Jew with a Catholic."

"My mother was a prostitute?" The air seemed to leave my lungs.

He smiled that terribly weak smile again. "What did you think she was, Patrick?"

I'd heard enough. I now knew who she was, what she was and where she might be. I left the office and walked out of a back door into the alley behind the dance hall. It was dark and a new snow had begun to fall. It was terribly cold. I stood there a moment and heard the door open behind me. Jacob Fine was standing there.

"What the hell is wrong with you?" he asked.

"I'm done with you," I said.

"I don't understand you at all. This is just a business. We help men find women. These women are whores. It's just business like it was for your mother. We just made a mistake."

"Don't use that word," I said.

"What word?"

"Whore."

He laughed. "It's just a word, Patrick. Prostitute or whore, what's the difference. It may sound a little bad, but your mother was a whore."

I didn't think about taking my gun out of the holster. It just happened. I don't think I knew what I was doing, but I saw the fear register on my father's face. His eyes widened and his mouth formed a small circle. He didn't say anything. I didn't give him a chance.

He wasn't more than three feet from me. It was an easy shot. When the bullet hit him between the eyes he seemed to stand there with that amazed look on his face for longer than a few seconds. Then he fell backwards against the door and his eyes closed.

I put my gun back in its holster and backed away from his body. It was still early, and I suddenly felt relaxed. I was hungry. It was still Christmas. I turned and walked down the alley in search of a restaurant where I could enjoy my Christmas dinner.

## About The Author

After over a thirty year career in the insurance business, John Sturgeon retired in 2010 and began to spend more time on his writing. In that time, he has completed nine short stories and the novel, *"Crimes in the Levee"*. It is entirely a work of fiction which was inspired by a class on the History of Chicago and Karen Abbott's excellent book, *"Sin in the Second City"*. Classes at the University of Chicago's Writer's Studio were a great motivator. His short story, *"The Murder of the Yipping Dog"*, was published by *Mysterical-E* in 2012. John currently lives in Wheaton, Illinois with his wife, Mary, and their family. He is currently trying to figure out what to do with the rest of his life.

© Black Rose Writing

CPSIA information can be obtained at www.ICGtesting.com
Printed in the USA
BVOW03s0949141113

336218BV00003B/136/P

9 781612 962665